The Adjustments

Ann Lineberger

full
fathom
five

(digital)

For information visit Full Fathom Five Digital,
a division of Full Fathom Five LLC, at
www.fullfathomfive.com

Cover design by Cow Goes Moo™

ISBN 978-1-63370-109-0

First Edition

For Dince

1

"Your vision will become clear only when you look into your heart.
Who looks outside, dreams; who looks inside, awakes."
–Carl Jung

Although they were meant to turn inward during yoga class, their focus was communal. They studied the mirror's reflection—a group of women clad in black, streamlined clothing, posed on a floor dotted with colorful mats. They looked and judged themselves and the others although the practice of yoga was not meant for such vanity. Each member of the class was virtually a carbon copy of the other, though made distinct by her story, her mishap. In a small town, nothing went under the radar.

Their instructor led them through the poses, first seated with deep breaths, then upright, and then onto all fours. *Sukhasana to urdhva vrikshasana to adho-mukha-svanasana.* They moved as one to *virabhadrasana I*—or warrior I—looking up through raised, sinewy arms. They moved as one to *virabhadrasana II*—warrior II—and gazed out over their second fingers into the mirror, well aware of the areas on their bodies that still needed work. They moved as one through additional sun salutations and balancing poses, noting who in the studio maintained stillness and who faltered.

They moved, and their instructor, Yogi Jack, studied them, occasionally reminding them to breathe, to lengthen. He traveled quietly through the studio, widening stances, increasing stretches, and spotting bends. He adjusted them all but repeatedly returned and lingered with a select few.

They watched him, too. Handsome. Athletic. Desirable. Who would be his favorite today? Who would be the chosen adjustment?

They moved until settling into the dark and quiet in corpse pose—legs extended and arms at their sides. *Shavasana.* It was a time of personal reflection, but Jack continued to engage them. He moved from body to body, catlike, pushing down shoulders, gently tugging on legs, massaging necks and foreheads. He realigned bodies that had become stiff and uneven from the stress unique to mothers in a wealthy suburb.

Prone with eyes closed, the women could no longer study the mirror's reflection. Their obsessive watching and their judgments—which were ultimately an avoidance of deeper thought—slowed. They finally relaxed. Similar to the moments before sleep, rational lines of thought blurred. Storylines intersected. Their personal censors were muted.

"Let go," Jack intoned. "Let go of who you think you are.

"You are not your car.

"You are not your house.

"Don't let material things define you.

"Don't let the acquisition of them confine you.

"Open your mind.

"Release your imagination.

"When you do, anything is possible.

"You are divine.

"You are a goddess."

They were here for more than a workout—they hoped to absorb an ancient, transformative wisdom, but their commitment to personal growth wasn't likely to last beyond the moment. They would exit the darkened room and turn their iPhones back on. They would walk to their luxury cars. They would return to their impressive homes. The physical manifestations of their blinding and damning materialism would once again envelop them.

But before leaving, they were instructed to sit on their mats, cross-legged, hands at heart center—the sacred *anjali mudra.* They turned to face each other while Yogi Jack positioned himself at the studio's center. The reflected view was gone. No more judgments buffered by darkness and indirect vistas. They were face-to-face.

"*Namaste,*" said Yogi Jack. "Honor and acknowledge your fellow yogis."

"*Namaste,*" They echoed. They bowed to Jack and to each other, one at a time. Remembering, as they did, each woman's story. Her flaw.

Beautiful and kind Kate Musto was raised by a drunk and saddled with a tenuous self-confidence. Her days were a juggle of masking a scarred childhood and an abusive marriage.

Spendthrift and drinker Leigh Gilding, the comical queen of a monstrous developer's McMansion—a gigantic, oddly designed structure—was on a quest to void her trailer park history. As her children languished in her attic, money remained her king.

Garish and angry Brianna Worth—no stranger to the community's police blotter—strived for approval in a town that would never embrace her. What lengths would she go to for acceptance?

And pretty and popular Adair Burns wanted nothing more

than happiness. She wanted her husband and kids to love her. She wanted the community to admire her. She wanted Yogi Jack to desire her. Rejecting reality time and time again, she wanted and wanted and wanted.

They sat in lotus position in the lingering seconds of the class, wishing the vibe could last. It carried with it the promise of change—a break from their manic, perfectionist lifestyles—but they were torn. They had all bought into the same dream: an easy life filled with beautiful things and karmic debts that never had to be paid. Their dream was blinding. It kept them from knowing their own hearts.

2

Elizabeth Kelly entered the yoga studio just before class started. She had already dropped off her daughters, Alexis and Alice, at school. After class, she would head into the magazine where she worked. But right now Elizabeth was looking forward to having an hour to herself.

Yogi Jack sat in lotus position at the front of the room. This was Elizabeth's first class with him, and she found that he was as handsome as she had been told. His thick, sandy-blond hair was parted to the side, and his features were perfectly proportioned. His hair was cut tight, which made him look boyish although he was clearly in his midforties. He was thin and toned, wearing loose, black Hind pants and a gray-blue Under Armour T-shirt. The outfit was a far cry from the typical male fitness instructor getup of tight shorts and athletic shirts.

He seemed gentle. Elizabeth knew very little about him, but just before class started, she surprised herself by thinking, *I would have dated him in college.*

The friends who insisted she try Yogi Jack's class said he began with a short, sobering, yoga-related teaching. He read a quote from Gandhi or Rumi and extrapolated, connecting it to something currently relevant. Jack appeared to be on a high that day; as Elizabeth rolled out her mat, she overheard him say that he was just back from a yoga retreat.

"It's nice to see all of you again," he said as he began the class. "And welcome to those of you who are new. As most of you know, I was away running a week-long yoga retreat in Costa Rica. Sixteen women attended. We had a marvelous time."

Jack went on with what sounded like an infomercial, describing days filled with yoga classes and other physical activities, naps and alone time, and meals of fresh fruit and seafood.

"Nights were spent leisurely at a long dinner table with food prepared for us by a personal chef," he said. "Even though it was a yoga retreat, there was no shortage of wine with dinner. During my retreats, we create the world we wish we could live in—a world based on giving and receiving love, of trust and of challenging ourselves, of questioning convention and following our hearts. We create strong emotional connections and stay in touch until the next trip, when we can all be together again. I hope some of you will join me next time."

It was February—freezing. For a group of mothers who'd felt somewhat housebound for months, Jack was describing the Garden of Eden. Elizabeth wasn't used to instructors like him. He spoke so personally. The instructors she had encountered always kept a kind of ubiquitous distance, especially those she had in Manhattan. It was obvious that Jack wanted to draw his audience in. He wanted to build a following.

Jack scanned the darkened room then, and his eyes settled on her. "You're new," he said. Wide-eyed, she obediently nodded up and down like a kindergartener on her first day of school. She blushed.

"What's your name?" he asked.

"Elizabeth," she replied.

"Welcome, Elizabeth," he said with a smile, amused that his attention embarrassed her. "Are you ready for the movement part of the class to start?" he asked.

"Yes," she said, feeling shy and wanting his eyes off of her.

Yogi Jack taught many different types of yoga—hatha, kripalu, bikram—in several Fairfield County studios and in his own personal studio in Cannondale, but his Wednesday morning class was ashtanga yoga, an often strenuous combination of standing and sitting movements linked to conscious breathing and meditation.

As Elizabeth had been told, Jack's class had a pleasant, gentle flow to it. Twenty minutes in, she was completely relaxed and in rhythm. Her mind had quieted, and that day's to-do list was temporarily buried.

Several times during the class, Jack stood behind her and adjusted her position. The adjustments were intended to teach proper alignment and maximize the position while building trust between student and instructor. Other times, when she sat in child's pose, he laid his hands on her lower spine. Elizabeth felt a complete sense of calm when he touched her back.

She wondered if his touch had some sort of power to it. She wondered if she was having a sexual response. Aside from a massage, it'd been years—more than fifteen years—since anyone other than her husband had touched her in this way. But it was more than the touch. There was something overtly sexual to Jack's class. She couldn't place it exactly.

Elizabeth looked at the clock as they neared the end of class. "Last position," Jack said. "Now it's time to move to *shavasana* or 'stillness.' Lay on your back. Allow your hands to fall to your sides with your palms up and your feet slightly spread apart. Relax."

Elizabeth lay down but clasped her hands over her stomach. At that moment, it was the position that felt most comfortable.

"Relax," he repeated in a whisper just loud enough for his students to hear. "Breathe. You have nowhere to go, nothing to do. Be still. Let go. Let go of who you think you are. Let go of who you think you need to be. Right now you are *you*. You are not a wife. You are not a mother. You are not a daughter or a sister. You are not an employee. You are who you are at your deepest core—a woman with individual wants and needs. Entertain those wants and needs. Embrace them; don't stifle them. Open yourself to new possibilities. Think about different ways of living your life."

Several minutes later, Yogi Jack's hands touched Elizabeth's forehead. He massaged it as well as her scalp. She noticed a faint scent of eucalyptus. Without thinking, Elizabeth's hands started to fall apart and glide to the floor. She was in a pose of complete stillness. For a person who felt guarded most of the time, she was shocked by what felt like submission.

After a few more minutes, the class was instructed to sit up in sukhasana pose. Next, they said the yoga-type "*namaste*" good-byes. The class was over.

As the women rolled up their mats and put on their shoes, Jack stood in the center of the room.

"I'll be here for a few minutes if anyone wants to speak with me," he said. "Please be sure to sign up for my email list. I'll send you updates to my class schedule and my availability for private sessions."

Elizabeth was in the corner tying her shoelaces. She watched the rest of the women as they left. A number of them fell into Jack's arms as he embraced them. One—an attractive, fit woman in her forties—smiled up at him during the hug and gave him a kiss on the lips. He kissed back and smiled. They shared a secret—they were lovers. The woman made a quick exit, and Jack continued on with his overly friendly good-byes.

Another woman approached him and, after a hug, showed him what appeared to be a hip tattoo. Elizabeth wondered how many women in the room were sleeping with him. Then it hit her. She knew why parts of Jack's class made her feel uneasy. Although the sequence was standard ashtanga yoga, Jack's version had its own spin.

He structured his classes like sex.

There was a friendly, gentle vibe as the students sat and waited for class to start. When Jack spoke in his intimate way, they mentally opened up. Lights lowered and movement started, which slowly built in intensity as Jack led the class through increasingly challenging poses, adjusting the women throughout. Classic arousing songs played softly. As the movements repeated, the students became heated. Jack added more challenging poses, and the women began lightly perspiring. The climax came during the difficult final pose—a backbend. The class ended with a rest period.

A Google search later revealed that other yoga instructors structured their classes in the same way. There were even students who used these classes as foreplay. This was news to Elizabeth, as she was not seasoned enough to know. What she experienced in Yogi Jack's class was different, and the entire scene—the talk, the well-run class, the attractive yoga instructor and his groupies—fascinated her.

Elizabeth was so bewitched that it preoccupied her for the rest of the day: during work, when picking up her children from school, and while making dinner. She tried to reach her sister,

Abby, to tell her about the class and ask whether she had ever been to one like it.

When she heard her husband's car pull into the driveway, she ran to the door to greet him. As he entered their home, her hands encircled his waist and pulled him close.

Looking him in the eyes, Elizabeth said, "I need to have sex with you *right* now."

Andrew looked surprised.

"I went to this amazing yoga class, and I've been incredibly turned on all day," she continued.

"Yoga?" he asked.

"Yes," she said.

"A *yoga* class?" he repeated.

"Yes," she said. "I can't explain it exactly, but it was a combination of the poses and the music and the dark room and the instructor and his adjustments… I haven't been able to stop thinking about sex since."

"*His* adjustments?" Andrew asked. "A guy?"

"He touches everyone," she said, "to guide us into the right positions."

Elizabeth pushed Andrew toward his office. Once inside, she kissed him hard and pulled him close, allowing their bodies to touch, and locked the door behind them. Elizabeth tugged him down to the floor and, while straddling his thighs, started undoing his pants.

Andrew's mind flashed to the last time she did this to him, during a drunken night on a vacation they took without their kids. Afterward they'd passed out on the beach and were woken by the hotel's security guard.

Elizabeth slid her underwear off, mounted him, and guided

him inside of her. She let out a happy sigh of relief as her day-long desire was satisfied. She rocked, her torso upright, her head tilted back slightly, her eyes closed, grinding against her husband. Andrew watched her.

A male yoga instructor? he thought. They had been married over ten years, and he still wanted her as much as he did the first night they met. *But does she?* he questioned. *Who is she thinking about right now?*

As if sensing Andrew's concern, Elizabeth leaned forward and kissed him. "I missed you today," she whispered in his ear.

Reassured, Andrew's hands moved to her waist, encouraging her movements. He wanted her to enjoy this, and he wanted her to initiate it more—with him. As Andrew pushed deeper into her, his mind flooded with endorphins. *She missed me today,* he thought.

Later that night, after their children had fallen asleep, Elizabeth was giddy telling Andrew about her yoga experience. "Jack's hand-some, he's suave, and he's definitely sleeping with a number of women in the class," she said as they lay in bed. "All this in con-servative, perfect Cannondale. Can you believe it?"

"Absolutely," Andrew replied. "Remember the personal trainer in Darien who was having affairs with seven married women at the same time? None of them thought he was sleeping with anyone else."

"I know," Elizabeth said. "I know. You're right. It's no different, but I still find it shocking. And this time I'm not just hearing a story after the fact—I saw how this guy operates firsthand. I can't wait to tell Abby about him. I'm going to bring her to his class the next time she visits. She'd like him. It's too bad he doesn't work in Manhattan. Private sessions with him might be just what she needs to get her mind off Colin."

"Are you serious?" Andrew responded. "You want to hook your sister up with a lothario within months of her husband's suicide? How is that a good idea?"

"He would just be a distraction for her," Elizabeth said. "She's seasoned and way too smart to fall for him."

"It's really an awful idea, Elizabeth," Andrew said, smiling. "Come to think of it, maybe I should have become a fitness instructor," he joked. "Having sex with lonely, beautiful women while someone else pays their bills sounds like a good gig."

Andrew had a point. Jack enjoyed the physical benefits from these unhappy housewives but dealt with none of the difficult relationships. These women weren't complaining about their kids to him. They weren't asking for a new car or a bigger house. They asked for nothing but sex—at least in theory.

Based on what Elizabeth discovered about Jack online after the class—his privileged upbringing, his sailing scholarship, his MBA from Georgetown—he would be prime marriage material for most of the women in his class. Jack's background allowed his students to feel instantly comfortable with him. His only apparent drawbacks were his relatively newfound status as a yoga instructor and his self-proclaimed rejection of worldly possessions. Those aspects of him didn't appeal to most of the women who took his classes. They needed someone who could and wanted to support their current lifestyles.

"I enjoyed my homecoming, but aren't there other yoga teachers you can go to?" Andrew asked Elizabeth, bringing her back to the conversation.

"Yes, there are, and I've taken classes with a number of them in town, but his class is exceptionally good," she responded. "Don't worry. I'm not interested in him. Oh, guess who takes private sessions with Jack?"

"Who?" Andrew asked.

"Adair Burns!" she said. "He comes to her home every Monday. She's into partner yoga, which is a very intimate form of body-on-body yoga. They use each other to get the best stretch out of the workout. She said it's amazing."

"No partner yoga with Yogi Jack for you," Andrew responded. "That sounds like a slippery slope."

"Oh, shut up, Andrew," joked Elizabeth, though she was aroused just by the thought of it. Looking coyly at her husband, she slipped off her nightie and tugged down his boxers.

Andrew's eyes brightened. "Round two?" he asked, instantly hard.

"Round two," she repeated as she slowly ran her hands up his legs and gently took him into her mouth.

3

Oh no! Elizabeth thought as she glanced at her iPhone a few weeks later. *Three texts and two missed calls from Abby in the last fifteen minutes? I hope she's okay.*

Elizabeth quickly speed-dialed her older sister. The phone rang once and then went to voice mail: "*Hello, you've reached the office of Abigail Davis-Powers. Sorry to have missed your call. Please leave a message or, if it's urgent, contact my assistant, Rebecca Burke. Thank you!*" Beep.

"Abby, it's me," said Elizabeth. "Call me. I hope everything's okay."

Elizabeth contemplated calling Rebecca but decided against it. Rebecca was Abby's new, fresh-out-of-college assistant. Odds were good that Rebecca wouldn't know what the missed calls and texts were about.

God, I hope it's not something with one of the kids, thought Elizabeth. *Maybe she ran into one of Colin's old colleagues; that always upsets her. Her last call was just five minutes ago. Why isn't she picking up?*

Colin had been married to Abby for eleven years when he jumped off the roof of the University Club in midtown Manhattan. Abby had been inside at Stewart Browning's forty-fifth birthday party.

It was a lavish affair with over three hundred guests—largely investment bankers and their perfectly groomed wives. Stewart's wife, Michelle, had spared no expense making the ballroom look absolutely beautiful. Individually spotlighted from above, the silk moiré-covered tables were decorated with large, artful arrangements of cherry blossoms, stargazer lilies, and trailing ivy. In honor of the year Stewart was promoted to managing director at J.P. Morgan, vintage 1996 Dom Pérignon was poured. After the cocktail period, a main course of filet mignon and lobster was served. Stewart's favorite childhood band, The Eagles, started up their set as dinner was ending.

Before excusing himself and heading to the roof, Colin commented that the event must have cost over $200,000. "I wanted to host a party like this for your forty-fifth birthday," he'd said to Abby. Abby didn't say anything at the time, but she'd felt it was inappropriately extravagant.

Parties like this were common until September 2008, but after the economic crash, even the word "luxury" seemed stricken from usage. The overnight disappearance of so many finance jobs negatively impacted bankers as well as those who provided services for them—contractors, landscapers, grocers, doormen, personal trainers. And yet here was smug Stewart and pretentious Michelle acting as if the world economy hadn't almost collapsed.

After slowly surveying the room, Colin looked Abby in the eyes and said, "I'm sorry I let you and the kids down." He then turned and walked away.

Sensing his distress, Abby had followed him to the ballroom's doorway. She grabbed his hand and looked pleadingly into his eyes. "Colin, what's going on?" she'd asked. "Talk to me."

"I'm okay," he'd said. "Really. Just going to get some air. I'll be back shortly."

Colin and Stewart met as undergraduates at Tufts University. They'd remained close friends since, but Abby had contemplated throwing away the party invitation when she first received it. She knew the gala would upset Colin.

He'd lost his job as the head of the Lehman Brothers' Credit Default Swap Desk along with most of the family's money the year before. Somehow Stewart and many of their friends were still employed and, although impacted by the great recession, few were in such a dire place as the Powers.

Colin appeared unemployable. No one was investing in the unregulated structured finance products that he had spent nearly his entire career managing. Dubbed "financial weapons of mass destruction," They were blamed for the crash. His expertise made him toxic. Big banks wouldn't hire him. Hedge funds didn't want to be associated with him. Fear was rampant in the financial industry.

For four months, Colin had been trying to get another job. He'd attended job fairs, which were beneath him even in his early twenties, but he was desperate. After one such fair, he contemplated stepping in front of a subway train. He pulled himself back from the yellow line, but the thought had nonetheless been planted.

Abby, a successful real estate broker with Benedict Mathews Farnsworth, was struggling, too. After the crash, all her seller clients pulled their listings. Her buyers were only interested in predatory deals from desperate sellers. Brokers used to years of escalating real estate prices were panicked and increasingly difficult to work with.

The Powers had decided on a plan: intending to downsize, they listed their apartment and would rent it if they didn't get the price they wanted. They rented their vacation home. They looked for alternative school options for their two kids. They asked for financial help from their parents.

On the day the Brownings' invitation arrived, Abby said, "Let's go just to be polite. He's a good friend and contact for you. When you want to leave, we will."

Within an hour of Colin's suicide, the story led the ten o'clock news: FORMER LEHMAN EXEC JUMPS, DISTRAUGHT WIFE AT SCENE. There was limited reporting but plenty of striking visuals:

A hastily taped-off crime scene between Cartier's flagship store and the granite façade of The University Club.

A body under a tarp on Fifth Avenue.

The suicide victim's black tie-attired friends cradling one another, tourists in denim and sneakers acting as a striking counterpart.

A line of chauffeured town cars waiting to take the victim's distraught acquaintances home.

In the following days, the Powers suicide received a lot of play. It was front-page international news and appeared in the Manhattan tabloids for a week. Not since the fall of Lehman Brothers had one news event so profoundly symbolized the impact of the financial market collapse on the one percent.

The night of Colin's suicide, Elizabeth and Andrew were sitting in a movie theatre. They had turned their phones to vibrate, planning to only pick up if their babysitter called. A half hour into the film, Elizabeth's phone started a perpetual quiver. She ignored the first few calls from her mother and one from Abby, thinking they were related to an upcoming family gathering. But when Abby's best friend's name appeared on her phone, Elizabeth picked up.

Today, two months after that awful night, Elizabeth was

panicking. When her phone finally rang with Abby's return call, she rushed to answer.

"Abby, what's going on? Are you okay?"

"Yes, I'm okay," Abby said, scanning the online Cannondale rental listings in search of a new home for her family of three. *My kids are finally going to have a yard to play in and a driveway to ride bikes in,* Abby thought, noting the listings' lush green expanses and long driveways. *That's good. Maybe we'll get a dog or two.*

"Yes, everything is okay, Elizabeth," Abby continued. "Nothing to worry about. I just wanted to tell you my news."

"What news?" Elizabeth asked, relieved.

"Guess who's moving back to Connecticut?"

"What?" Elizabeth exclaimed. "No way!"

"Yes, way," said Abby. "That is, unless I pull a Colin and jump off a building. I have no other choice."

"But you hate suburbia," said Elizabeth. "Even as a child, you hated it. It's too staid for you."

"Well, life has a funny way of playing out, doesn't it?" Abby quipped. "It isn't public knowledge yet, so don't repeat it, but Benedict Mathews Farnsworth is acquiring White's Realty. The Bloom Brothers asked me about the firm a month ago—they know I grew up in Cannondale. I asked them if they're going to keep the firm's current manager. They aren't, so I asked for the job."

"You? A manager and mentor of other real estate agents?" Elizabeth said incredulously. "Really?"

"It's a salaried job," she responded. "I need a steady income, so I'm going to have to learn how to mentor. I start in two weeks."

"Wow! That is fast. What about dealing with the suburban clients and your neighbors? You can barely hide your disdain for people out here, especially the Cannondale women."

"I can fake it when I have to," said Abby. "I've had to work with a number of them over the years. And I'll have you nearby to meet for coffee so that we can have a good laugh over it. One upside to the move is that I can live near you again, and our kids will get to be together more often."

"I'm sorry to say it, but I'm selfishly kind of thrilled by your news," Elizabeth admitted. "What are you going to do with your apartment?"

"Rent it. Even in this market I can easily get $20,000 a month for it, which will cover the building's maintenance and its taxes plus some. I'm definitely returning to the city when the New York market rebounds and the kids are older."

"Abigail Davis back in the 'burbs... Is there anyone we should warn?"

"Maybe Mrs. Harris, if she's still alive," joked Abby.

"Oh my God," laughed Elizabeth. "The muffins. That poor woman."

The day Abby and Elizabeth's family moved into their second home in Stamford, their neighbor Karen Harris baked them blueberry muffins. She put them in a wicker basket and left them on their front stoop with a colorful "*Welcome to the Neighborhood*" note. Abby got to them first, and within an hour all of the muffins and the basket were littered across the Harris' driveway. Abby and her best friend, Gigi Tollbrook, had thrown them at the house from Abby's bedroom window. Little round stains appeared on the exterior paint where the muffins hit the home.

"I was horrified when you did that," Elizabeth recalled. "Mrs. Harris was so sweet."

"Her son used to follow me around at school," said Abby. "He was totally creepy. I didn't want anyone in the Harris family to think they could come over to our house just because we were neighbors. Is my old Confraternity of Christian Doctrine teacher, Mrs. Clement, still around?"

"Yes, Mom hangs out with her," Elizabeth said.

"Remember when Gigi and I snuck onto her property and cut all the heads off her flowers the night before Mother's Day?"

"I do," Elizabeth said, smiling. "Her beautiful garden was transformed into a sea of green stalks. That was really mean, too."

"She was so uptight," Abby insisted, "and she told Mom that I skipped her classes."

As a child, Abby was always in some kind of low-grade trouble. She was mischievous and fun, and boys loved hanging out with her. But as she got older, she became increasingly irreverent, and the trouble turned real. Abby spent her teens doing the exact opposite of what their prim mother wanted: she got kicked out of two private schools, she totaled her new car by driving it into a parked vehicle on the family's street, she partied before coming home to their family's daily formal dinners, and she never made curfew. Abby was so bad that when she left for college, the relief in their house was palpable.

Paradoxically, what saved Abby in adulthood was a desire to feel as powerful as she had felt in her family. After college, she moved to Manhattan, a place where money equals power, and realized that bravado without a career would get her nowhere. Not one to rely on someone else for support, Abby dabbled in the fashion industry before turning to real estate. In a business where most everyone you meet can be considered a potential client or point of referral, Abby started to care what people thought of her. In the ways that would directly benefit her, Abby conformed.

"Mrs. Milburn must be dead by now," Abby continued. "She was old when she was our babysitter."

"Yes, she's long gone," Elizabeth said. "Those clear glass marbles at the top of the stairs… She knew to be wary of you."

"She was awful," added Abby of their mother's favorite and strictest babysitter. "If she had fallen and broken something, we would have been free of her for a few months. You would have been thanking me."

"Thanking you?" Elizabeth repeated.

"Well, I'm tamer now," Abby asserted.

"Only around people you want to make money off of," responded Elizabeth. "Real estate was the best thing that happened to you."

"Will you house hunt with me?" Abby asked Elizabeth. "I'm looking at rentals online now."

"Of course," Elizabeth said.

"What gym should I join?" she asked.

"FIT is good, or there are lots of boutique gyms," Elizabeth offered. "Oh, and I definitely want you to come with me to Yogi Jack's classes. Do you remember when I told you about him? The hot one with the groupies? He also offers private sessions that are supposed to be amazing. My friend Adair said her sessions with him are the best two hours of her week."

"Sign me up," Abby said.

4

"Are you excited for your first yoga class in Connecticut?" Elizabeth asked Abby, watching her exit her black BMW 650i. Wearing nude-colored FitFlops and an all-black ensemble of Lululemon yoga pants, fitted tank top, and Patagonia fleece, Abby looked pretty and polished.

"Absolutely," said Abby. "I was up until two o'clock this morning unpacking boxes. My back is in knots."

"Based on the number of cars already in the parking lot, it looks like the class is nearly full," warned Elizabeth. "We better go in and put down our mats."

Yogi Jack's studio was on a small, one-way side street off of Cannondale's main avenue. It was located in a converted art deco-style bank that dated to the 1930s. Its design—a fortified one-story, four-bay rectangular brick building with a large, open interior space—was ideal for yoga.

"Nice building," Abby said as they walked up the worn granite stairs to the original bronze doors. "I love when towns preserve vintage structures like this."

"The vault is used for the daycare," said Elizabeth.

"Quinn and Lily would love that," said Abby. "Let's come back on a weekend."

Hearing the hum of accumulated whispers in the studio, Elizabeth said, "Prepare yourself. Until class starts, there's nothing 'Zen' about the atmosphere. It's ladies' social hour."

"Got it," Abby noted.

The room was nearly full. Elizabeth and Abby found an open space in the back right corner. As they settled in, Tory Blume entered and rolled out her mat next to Elizabeth's.

"Hi, Elizabeth," she said. "Late this morning? You never sit this far back."

"Yes, Tory, a bit late today," said Elizabeth, annoyed to see that Tory would be next to her during class.

"Who are you with?" Tory whispered as she peered around Elizabeth. "You two could be twins."

"Tory, this is my sister, Abby," responded Elizabeth. "She just moved to town with her two kids."

"Abby!" Tory said incredulously. "I should have known. Now I understand why you're in the back corner. Trying to keep a low profile, huh?"

Abby smiled warily at Tory and waited. She knew what was coming next.

"I heard about your husband, Colin," Tory continued. "I followed the story really closely. I'm so sorry for you. To be left with two young kids and no life insurance money... It must have been terrible for your kids to see their dad's suicide played on the news over and over and over again. I was praying for another tragedy so that the reporters would have a new story to focus on."

Abby, who was used to passive-aggressive-type condolences from strangers and friends alike, simply smiled and said, "Thank you."

"Few of us in Cannondale knew Elizabeth was related to you until several days after it happened," Tory continued. "Your sister can be infuriatingly private. I was the one who organized the dinner drop-off for her. Elizabeth, did you tell her about it? We had thirty-seven women sign up. Elizabeth didn't have to worry about making meals for over a month."

"I appreciated that very much," Elizabeth said, still angered by how this unrequested act indebted her to Tory and a number of other women she barely knew. "The lemon chicken your housekeeper made was delicious."

"You're welcome," Tory said. "Isn't Lucy a good cook? I'm hopeless in the kitchen… So why did you move to Cannondale?" Tory asked Abby.

"Work. I'm running White's Realty," responded Abby.

"Oh, that's fortuitous," said Tory. "Gene asked me to get a price opinion on our house just last night. He wants to go to town hall with it and dispute the taxes on our home. The last assessment was done in 2007 when home prices were sky-high."

"I'd be happy to introduce you to one of my colleagues," said Abby. "I'm having lunch tomorrow with one of our top producers, Cecily Morgan. Do you want to join us? She could tour your home after lunch."

"Can't tomorrow," said Tory. "I have a private session with my trainer at noon."

"We're scheduled for a late lunch, though, starting at one thirty," said Abby.

"Still can't do it," said Tory. "By that point, I'll be fucking him."

"You'll be doing what?" choked out Elizabeth. Abby laughed.

"Was that too blunt?" Tory asked, feeding off Abby's amusement. "I assumed you knew, Elizabeth," she added. "Mitchell has sex with all his private clients. It's the perk he offers to make up for charging $350 a session."

"He must be good," joked Abby. "Anyway, let's exchange numbers after class and then we can find a date that works for you to meet Cecily."

Elizabeth had met Tory two years before through a mutual friend who thought Elizabeth's career in journalism and Tory's background in media would be a good connection point. Elizabeth was eager to meet likeminded women in town, having not met many since relocating from Manhattan. Being career-focused put her in a different mindset than many local women.

Their original introduction happened during a party, and Elizabeth initially found Tory's frank personality funny and refreshing. Afterward, Tory invited the Kellys over for dinner.

Several weeks later, Andrew and Elizabeth stood on the porch of the Blumes' new home. It was an updated antique, similar in style to the home the Kellys purchased. Unlike the slew of large, generically designed homes that were currently being built in Fairfield County, Elizabeth and Andrew admired its details and proportions.

"Hi, kids," said Tory as she and her husband, Gene, greeted them at the door. "So glad you could make it."

"Thanks for having us," Elizabeth replied.

"We cracked the wine a few hours ago and need you to join us before we get in trouble," said Gene. "Anna and Devin are at my parents' home for a sleepover, so we'll be enjoying tonight to the fullest!"

"That sounds promising," Andrew replied.

After a tour of their home and a few pleasantries, Andrew and Gene went outside to grill the main course. Elizabeth helped Tory make a salad.

"So how did you meet Gene?" Elizabeth asked as she chopped a pepper.

"In college," Tory replied. "He was the guy who always followed me around. It was love at first sight for him."

"How nice," Elizabeth responded, feeling instantly uncomfortable and hoping she was joking.

"But I wasn't into Gene during college," Tory confessed. "I dated a guy named Brad Hagerty. Brad and Gene were fraternity brothers. Brad is one of those perfect guys—handsome, rich, fun. We dated on and off for years after college, but he wouldn't get serious with me. We'd break up, and I would date someone else, but his trust fund always lured me back. It took me a long time to realize he was never going to marry me."

Tory went on to explain how, as her thirty-fifth birthday approached, she started to panic that she would never marry. At the same time, Brad was planning a move alone to the West coast. "I called Gene—we'd stayed in touch—and asked if he wanted to go out," she said. "He was freshly divorced. We went to dinner, and that was that. We've been married six years."

"Oh!" Elizabeth said, more accustomed to sugarcoated, humorous versions of how married couples first met.

"The good news is that Gene will always love me more than I love him," she went on. "That's a guarantee."

Elizabeth's startled eyes wandered to Tory and Gene's wedding portrait. There stood doughy, awkward Gene enthusiastically embracing petite, pretty Tory. After all those years, he'd finally landed her. How sad the truth was for him.

Elizabeth changed the subject.

"So do you ever think about freelancing or consulting?" Elizabeth asked. "You had such a great career in sports' television."

With a look that indicated Elizabeth was completely off the mark, Tory said, "Not at all. I was becoming one of those tough spinster types with a furrowed brow. I was embarrassed to still be working over the age of thirty. I wanted to be married and quit working altogether."

Again, all Elizabeth could say was "Oh." Elizabeth thought about how much she enjoyed work. How, if she ever quit, she would use her skills volunteering. *Who decided that a woman having a successful career is embarrassing?* Elizabeth thought.

"Don't you hate going into the office?" Tory asked.

"No, I actually like my job," Elizabeth asserted. "It gives me a lot of fulfillment, and I work with interesting people. I'd be bored otherwise."

Knowing that comment wouldn't lead to anything with Tory, Elizabeth changed the subject again. This time, she picked a safe topic, something every woman she encountered in Cannondale liked to discuss.

"I love your new home," Elizabeth said. "It's enchanting."

"*Enchanting*," Tory quipped, "as in a charming little cottage?"

"No," responded Elizabeth. "Enchanting as in delightful. I love antiques. Your home is similar to ours."

"Well, I don't think our home is big enough for our family of four, but Gene put me on a budget when I went house hunting. We have plenty of money, but Gene wants to keep some of our money liquid."

Am I supposed to feel sorry for her? Elizabeth thought. She only knew a handful of people who didn't have a limit to what they could spend on a home.

In the blink of an eye, Tory rolled out architectural plans, chattering about the large addition she was planning. As Elizabeth listened, she wondered why Tory felt the need to immediately add two more bedrooms, a library, and a large sunroom with a terrace to the four thousand square foot, four-bedroom house. In order to do so, the fully landscaped pool would have to be moved.

Then, looking conspiratorial, Tory abruptly stopped talking about the addition and leaned in toward Elizabeth.

"Can you keep a secret?" she asked.

"I think so," Elizabeth replied, equally curious and afraid of whatever confidence Tory wanted her to keep.

"I've told Gene that I'm pregnant and that we have to add an addition to the house as soon as possible!"

"Congratulations," Elizabeth perfunctorily said, noting Tory's nearly empty wineglass. Since Gene and Andrew went outside, Tory had downed two glasses of Pinot Grigio. "That's exciting news. You're not even showing yet. How far along are you?"

"I'm not pregnant," Tory said with the largest smile Elizabeth had seen on her face to date. "Being pregnant was the only way I could convince Gene to let me go ahead with the addition. After playing the morning sickness act for a few more months—which will also justify my hiring a live-in nanny—I'll fake a miscarriage. By that point, our addition will be in full swing."

She is actually faking a pregnancy to get a bigger house and a nanny, Elizabeth thought.

"Wow!" she said, finding her words. "That's quite a lie. Now I understand why it was important for you to marry someone who loves you more than you love him."

"Exactly," Tory replied.

5

Just before 10:00 a.m., the lights lowered and Yogi Jack entered the studio. He was simply dressed, wearing a fitted sage-green T-shirt and a pair of loose black Nike shorts. Already in place in the front of the room was Jack's trademark mat, imprinted with a female silhouette in meditation Buddha pose. He settled onto it, moving into cross-legged sukhasana. As Jack looked around the room and silently greeted his students, he rocked his hips back and forth, getting into full position. He closed his eyes.

Abby shot Elizabeth a look of approval. "He's a better-looking Andrew McCarthy," she whispered, referring to the eighties teen idol in the movies *St. Elmo's Fire and Pretty in Pink.*

Elizabeth smiled and nodded.

"No wedding ring," Abby noted.

"No," Elizabeth whispered.

"Good morning!" Jack said, opening his eyes and surveying the room again.

"Good morning!" The women echoed back.

"I hope everyone is well today," Jack cooed. "I've missed you. It's nice to see so many friendly faces.

"Today's practice will be ashtanga yoga, but first I would like to share information about a yoga practice I'm studying. As those of you who regularly take my classes know, I am close to becoming an official *kundalini* yoga practitioner. I have been studying under Dr. Guru Giani Ghan Khalsa Singh, a visiting scholar from the Mendocino Academy. He's the head of the International Kundalini Yoga Teachers Association. I have eight hours left in the over two-hundred-hour teacher training program. In two weeks time, I will start the first of a series of kundalini yoga workshops. I'll be running them here, in my studio, from eight to ten o'clock on Thursday nights."

He paused and looked for responses from his students.

"Who in the room has heard of kundalini?" Jack asked.

A few hands shot up.

Yogi Jack lips ticked up in an amused smile. "Okay, I'm glad it's not a new concept for everyone," he said. "For those who are unfamiliar, let me explain.

"Within each of our bodies, there is an energy that has infinite capabilities. The Hindus call this energy kundalini, and, in their beliefs, it's coiled like a serpent at the base of the spine. Kundalini is the body's unconscious libidinal energy. It lies dormant, awaiting an awakening stimulus to unfold its potential. Kundalini can be woken in many ways, including through kundalini yoga, which employs a yogic combination of movement, breathing, chanting, and meditation. Once aroused, it travels through the body and, with proper guidance, eventually reaches the mind.

"My workshop will be distinctive in that it unites kundalini with Western tantra practices. The goal of my classes will be to build physical, mental, and spiritual strength while uncoiling the sacred, sleeping sexuality that exists in all of us. Once woken, this sexuality allows for the discovery of personal potential and vitality.

"For those of you interested in my workshop, please speak with me after class or visit my website."

One woman's hand rose. Yogi Jack turned to her. "Hi, Rachel, nice to see you here today. Do you have a question?"

"Yes, I do," she said. "I've heard of kundalini awakenings and that they can be quite intense. One description I read described it as feeling like you're plugged into a wall and lit up like a Christmas tree. Have you personally experienced kundalini awakening?"

"Yes, I have," Jack replied, "and what you describe would be an accurate way to illustrate my experience. My awakening was electric, but not all of them are intense. Some of you may have already experienced it without knowing. Those who have now need guidance to move the energy through the body, which leads to divine wisdom. Kundalini awakenings can be brought on by many things, including childbirth and other traumas, a guru's laying of hands, a love affair, or guided meditation. The kundalini awakening experience varies greatly."

Another hand went up.

"Hi, Claire," Jack said, turning toward her.

"Will you share your kundalini awakening experience with the class?" she asked.

"Yes," he replied. "Mine occurred last summer, during a three-day-long retreat called 'Taste of Tantra' in Johnson, Vermont. It was led by Joh Eagle, a world-renowned tantric expert. The first few days of the retreat involved exercises meant to strip away ego defenses, enabling the participants to get to a real place that allows for exploration and growth.

"With various partners over the first two days, I did breathing, prolonged eye contact, 'soul gazing,' visualization, and therapy-like exercises. Each activity made me feel more open, more vulnerable, and more revealed.

"On the morning of our third day, after breakfast and a five-mile hike up Madonna Peak, we met at the top of the mountain for tantric movement exercises. We did a series of classic partner poses: downward-facing dogs, pelvic tilts, and Hercules with one partner. They were all body on body and very intimate. The last exercise was the *yab-yum*. It's a tantric position where partners sit in each other's laps and wrap their legs around one another so that the bodies are lined up heart-to-heart and eye-to-eye.

"My partner Jackie and I were in yab-yum doing the related tantric breathing exercises and hip undulation. That's when it struck. My body lurched forward at her, and then, as if pulled by a force, plunged backward. I started to shake uncontrollably. Initially, I thought I was having a full-body orgasm, but then I realized it was something much more powerful. I trembled for about two minutes. During most of it, I felt like I was going to die, that my heart would stop. But then it passed and, in my relief, I started to weep, crying uncontrollably. Jackie cradled me until I calmed down.

"Later, when we were back at the retreat center, I met with Joh Eagle. He told me that what I had experienced was a 'kundalini crisis,' which is when the awakening is so sudden it completely overwhelms the body. I have since learned that these 'crises' can be very dangerous, so the goal of my workshop will be to slowly awaken my students' kundalini."

Claire asked, "Are you different since your crisis—I mean, awakening?"

"Oh, yes," Jack enthusiastically responded, "in so many incredible ways. It was well worth the two minutes of wild panic. Since that day, there is an overall clarity to my thoughts and perceptions. It's as if I am finally seeing the world clearly, which can be upsetting, but my lucidity is coupled with a calmness and a feeling that I can handle whatever happens. There is a divinity to it. After kundalini awakenings, people claim to have greater sensitivity, creativity, spirituality, and wisdom, as well as psychic abilities, alpha sexual attraction, and newfound charisma."

Jack looked around the room again, noting the reactions. He smiled and asked, "So who is ready for the movement part of class to start?"

"I am," several women in the class called out.

"Okay, let's move to downward-facing dog and walk the dog out," he said, referring to a version of the pose where legs alternatively bend and straighten to make the stretch less intense.

From that pose, Jack led the class through a series of standing positions and sun salutations. He moved through the studio, silently adjusting his students. The women were then instructed to move from downward dog to cat pose.

Once everyone was on all fours, Yogi Jack intoned, "Close your eyes. Don't think about your mat neighbors. Move your body the way it wants to go. Give yourself over to what the body wants, what the body asks. Allow your movements to be driven from an unconscious place within. Then, when you find your happy spot, stop and settle."

Collectively, all the women in the room swayed in a slow, rhythmic way—forward and back and side-to-side. To release the neck, their heads moved in half circles. Eventually, some women leaned backward and sat in child's pose. Others lay prone in plank.

Abby sat in child's pose. To release her back, she stretched her arms in front of her. Jack moved behind Abby and rested his hands at the base of her spine. A few moments later he turned and sat so that his bottom was back to back with hers. Jack leaned his body backward, covering her. His arms reached over her head so he could lay the backs of his hands on top of hers. He slowed his breathing to be in sync with Abby's.

They sat together like that for several minutes, breathing united, rising and falling. Jack slowly sat up and turned. He gently laid his hands on her lower back again. Silently, he rose and returned to his mat.

At the end of class, Elizabeth turned her head toward Abby's prone body. Abby's eyes were closed. She looked like she might be asleep. Elizabeth smiled. It was rare to see her intense sister so relaxed.

Elizabeth closed her eyes again, hoping Tory would leave without saying good-bye. Soon she felt a small burst of air as Tory lifted her mat, and she thankfully heard her footsteps leading away.

Phew, Elizabeth thought.

The noise level in the studio increased as more women stood, chatting and rolling up their mats. Elizabeth looked at Abby again and saw her eyes start to flutter. "So what did you think?" she asked her.

"Really good," Abby replied, fighting full consciousness. "I fell asleep during shavasana. I haven't felt this relaxed in over a year."

Elizabeth got up on her knees and started rolling up her mat. She walked to the wall where she and Abby had left their shoes and retrieved them. She handed Abby her sandals and sat to put her own shoes on.

Jack was in the center of the room saying good-bye to his students. As usual, there was much hugging and kissing as the women thanked him and told him they would be back. Abby watched. With shoes on, the two sisters picked up their rolled mats and walked toward Jack. There was a short line of ladies waiting to speak with him.

Elizabeth looked at her watch then and realized she needed to go. "Abby, I've got to run," she said.

"Do you have just a minute to wait with me?" Abby asked. "I have a quick question about kundalini."

Elizabeth was shocked by Abby and agreed. The Abby she knew—the Abby before her husband killed himself—would never buy into the concept of a dormant, infinite energy in her body. If anything, Abby always seemed to have too much energy pulsing through her veins, making her mind race and propelling her into action. She was one of those people who got up in the morning with a start and was on the go until she exhaustively crashed at the end of the day.

Abby also thought organized religion was a "bunch of crap," a way to control the masses. Abby wasn't privately spiritual, nor did she believe that the universe gave out signs.

"My friend Marty believes that every time she sees a cardinal, it's her deceased sister communicating with her," Abby once told Elizabeth. "Can you believe that? Marty has six birdfeeders and buys seed that attracts cardinals. And it's not like those birds are rare in this part of the country."

Abby thought gurus and zshamans were for lost souls. "It's all about sex and money," she had said in the past. "Those shaman types just want to sleep with their 'flock' and be financially supported by them."

Elizabeth wondered if Abby's opinion of yoga instructors who had a guru-like following were the same.

Once it was their turn to speak with Yogi Jack, Abby introduced herself. Jack smiled and extended his hands, encircling her right one with both of his own. "It's wonderful to have a new student," he said. "I enjoy having your sister, Elizabeth, in my class."

"May I ask you a question about kundalini?" Abby said.

"Of course," Jack responded brightly. "It's one of my favorite subjects."

"I'm interested in learning more about the practice," she said. "I will sign up for your workshop but, in the meantime, do you recommend any books on the subject?"

"I do," Jack responded. "I've read a lot about it. I enjoyed *The Serpent Power: The Secrets of Tantric and Shaktic Yoga* by Arthur Avalon, who is an expert on tantric. Or *Awakening Kundalini: The Path to Radical Freedom* by the scholar Dr. Lawrence Edwards. Another good book is *The Psychology of Kundalini Yoga* by C. G. Jung. If you are interested specifically in learning about our bodies' various energies, Anodea Judith, who is an expert on the subject and a healer, wrote a book called *Wheels of Life: A User's Guide to the Chakra System*.

"Thank you," said Abby. "Authors Avalon, Edwards, Jung, and Judith. I'll look them up."

"Why don't we get together over coffee to discuss it more?" Jack offered. "I have some time open tomorrow morning. Want to meet at Brioche?"

"I'd like that," Abby responded. "Elizabeth, will you join us?"

"Sure," Elizabeth said, completely surprised.

The following morning, Elizabeth arrived early to Maple Street, entered Brioche and picked a table near a window that looked out at the bustle on the late morning street. The town center radiated off of two adjoining streets: Maple and Main. Main Street was the Cannondale's primary thoroughfare when the town was founded in 1731, but as it grew, city planners allowed retail business to spread to Maple and then adjoining side streets.

Once a prim town of lovely, privately owned shops, restaurants, and a small two-screen cinema, it had been invaded in the last few decades by chain stores such as CVS Pharmacy, Ann Taylor, and Sleepy's. Despite the infiltration necessary to fill the overdevelopment of the late 1990s, the town retained its quaint appearance through strict zoning laws—as a result, even the Dunkin' Donuts looked picturesque. The retail establishments were housed in charming one- and two-story buildings of alternating red brick and white clapboard. Their first stories had tastefully framed plate-glass and were often adorned with colorful awnings. Hinting at the safety of its streets, large potted plants and topiaries dotted the sidewalks and remained unchained overnight. The second stories were ornamented with shuttered nine-over-nine sash windows and were topped with slate roofs and cupolas. An occasional metal-vented air conditioner jutted from a second-floor window, its bulk and awkwardness hinting at the continued existence of the town's thrifty old-timers.

Despite the overall sense of calm one felt while shopping in a town of historically inspired architecture with a well-funded police force, there was also an obvious tension between what was old and what was new.

The town was founded by a group of Protestants, many of whose offspring still subscribed to their parents' conservative beliefs and prudence. When it came to money, a strong dichotomy fueled by guilt and fostered by righteousness existed within them. They owned several homes in various locales but refused to drive a car that fell into the high-end luxury category. They were members of multiple country clubs but recycled soda cans religiously for the five-cent deposit. They were as likely to find a winter coat in a local consignment shop as they would a department store, and finding one secondhand qualified as a major victory. Words like "democrats," "soup kitchens," and "welfare recipients" slid from their mouths with a hiss.

In exact opposition to the WASPs were newer arrivals who moved to Cannondale for its Mayflower cache. They'd made their mark in the world more recently and hoped that a number of years in an affluent town would shed them of their "new money" status. This group, which tended to enjoy luxury and excess, brought profound changes to the town.

The de rigueur Chevy Malibu Classic wood-paneled station wagons that once filled Maple Street parking lots were replaced first by BMWs, Saabs, and Mercedes and then by larger, showier Range Rovers, Porsche Cayennes, and Escalades. The new arrivals' varied tastes also brought a greater variety of restaurants—Indian, Thai, crepe, Brazilian, sushi, and upscale Mexican restaurants settled alongside the diners, Chinese takeout, Italian, and French restaurants that had dotted the town for years. Also, to appeal to those with higher expectations, a new YMCA with state-of-the-art equipment and better facilities replaced a dated, but sufficient, version. It was solely for the kids. This group of parents exercised at boutique gyms and with personal trainers.

When spending time with people from either group, there was a depressing feeling that they lacked control of their lives. They both felt entitled, but the originals were driven by restraint and the newer arrivals were driven by self-indulgence. They didn't fully comprehend their own motivators, which made them ripe for manipulation.

It was while Elizabeth was watching the driver of an Escalade ESV attempt to park in a spot several feet shy of the space needed that Jack entered Brioche. He wore a collared shirt, navy V-neck sweater, and olive-colored wide whale corduroys. Elizabeth realized this was the first time she had seen him dressed in something other than exercise clothing. *He is extremely handsome,* she thought.

Jack held the door open for a woman behind him, chatting as they moved into the café. He saw Elizabeth and, as he neared the table, extended his arms widely, offering her a hug. Elizabeth stood and embraced him but wasn't totally comfortable with their growing familiarity. She'd learned too much about him since beginning his classes.

"May I get you something?" she offered, feeling the need to create space between them until Abby arrived.

"Green tea, please," he said, "with one raw sugar."

"I'll be right back," she responded.

While Elizabeth stood in line, Abby entered the café. She was dressed for work in a fitted navy Hugo Boss suit, a matching navy collared shirt, and brown heeled Jimmy Choo boots, which made her look much taller than her five foot five frame. Her long, straight, chestnut-colored hair was pulled back into a neat ponytail, and, as always, her makeup was light.

She saw Jack before she saw Elizabeth and headed over to him. He greeted her in a similarly warm way. As Abby settled into a chair next to Jack, she made eye contact with Elizabeth. She mouthed the words "cappuccino" and "lemon scone." Elizabeth smiled, thinking that was exactly what she would have ordered for her.

When Elizabeth returned to the table, Jack was talking about an upcoming charity event he was organizing. "All the proceeds will go to a village in West Bengal near the border of Nepal," he said. "I'm hoping to raise enough money to build a large gathering space for the women so they can produce handmade goods. It would also have dual use as a daycare and school for their children."

"Oh, is this the event you mentioned in class recently?" asked Elizabeth as she sat down and passed their drinks and Abby's scone. "The Auntie Arts charity benefit at The Glass House?"

"Yes," said Jack, nodding thankfully to Elizabeth and wrapping his hands around the warm teacup. "It's going to be take place in peak foliage season—November seventh. As long as there are no storms, the property will be aglow with autumnal colors."

Jack went on to explain how the party would take place in The Glass House estate's various buildings. Each building was relatively small, so most of the estate's structures would be used.

"When the guests first arrive, they will be directed to the sculpture gallery, where a small orchestra will be playing classical Indian music and cocktails will be served," he explained. "From there, guests can go to any of the other sites. Heavy *hors d' oeuvres* and cocktails will be served in the painting gallery and library, and the silent auction tables will also be set up those spaces. Dessert and champagne will be served in the Glass House. There will be a hookah lounge with henna stations in the guest house and an Indi-Pop band and dance floor in the lake pavilion building."

"The auction items are impressive," Elizabeth added, buttering her croissant. "A MINI Cooper, a private yoga session with Rodney Yee, an interior design consultation with India Hicks…"

"Yes, we have amassed a nice selection," Jack agreed, taking a sip of tea. "The full list will be posted on my website next week."

"Are you looking for sponsors?" asked Abby. "I can suggest it to the Bloom Brothers. They're trying to make inroads into the community since acquiring White's Realty."

"That would be wonderful," he enthused. "We already have a number of sponsors, including Longchamp, Baccarat, Ralph Lauren, and *Fairfield County Lux Magazine*, but we can always use more. I'll send you a link to the sponsor form on my website."

"Your charity is called Auntie Arts, right?" asked Elizabeth.

Jack nodded. "Yes. 'Auntie' is an affectionate term used for Indian women. Right now I'm working with women in West Bengal, teaching them how to adapt their handicrafts to appeal to the American market. Before I became a yogi, I worked for a nonprofit called CANstruct. I oversaw school development of impoverished areas in that state. My time there developed both my love of yoga and my fondness for the locals, including their crafts. I've missed nonprofit work, so about five years ago I set up this charity and have been slowly building it. Its goal is to empower and educate women in the poorest areas of India, starting with West Bengal."

"What do the women make?" Elizabeth asked, breaking off a small piece of scone.

"Hand-embroidered silk tunics and shawls," Jack responded, his expression brightening. "They are really beautiful. Detailed. Colorful. Made from the finest Indian silk. And what makes the product unique is how the traditional Indian designs are adapted to suit current American and European trends."

"Where do you sell them?" asked Abby, wondering if she had already seen them on a sales rack somewhere.

"I coordinate with buyers at high-end stores like Barneys and Henri Bendel, as well as with boutiques, exclusive resorts, and hotel chains that have shops in vacation areas like Palm Beach and the Caribbean," he responded. "Getting it into the right stores has granted me a few fun trips."

"What about the profit? Where does it go?" inquired Abby, sipping her cappuccino.

"The artisans are paid a salary," Jack said, "and whatever is left over is used to aid the community in various ways—mostly with infrastructure, food, and medical aid. It's been amazing to see how the income empowers them within the community. Here, I have some pictures on my phone of the artisans." Jack pulled his phone from his pants pocket, queued the images, and handed it to Abby. "The women I work with specialize in a type of embroidery called sozni," he explained as Elizabeth leaned in to review the images with Abby. "It's a centuries-old tradition. Colorful silk and metallic threads are sewn into dyed silk fabric."

The first image was of a beautiful Indian girl dressed in layers of brightly colored, embroidered shawls. She looked about six years old and smiled shyly for the camera. "Her mother is one of my best embroiders," Jack noted.

The next picture showed women posing, wearing silk tunics and veils. "Note the garments' level of detail," Jack said, reaching over and zooming in on the image for the sisters. "It takes one woman two weeks to make a shawl," he added.

The next photo was of the women at work, seated under a tented structure on what appeared to be a scorching-hot day. They were dressed in a riot of colors and sitting cross-legged on mats in a large circle. "Working outside is far from ideal," Jack stated. "It can be unbearably hot and dusty, especially during the summer. That's why I want to build them a facility." The next images demonstrated the difference in garments made to appeal to Indian markets compared to international markets.

"Just one more," Jack noted. "This last one is of a family standing in front of their home, which the wife, who is one of my embroiders, helped purchase."

"That's so admirable," Elizabeth said, taking in the woman's proud expression. "Where do you find the time to run it in addition to your yoga business?"

"I get a lot of help from friends, including some of my students," said Jack. "Do you know Adair Burns? She's a huge help to me. In fact, she and several of my other students organized the entire benefit."

Tucking his phone back into his pants' pocket, Jack said, "Now, aren't we here to talk about kundalini?"

"Yes," Abby responded, nodding. "I signed up for your workshop last night."

"I know," Jack said. "I saw this morning. Thank you. Elizabeth, will you be signing up, too?"

"I'm not sure yet," she said. "My kids have after-school commitments on Thursdays. I need to think about it."

"Okay. I hope you will," Jack responded. Turning back to Abby, he said, "And what are your questions? I'll try my best to answer them."

Abby stared down into her cappuccino for a moment before answering. "Kundalini is one of those 'leap of faith' concepts, and I'm traditionally not one to take a leap. I've never been religious, but I do find solace in yoga," she hesitated for a moment, "...especially since my husband Colin died several months ago. So when you mentioned kundalini and its relationship to yoga, it intrigued me. I've always relied on myself, so the idea of something existing within me that, once nurtured, would give me greater insight and peace appeals to me. I'm still struggling with Colin's death, and I have two children who miss their father. I need to be in a good mental place for them."

"I can't think of a better reason to seek help," said Jack as he reached out and momentarily cupped her hand in his. "I like to tell my students that there is no downside to believing in kundalini. If you discover it within yourself, the benefits are amazing."

"I know you explained a bit about it in class yesterday, but I'm still unclear on how exactly it works within us?" Abby asked.

Jack settled back into his chair. "As the libidinal energy in the body, kundalini is our universal life force," he explained. "Releasing it allows us to connect to a loving and benevolent energy bigger than our individual selves. The connection to something outside of the self gives a sense of happiness and security that otherwise can't exist. This well-being frees the mind of anxiety and allows it to focus on the discovery of personal potential."

"Do kundalini masters believe most of us live our entire lives without its release? With it stalled inside our bodies?" she inquired.

"The masters generally don't comment on that since it can't be known for sure, but if you look at the level of unhappiness in the world—even in the developed world where we have so many conveniences and luxuries—one would think it's still locked or blocked within most of us. We don't appear to be as psychologically and emotionally evolved as we are in other ways."

"That makes a lot of sense," Abby commented, pausing to think for a moment. "Can you give me a sense of how your workshop will encourage kundalini's release and movement through the body?"

"Kundalini yoga is specifically designed to encourage release because it involves a series of poses that stimulate the entire spinal cord and pelvic regions," Jack explained. "The practice's related breathing exercises and mediation help aid passage through the various chakras, which are the body's subtle energy points. There are a total of seven," he held up seven fingers and then pointed to the base of his head, "with the last one called 'the crown,' located behind the skull. The books I recommended to you yesterday go into great detail about the chakras. Anyway, the movement of the kundalini energy through the body isn't a quick path, because people carry their pain in different ways and in different places in the body. Personal trauma, for instance, creates blockages within the chakras that stop the kundalini energy flow. You may not be aware of it when your energy hits one of these obstacles, but a kundalini master would be. His job—in this case, my job—is to guide you through the related distress so the energy can flow through."

"In yesterday's class you mentioned that there's a tantric aspect to your workshop? Can you tell me about that?" Abby asked.

"The reason my workshop combines kundalini yoga with Western tantric practices is because the primary way to move the libidinal energy through the body is by embracing desire. Once your kundalini is awakened, it will be active every time you are sexually aroused." Jack leaned forward in his seat, explaining, "Every time you have sex, there is the potential for its movement in the body. But not all sex is the same. When you engage in what I like to call monotonous sex, which is intimacy with a long-term partner, the body's emotional, intellectual, and spiritual systems harmonize—there is nothing new, no heightened awareness in the body. But when you engage in one of your sexual fantasies, there is higher sexual energy and sex hormone production. It's caused by the thrill of doing what our society has labeled as forbidden, but is, in fact, what the body and mind craves. Engaging in a sexual fantasy best facilitates kundalini's movement through the chakras. It's believed that you can even bypass an energy blockage when in the throes of acting out a fantasy."

"Acting out a fantasy?" Abby inquired, exchanging a look with Elizabeth.

"Yes," said Jack. "If you're as interested as you sound, why don't we start meeting once a week for private kundalini yoga sessions? I believe you would find private sessions very helpful in combination with my workshop."

"I'd like that," said Abby, smiling.

7

After Jack left Brioche, Elizabeth leaned toward her sister. "Before you sign up for private sessions with Jack, I think you need to know more about him," she said in a hushed voice.

"Okay," Abby agreed, "but I thought you liked him?"

"I like his yoga classes," Elizabeth corrected.

"If I sign up for a private session, is he going to think I definitely want to sleep with him?" Abby asked.

"He sleeps with a lot of his private clients," Elizabeth disclosed. "Maybe all of them."

"Well, the potential of getting an STD aside, it wouldn't be such a bad thing," Abby assessed. "With Jack I wouldn't have to worry about a commitment, which is the last thing I want right now."

"But there's more to him that you should know before getting involved," said Elizabeth. "During the latter part of your conversation, he…alluded to it."

"Okay," she responded. "What is it?"

"You can't tell anyone," insisted Elizabeth, starring into Abby's eyes. "You have to absolutely swear to me that you will never repeat what I'm going to tell you."

"I won't," she replied.

"Promise," Elizabeth demanded.

"Okay, I promise," Abby insisted. "Sheesh!"

"Jack offers a service beyond yoga instruction that's tied to kundalini and embracing one's desires," she explained. "He literally facilitates his private clients' sexual fantasies: lesbianism, threesomes, orgies, BDSM... Basically anything his clients want. Jack calls the service 'sexcapades' and only offers it to his private clients. You know my friend Kate, the one with the catering business?"

"Yes," said Abby, her interest piqued.

"He does it for her, and I *know* he does it for other clients, too," Elizabeth continued.

"How did she get involved with him?" Abby asked.

"Kate became friends with Jack about a year ago, which led to private sessions," Elizabeth explained. "Several months ago Jack asked her about her sexual interests, and she admitted having developed a curiosity about lesbians. Kate's husband is abusive, and she wondered if she could form a stronger bond with a female given the inherent like-mindedness. That's when Jack told her about his sexcapades service. About once a month, she visits an estate he takes care of. There's a converted safe room-type space on the third floor. That's where she meets with a woman named Carly.

"Are you serious?" Abby asked.

"Yes, but again, you can't tell anyone," Elizabeth said. "Kate had to sign a confidentiality agreement."

"Wow," said Abby. Then, with an edge of gossip to her voice, she asked, "Do you know who else who uses the service?"

"When Jack first explained it to Kate, he told her about a young Greenwich widow who witnessed her husband's violent death," Elizabeth responded. "They were walking across a street, and he was hit by a car. The wife feels incredibly guilty because she was the one pulling him across the road. Jack didn't go into more specifics because of the confidentiality agreement, but he did explain how sexcapades helped her work through her grief."

"That scenario sounds familiar, doesn't it?" Abby said, annoyed. "Anyone else?"

"Kate thinks a woman named Leigh Gilding is a client, but she isn't positive."

"I know a Leigh Gilding from New York," said Abby. "Is the one you know a landscape designer?"

"Yes," acknowledged Elizabeth. "Petite, blonde, pretty, and can be a total bitch."

"That's got to be the same one," Abby laughed. "She was a client of mine a number of years ago. I heard she moved to a suburb, but I don't know where."

"Here, evidently."

"Do you know what other fantasies he enables?" asked Abby.

"No, but according to Kate, he has done the other ones I mentioned. And he suggested that, in addition to meeting with Carly, Kate should entertain the idea of a threesome *and* an orgy. He said she needs to learn how to trust men again, and he wants to slowly introduce men into the trysts he arranges for her."

"An orgy as a way to trust men again?" scoffed Abby. "How does that work?"

"I'm just repeating what she said," Elizabeth responded, raising her hands.

"How does Kate know about Leigh?" Abby questioned.

"She overheard Jack on the phone one day," Elizabeth said.

"So where's the house?" Abby asked.

"It's on Old Farm Highway," Elizabeth divulged. "It's called Le Beau Château. An elderly Manhattan heiress named Georgette Ark owns it."

"Have you ever been there?" asked Abby.

"No, but it was featured in *Cannondale Cottages & Gardens Magazine* before I started working there, so I've seen pictures of its interior and the satellite buildings—did you know it has a large carriage barn? It's a gorgeous French chateau-style white-brick manor house with a mansard roof set on seventy acres. Shortly after it was featured in the magazine, there was a home invasion that turned violent." Abby's mouth dropped open, and Elizabeth nodded, continuing, "I know. Ark was tied up, and the intruders savagely beat her butler. She had to watch the whole thing—apparently she thought he was going to die. The housekeeper found them the next morning."

"Oh my God!"

"The experience terrified Ark, understandably, and she contemplated selling the house but instead had the third floor converted into a safe room. According to Kate, it can only be accessed from the closet in the master bedroom or from a secret rooftop hatch. Kate said it's tastefully decorated and doesn't feel much like a safe room. And, when looking at the home from the exterior, you can't even tell it has a third floor because of the mansard roof design."

Abby sat in silence for a minute before responding. "I wonder what Leigh's fantasy is."

Elizabeth shrugged noncommittally.

"What would you pick?" Abby asked Elizabeth, raising her eyebrows.

"That's a good question," she responded with a laugh. "There certainly are a lot of options. I would probably go with something straightforward and uncomplicated like…sex with a stranger."

"You don't need Jack to set that up," Abby responded. "Just go out to a bar alone."

"Oh, stop. How about you?" Elizabeth asked. "There can't be much that you haven't already tried."

"That's mean," said Abby.

"No!" protested Elizabeth. "Honest."

"Well, I do have an idea," Abby began. "Ever since Colin died, I've been having dreams about sleeping with the policemen and firemen who were at the scene that night. It's weird, though, because the sex always happens inside or on the roof of the University Club. Colin's not there, but he isn't dead, either...or at least I don't think he's dead because I never feel the panic I felt that night."

"Sounds like you think Colin's death could have been prevented if they were at the club before he jumped?" offered Elizabeth.

"But why would I be screwing them?" Abby asked.

"Because it's a dream," Elizabeth reasoned. "You associate feeling safe with them."

"Sergeant Morello still calls me every few weeks to check in," Abby said. "It's very sweet."

"I remember him," said Elizabeth. "He's cute. And single, right? If you're into policemen, why don't you ask him out?"

"He's not my type. What I need right now is something light and fun and distracting."

"Right, like sex with a yoga instructor or a sexcapade with an anonymous civil servant?" Elizabeth suggested.

"Or both," optioned Abby. "How could you have not told me sooner about the sexcapades going on out here?"

"I actually didn't even think to," Abby said. "Kate confided in me a few weeks ago, and you've had a lot more important things to focus on lately."

"So does Kate like having sex with a woman?" Abby asked. "Did she make the emotional connection she was looking for?"

"I know she likes being with Carly because it's so different from what she's used to," Elizabeth said.

"Has she gone into detail about it?" Abby asked.

"A little bit," Elizabeth responded. "I know they do the marathon foreplay that you hear about with lesbians. I would think it gets tedious, but she's into it."

"How do they orgasm?" Abby asked in a whisper. "Do they do that scissoring thing or oral or use toys?"

"I don't know," Elizabeth said, blushing. "She didn't go into *that* much detail with me."

"Why don't you ask her?" Abby responded.

"Because that's a totally inappropriate question!" said Elizabeth. "It implies that it's hard to achieve because there isn't a penis involved."

"I don't think so," said Abby. "It's just a question following a natural stream of thought."

"But I wouldn't ask *you* that," objected Elizabeth.

"And who said there isn't some kind of a penis involved?" asked Abby, ignoring her. "Have you ever seen one of those double-penetration dildos? They're these long—like, twenty-inch long—attached double dildos. Lesbians use them to screw each other at the same time."

"Oh my God!" Elizabeth stage-whispered. "How do you know about them?"

"Because," said Abby, smiling mischievously, "straight people can use them, too."

8

Jack always comes to me. He comes to me during the dead of night. I never know which evening it will be; the mystery elevates my nighttime routine to a thrilling ritual. I think of him in bed with me as I turn down my comforter, as I choose a petite silk nightie, as I moisturize my skin. Maybe tonight?

He knows my house well. He enters through the front door, walks through the foyer lined with the broad-stroke oils that my work has become known for, and up the twelve steps that lead to the second-floor landing and, eventually, my bedroom. He travels it easily in the dark and silently slips into my bed. He gently wakes me as his hand travels up my thigh and encircles my waist, pulling me close to him.

Some nights we lie together like that for hours, like two stacked spoons blanketed neatly in down. All nights we have sex, slowly, mindfully, guided by sensations.

He is always gone in the morning, which allows our intimacies to feel like a dream—a sweet, sensual dream. I savor that time, alone in bed, my memory full of the night before, devoid of the jarring visuals that often haunt me after a night's sleep. I can think of him and his warm body and his tenderness. I can think of his full lips on mine, of his slightly weathered hands touching me, of his kind murmurs.

I lie in bed for as long as that day's demands allow, drinking in the tangy scent of perspiration he leaves behind.

The night visits were his idea. I'd been his student for several months when the accident happened, when my private life was splashed all over the papers as a terrible tragedy. My husband Michael and I were crossing a street, holding hands, our arms stretched as I pulled him along. I'd seen a puppy on the other side of the street—a mutt that looked like a combination of basset hound and corgi, long ears dragging on the pavement, a short, stout, tailless form. An adorable misfit.

We were holding hands; I was pulling on his to get him to walk faster, and then my hand was empty. I hadn't seen or heard the car. It wasn't there when I scanned the streets and stepped off the curb.

I was told that the driver had turned onto the street that we were crossing and drove straight through a four-way stop. The driver was texting a friend, another teenager, when it happened. There was no warning, no screeching tires to attract my attention. Maybe Michael saw the car just before impact? I'd been smiling and looking toward the puppy, a childlike reaction that animals bring out in me. I was feeling nothing but pure joy at the moment I heard the impact. How can that be? How can those two things exist at the same time? There was only a sound, a horrible sound of two things colliding. A slam.

And then nothingness. An empty hand.

I turned and saw a blue Highlander driving away, revealing the broken body of my husband as it went. Michael. Facedown with his head turned to one side, a steadily growing puddle of blood around him. The hand I had been holding was awkwardly twisted, the arm outstretched with the palm facing up. His athletic legs splayed, his feet facing out, one shoe on, one shoe off.

By the time I got to him, he was gone. Lifeless. His eyes were frozen with half lids and, amazingly, a look of calm. I found solace in his expression.

Two weeks after the accident, after the funeral, after my family and friends had returned to their homes, when I was most despondent, Jack came unannounced to my home. He offered counseling and, eventually, after asking about my sexual fantasies, offered the night visits. He said he wanted me to learn how to trust again, to love again. He told me that we could start with this fantasy and, once I was ready for others to be explored, that he would help facilitate those, too. He told me it would change my life. That it would free me.

I'm not ready yet for my other fantasies. I'm not ready to move too far from the place where I am. But I need intimacy, and I need distraction. I need new, happier memories to slowly blot out the old.

Right now, I need him with his compassion—real or manufactured, I don't know for sure, and I don't care—and his discretion to come and then to go.

9

Within a few months of moving to Cannondale, Elizabeth met Kate Musto. Even though they appeared to have little in common, Elizabeth instantly liked her. She was quick, funny, and upbeat. She always seemed a bit frazzled. The two women were put together in a mothers' social circle that was part of the Cannondale Newcomers Group.

It was made up of twelve moms, and the weekly gathering offered them an opportunity to spend time with women going through the same infant-related experiences. Elizabeth had just given birth to her second child, Alice, and Kate to her third child, Madeline. The two women originally met at Svelte, a local trendy dress shop, a few weeks before the group started. Madeline had started screeching at the checkout. Kate was second in line. Elizabeth offered to help, and she and Kate tried to soothe the baby.

"I'm not leaving without this dress," Kate had said. "I have to go out tonight, and I'm still wearing maternity clothes. Nothing else fits." Kate started to push the stroller back and forth in a manic way that looked more agitating to the baby than soothing.

"Maddy, you are just going to have to wait today," she'd said. "Babies are so unpredictable."

Once Kate signed the receipt, she turned quickly and, holding the bag like a trophy, waved at Elizabeth.

"Mission accomplished!" she cheerfully said as Madeline wailed.

Kate had scurried for the exit, and in doing so, bumped into a table that was filled with hanging costume jewelry. She was out the door before the necklaces and bracelets crashed to the floor.

The first mothers' social gathering was at Karen Whitney's home. She was the President of the Cannondale Newcomers Group as well as the lady in charge of playgroups. She was polite to a fault but equally rigid and compulsively organized. On the day of the first meeting, petite, red-haired Karen—wearing crisp khakis and a matching fitted polo—met the women at her front door. She lived in a new mini-McMansion on a cul-de-sac.

The home was narrow with multiple rooflines that shot into the sky. It was painfully perfect, a sort of Barbie Dream House but colored in a more-fashionable beige shade with saffron shutters. The grounds were excessively manicured. Not even a leaf was out of place.

The interior is going to be perfectly ordered, Elizabeth thought as she lifted Alice from her car seat.

"Hi, ladies," Karen cooed. "What adorable infants!" Karen was friendly but all business. As the mothers struggled into her home with their babies and brimming designer baby bags, she placed a thick handout in their free hands.

"Now don't forget to remove your shoes," she said. "I don't want anything tracked inside."

Karen directed the women to a finished basement decorated in a tasteful version of Ralph Lauren's signature cottage-chic style. The walls and slip-covered furniture were ivory, the wool wall-to-wall carpeting was tan, navy pillows with tan piping dotted the upholstery, and the tables and cabinets were stained dark. Toys were neatly stored in labeled, dark wicker baskets.

Karen's children were older, and she had trademark *I-spend-a small-fortune-to-have-my-family-professionally-photographed* photos lining the walls. Hung were photographer Richard W. Scott-signed images, which Karen had blown up into huge poster-size photos. There was radiant Karen tossing a smiling toddler in the air. There was her husband, Gary, lying on a blanket with a sleeping infant under his arm. There were their four kids—age two, three, four, and five—walking in a line atop a stone wall, arms outstretched to keep from falling.

This particular photographer was insanely expensive. Additionally—and most comically—he chose photo framing and placement in each of his clients' homes per a written contract. He charged $350 an hour on top of the thousands of dollars necessary for the photography session itself.

As the women in the baby group made small talk, Karen asked them to arrange in a circle on the floor. The group was a mix of personalities and ages, and the anxiety level in some women appeared to be high given that they were strangers and that the babies were in various moods.

Rather than letting the conversations progress naturally, Karen instructed the women to go around the circle and share a bit about themselves with the group. Up next on the itinerary, she explained, would be a review of the thick handout, which was a compilation of local infant-related resources: pediatricians, preschools, and kid-friendly restaurants.

Elizabeth wondered how quickly Karen would be interrupted by babies needing to eat or be changed and soothed away from the others.

How old are her kids now? she wondered. *Has she completely forgotten what a newborn is like?*

Just as Karen, who had decided to share first, was telling the group about her impressive former career as a trial attorney, a late arrival appeared.

Kate Musto had let herself in and was starting down the stairs with Madeline. Standing at almost six feet tall, she had to bend slightly to see into the low-set room and stumbled down the last two steps. Her bulky baby bag swung forward, and she nearly dropped Madeline. Completely embarrassed, Kate made a joke about her entrance.

Then she saw Elizabeth.

"You must think I'm a complete mess," she said. "First you see me with my baby screaming uncontrollably in Svelte while I buy a dress for myself, and now you see me almost drop my baby on her head." Kate retold the Svelte story with funny exaggerations to the room. She had every mother—even uptight Karen—laughing hysterically.

"Did you realize you bumped into a table on the way out and toppled all of the store's costume jewelry?" Elizabeth asked.

"Well, I thought I did, but I was too afraid to look back," said Kate. "Now I'm really glad I didn't. Those salesgirls must hate me."

Before long, everyone was recounting their most humiliating stories since childbirth.

Hannah forgot to wear breast pads to a dinner with her male boss and unknowingly started leaking through a white blouse. "I wondered why he kept averting his eyes," she said. "I thought he found my huge rack embarrassing. No such luck. I was leaking like a cow."

Susan started crying uncontrollably in Target after forgetting to pack diapers in her baby bag. "It didn't dawn on me that they sell them in the store," she said. "I was just so frustrated and so exhausted. An outing, planned for weeks, could be ruined because you forgot to pack an extra bottle or pacifier or diaper."

Monica couldn't get her pricey imported stroller to close during a rainstorm. "It was one of those days when nothing was going right," she said. "Natalie was fussy and had been up most of the night. I was exhausted. As we were leaving the Cannondale Library, which was closing, it started to pour. So I'm walking and trying to keep Natalie dry by holding an umbrella over her in one hand and pushing her stroller—whose wheels were catching, by the way—with my other hand. Once I get to our car and Natalie is safely buckled in, I turn to collapse the stroller. It won't fold.

"I think about leaving it open and stuffing it into the Mercedes, but then remember the car is full with a Pack 'n Play, a portable swing, *and* a Tummy Time pillow and mat we used for last weekend's overnight. So I picked up the stroller and threw it, hoping the impact would close it. It didn't. I tried again. No luck. I decide to abandon it and turned to get into our car. That's when I see the head of the library's children's department staring at me. I explained why I was throwing the stroller, but she just stared at me like I was crazy. It was mortifying."

Elizabeth shared her first running post-birth story. "Six weeks after Alexis was born, I was so psyched to get back to running," she said. "As parenting magazines suggest, I wore a maxi pad just in case there was a little leakage. By the time I'd run less than an eighth of a mile, my pad was soaked through. I was so mad that I ran into the woods and threw it out. I was determined to get a run in and, luckily, didn't see anyone the rest of the way."

For the next two months, the group met once a week in each

others' homes, in coffee shops, and at the library. Soon they branched out and gathered at places like Bridgeport's Beardsley Zoo and Norwalk's Stepping Stones Museum for Children. The mothers enjoyed watching their babies' eyes brighten at the sight of animals and the activity of older kids. A ladies' night out was inevitable. Hadley Sayers suggested it during one of the gatherings.

"Brilliant idea," They all replied.

After the women debated and then voted down the idea of including Karen, an Evite titled "A Night on the Town" was sent out. On the assigned date, Elizabeth and Hadley were ensconced in a large booth at Poquitos, a lively tapas restaurant. As they sipped sangria and waited for the others to arrive, they saw Kate enter the restaurant.

"She looks upset," Hadley commented. Elizabeth noted Kate's expression, too. Something appeared to be very wrong.

"I'm furious," Kate blurted as she settled into the booth next to Elizabeth. "Lorenzo made me fuck him in the mudroom. He grabbed me as I was trying to leave the house and wouldn't let go. The kids were in the playroom. Thank God for the baby gate."

Elizabeth and Hadley's eyes widened and they became speechless. Kate continued.

Apparently, Lorenzo made Kate have sex with him every night. On the few nights she went out with her friends, it had to happen before she left as an unspoken form of punishment for leaving him alone to watch the children. It always took place in a location that made Kate feel compromised. The powder room, the hall closet, the laundry room—all with their kids feet away. It was humiliating. If she didn't sleep with him every night, he threatened to cheat on her.

"I'll get it somewhere else," he'd tell her. "You are my wife."

Kate called the waitress over and ordered a pomegranate martini.

Having just been raped by her husband, it was obvious she needed to talk and drink.

Prior to that night, Elizabeth assumed Kate was basically happy with Lorenzo. She'd grumbled about some of the things that most wives do, but it didn't seem indicative of a larger problem. It was obvious that Kate was responsible for the majority of parenting duties, but she seemed to embrace it.

As a couple, Kate and Lorenzo shared a background, and both had an obvious desire to rise above their origins. They had both grown up in the largely blue-collar town of Waterford. Living in affluent Cannondale and running in the circles that they did, Lorenzo and Kate were self-conscious about a past where they spent summers at the town pool, attended low-rate public schools, and never traveled farther than the state line. Also, and perhaps most damning given the well-educated group the Mustos were trying to pierce, Lorenzo had dropped out of high school. During baby group gatherings, Elizabeth witnessed Kate masterfully skirt questions about their upbringing and his lack of a college education.

Lorenzo was fifteen years older than Kate. They met just after Kate graduated from Roger Williams University with a degree in culinary arts. At the time, Lorenzo was running his uncle's septic business, which he later took over. Soon after, he acquired the competing septic businesses in the area. Kate was working at an entry position for a catering firm. Lorenzo courted Kate hard, and their relationship developed quickly. He took her out to dinner regularly, bought her lavish flower arrangements weekly, and eventually paid for an apartment so she could move out of her grandmother's home.

"I was raised by my grandmother," Kate told Elizabeth. "She was sweet but a drinker. She started every morning with breakfast:

eggs and a Bloody Mary. It was hard for me to move back home after college. Her drinking had gotten worse. Lorenzo took me away from her."

Kate explained how happy they had been early in their relationship. "When we were dating, I would make elaborate dinners, and then we would go out to meet our friends in bars," she said. "We were having so much fun. We had great sex. It was never forced then.

"And I still love the way he proposed to me," she added through sniffles. On Kate's twenty-third birthday, Lorenzo bought her a BMW convertible. He had it custom painted to match her green eyes. In the glove compartment was an emerald-cut four-carat diamond ring.

"I said 'yes' without even thinking," Kate said. "I was so young. I had no parents and no one else to trust. Lorenzo swept me off my feet." Kate twisted her large diamond ring. When it caught the light, its flawless quality made it glow like a beacon. With a large sigh, she went on to explain how the relationship changed after their first baby was born.

"Lorenzo said he wanted kids, but he didn't realize how much our lives would change," she said. "I adapted to the new life Lorenzo Jr. and our other kids brought with them, but Lorenzo still operates like he doesn't have children. It's all about him. I've threatened divorce, but he said he'll fight me to the death over custody rights."

"I'm so sorry to dump all of this on you two," Kate said, starting to cry again. "I try to keep it all in and hold myself together. Lorenzo would kill me if he knew I was telling you all this." Then Kate excused herself to go to the bathroom and wash her face.

"I want to tell her to leave him but don't know her well enough to say it," said Hadley. "Why does she stay with him?"

Elizabeth knew why Kate stayed. Her parents were dead. She had no siblings. All she had were her kids and Lorenzo. Kate's upbringing had been filled with uncertainties, in large part because a drunk raised her. Now, she was married to a guy who kept her equally off-balance. The only certainty Kate presently had was that her likely cheating husband would fuck her every night.

10

"Good morning, everyone," Jack said to his students in the studio later that week. "How are we today?"

"Good" resounded in the studio.

"Glad to hear it," Jack responded. "Personally, I'm on a high. My Auntie Arts charity benefit at The Glass House is coming up. I'm so excited for that night and to deliver the money raised to the women and children of West Bengal. And I'd like to say a special thank-you to Adair, who has devoted so much of her time and energy to making the event a success."

Jack looked over at Adair and smiled warmly. She looked haggard but beamed, obviously thrilled by his acknowledgment.

"This morning I'm going to share with you what brought me to yoga and how it redefined my life. It may help you on your journey to find greater daily peace. I know from our interactions that many of you sought out yoga as a way to find greater happiness in your life. I sought it for the same reason. I was at a desperate breaking point when I did. Nothing in my life had worked out as I had hoped and planned.

"I grew up in a wealthy suburb in Massachusetts very similar to Cannondale. My father was a general practitioner, and my mother didn't work outside the home until my four brothers and I were in middle school. Then she started selling real estate, which she still does today. Sadly, my father passed away several years ago.

"As a child, we lived near Nantucket Sound, and I spent most of my free time sailing. I was fortunate enough to attend Georgetown on a sailing scholarship. Needing to get serious about a career, I went back to school for an MBA, and at the end of my second year at Georgetown, I started my professional career on Wall Street working on the floor of the New York Stock Exchange. It was brutal.

"I quickly realized that I was not cut out for it, and although I worried about disappointing my parents, I quit. After some soul searching, I decided to work for a nonprofit. I knew I wouldn't make enough money to support the same lifestyle I had growing up, but it was the beginning of my awakening to how limiting that life is; the myopic focus toward making more and more money it creates, the related limitations, and all the things you miss when money is your goal.

"So I joined Boston's CANstruct, which builds schools in impoverished countries, as a product manager. Time passed and I eventually rose to be the head of Global School Production in its India division. I enjoyed the people I worked with and felt I was doing some good although the poverty and disease there is endemic. But we were providing education to a number of them and employing others.

"Then there were a series of very violent monsoons that caused flooding. Buildings were destroyed and hundreds of people died. We lost a number of our Indian and American workers, including my fiancée, Sarah Wells, who was the VP of Global School Production.

"I was devastated by her loss, and I sank into a depression so deep that I was eventually asked to leave CANstruct. I moved home and, thanks to a combination of therapy and yoga classes, I started to get better. I knew of yoga's physical benefits—I practiced in college with my sailing team and developed a love during my time in India—but during this awful phase of my life, when I felt so lost and like such a failure, it gave me great peace.

"I wasn't raised to run away from a tough job, but I did. I wasn't raised to get fired from a nonprofit, but I did. I wasn't raised to turn into a lost soul when someone I love dies, but I did. Everything had gone opposite of the expectations placed on me. I knew my parents loved me, but when I was growing up, my achievements were always closely tied to that love and their reactions to me. I was supposed to become a success in the classic New England way and accumulate a bunch of adjectives that would define me as a winner: educated, esteemed, athletic, and successful—all the things praised in men in our society.

"At that time, I felt nothing but athletic. Yoga and its teachings taught me to value myself simply for myself, beyond my adjectives, my accomplishments, beyond societal expectations. It taught me to not fool myself into thinking that impermanent things are permanent. To not place importance or faith in them. That was about fifteen years ago.

"Although I will never go back to working in the financial world, I have missed my nonprofit work since becoming a yogi. To fill the void, I set up the charity I've been telling you about called Auntie Arts. Its first major benefit is coming up and the night is going to be fantastic! Amazing people just like you mingling in the beautiful setting of the historic Glass House, enjoying classic and pop Indian music, hors d'oeuvres provided by Katherine's—my good friend Kate Musto's catering company—and cocktails, all for a good cause. The event's proceeds will fund a large building where the women will work as well as an on-site daycare and school for their children. I'll tell you more about it as we get closer."

His speech finished, Jack smiled broadly. He glanced around the room before positioning himself onto his knees. "Now, let us begin the movement part of class by shifting into the gentle child's pose, *balasana*."

From that pose, Jack led the class through a series of sun salutations: mountain to tree to triangle to half moon to warrior. With each pose, with each repetition, the students' bodies became a bit more limber, their stretches a bit deeper. Eventually, Jack instructed his students to move into downward-facing dog.

"Stay in this pose for a few minutes," he said. "It's one of the best shoulder stretches in yoga." Minutes passed. The class was then told to move to plank and then to cobra, and finally to rest prone on their stomachs with their heads down on the mat.

"Given the difficulty of holding downward-facing dog for that long, we are going to indulge in two rests during class today," Jack said in a loud whisper. "We are going to take five minutes here and then do a series of seated poses for fifteen more minutes before shavasana. Close your eyes. Breathe. Take this opportunity to be still. You have nowhere to go. You have nothing to do. Allow your mind to wander. Dream."

Jack moved to Kate. He straddled her, first massaging her lower back and then moving his hands to her buttocks. He pressed his thumbs deep into her gluteus medius muscles.

"A few more moments," Jack shared with the class. "Breathe in long, deep breaths," he said, stressing "long" and "deep." Jack's hands curved under Kate's body and, as he leaned forward, moved toward her breasts, lightly brushing them.

With the exception of breathing, the room was silent. A few women had fallen asleep.

As Jack pulled his hands back along Kate's torso and rested them on her hipbones, he said, "Let go of who you think you are. Let go of the stories you tell yourself—the stories that you think define you. You are not just a wife or a mother. You are not just an employee or a daughter. You're not the sum of your possessions. You are you. Embrace the beauty of who you really are, who you really want to be."

Jack gently lifted his hands from Kate and moved back to the front of the room.

//

Le Beau Château

Kate Musto

Kate was nervous—very nervous—when she pulled into the Le Beau Château estate for the first time. *Am I really going to sleep with a woman?* she'd asked herself. *I can't believe I'm doing this. I can't believe I requested this.*

She'd punched in the gate's security code, which Jack had texted her the night before. Slowly, the impressive wrought-iron gates opened.

I can do this, she'd thought, trying to bolster her courage as she pulled into the long, winding driveway. *I need to do this.*

Jack had met her at the front door. *He looks so handsome,* she thought. "I like you in your civilian clothes," she said. He'd smiled and silently taken her hand, leading her through the impressive foyer, up the gently winding staircase, through the master bedroom, and to the safe room entrance.

"She's waiting for you," he said. "Her name is Carly. I'm going to let you go in alone. Don't be afraid. She's sweet and gentle."

And she was, Kate had thought later that night. *When Carly slowly moved her fingers on my skin, she told me she was tracing me.*

Her feather-light touch started at my temples and then moved to my cheeks and my chin, creating a soothing circular pattern. From there, her fingers traveled to my shoulders, my hips, and my toes before reversing so unhurriedly that my body ached for what would come next: my breasts, my belly, my inner thighs.

Carly's eyes were curious and amused, Kate remembered. *They followed her fingers and noted my reactions. She encouraged me to be present, to not fear the intimacy. I wasn't afraid. Not with her.*

Kate had always seen hunger in the eyes of men. She didn't understand it in her adolescence. Not at first. The stranger at a neighborhood party. The gas station clerk as he passed her the bathroom key. The old man who picked the seat next to her on an empty train. It was the curse of being an adolescent girl. The curse of being attractive.

Kate grew to mistrust her body. It changed and developed, and by doing so, it betrayed her. She wondered why the boys she'd once ridden bikes and climbed trees with grew distant and started to watch her. She tried to mentally detach from her body, to ignore it and the unwanted attention it brought. She didn't understand that most of the interest was innocuous, a blanket desire directed at girls once they hit a certain age. She didn't have anyone to teach her how to distinguish the looks and figure out which ones were harmless and which were menacing; to demonstrate how to instantly register and understand the danger of walking into the bathroom at an empty, isolated gas station; to prevent what can and does happen so quickly to girls.

And, now, as an adult, after Kate learned how to expertly read eyes and to acknowledge that her own eyes could leer and burn with desire, she became crushed by the eyes that followed her most. They had grown so cruel. His eyes revealed a desire to control her, to conquer her.

Lorenzo made Kate hate sex, but when Jack touched her in her first yoga class, when he adjusted her, she changed. She instantly remembered a time when she enjoyed sex, when she longed for it. Jack understood her. He knew what she needed. He offered private sessions, and was kind and respectful during them. And then he offered Carly.

12

As Kate waited for Jack at Le Beau Château for her fifth session with Carly, she thought about her burgeoning relationship with Jack. *It started innocently enough,* she mused.

Kate had been at Westport's Brie discussing cheese with the owner when Jack walked in and joined their conversation. Not knowing he was a gourmand, she was impressed by Jack's knowledge of French cheeses. Noting their interest, the owner invited them both back to a cheese and wine tasting he was holding for his regular customers the following Friday evening. When they left the shop, Jack walked Kate to her car. He was headed to Miami for a long weekend. One of his private yoga clients was taking him to practice yoga with her while she was on a business trip.

"She's running a four-day convention and is very wound up at the end of each day," he explained. "Yoga is the only thing that helps her sleep."

The following Friday, Kate was excited to get ready for her night out. After trying on and discarding multiple outfits, she settled on her favorite white, fitted Diesel jeans and a slightly translucent white top over a turquoise tank top. She added black and cork mules and trendy turquoise and gold jewelry. Kate had asked Lorenzo's mother to watch the kids, adding that she should be there well before Lorenzo would be home. He wouldn't care if Kate wasn't at home as long as his mother was there to take care of their children and baby him.

Kate arrived at Brie a few minutes after the tasting started. No Jack. She scanned the crowd and, to her pleasant surprise, realized she didn't know anyone but the owner. She had hoped for as much.

Ten minutes in—still no Jack. Her disappointment was building. *Maybe he isn't coming*, she wondered. She had missed the Wednesday class and hadn't checked in with him. Maybe he forgot. She started to feel the awkwardness of being stood up.

As Kate repeatedly checked the door, the owner sensed her unease. He asked her to help him with the tasting. She happily obliged and began passing out platters of cheese to the crowd. Jack arrived about twenty minutes later. Kate didn't see him enter.

Their first contact was touch. Jack brushed up against her as she arranged a platter of aged blue cheese. He leaned in and whispered a quiet, "Hi, Kate" as the shop owner discussed the intricacies of the aged Gouda she had just passed.

Kate turned toward him to see his tanned face inches from hers. His gray-blue eyes were piercing. Devoid of his standard yoga gear and wearing fitted taupe khakis and a white-and-baby-blue checkered oxford, he looked strikingly handsome. Kate smiled and quickly stepped back from him, afraid of her attraction. As she delivered the platter, Jack stayed at the table where she was working until she returned. The crowd turned out to be a combination of Jack's clients and acquaintances, but he stayed by Kate's side throughout the evening as women walked up and greeted him. Kate felt like she was with a celebrity.

After the tasting, Jack suggested they get a drink together. It was a warm evening, and they walked to Asado, a quiet bar not too far away. Kate felt a sense of ease with him and an attraction that most men didn't evoke in her anymore. With age came trepidation for her with everyone, including the opposite sex. Despite how unhappy she was with Lorenzo, she envied none of her friends' marriages. Kate knew too much personal baggage about their husbands for any of them to appeal to her. Bad father. Cheap. Wandering eye. Perfectionist. Workaholic. Angry. Egocentric. Alcoholic. Manic. Strange. Meddling ex-wives. Too many kids. Dysfunctional parents…

Kate had also witnessed enough men go through midlife crises and ditch their families, either by mentally checking out or literally for their own self-preservation—a preservation of an unfulfilled self, a fantasy self. One who didn't have to think about the kids he chose to have and the impact of his abandonment. As a result, Kate hadn't found any man more than physically attractive in years.

But Jack was different. When Kate was with him, she felt like she was with a kindred spirit, a friend who could be a lover. She was able to speak freely and easily with him. And, unlike Lorenzo, Jack listened to her. Kate sensed that if she wanted someone other than Lorenzo to sleep with, Jack would be the right choice. He would appear and then disappear, never exposing the relationship. Given that she had children to think of, that appealed to her the most.

Over a pitcher of sangria, Jack and Kate discussed the subtlety of fresh butter and fine olive oil versus the standard varieties, the outrageousness of Pam in cooking, and their favorite gelatos. Since leaving Roger Williams, Kate rarely had anyone other than gourmet storeowners or clerks to speak to about such things in such detail. Many women in town knew good food, but they had chefs or other staff who cooked for them. Others bought prepared meals from gourmet stores or had caterers deliver meals weekly. Jack encouraged Kate to expand her small catering business, but she told him of Lorenzo's objections to her working outside the home.

"I only take on a few parties a year," Kate said. "Lorenzo doesn't let me take on more. He wants me to focus on the work that's needed in the home."

"Sounds like he feels threatened by your independence," Jack said.

Kate knew he was right. Their conversation moved to Jack's yoga studio. He suggested she take her practice to the next level with private sessions. "You aren't like many of the other women in Cannondale," he said. "The Fairfield County lifestyle doesn't fulfill you. Your kids are your priority. You want your own professional success. You need to spend time discovering who you are meant to be. I think yoga is the key for you, kundalini yoga specifically. Are your familiar with kundalini?"

It was one of the nicest evenings Kate could remember having since moving to Cannondale. She was so accustomed to Lorenzo's intensity as well as the nature of the women in town—everything was a competition. With Jack, there was no competition. There was no mention of material acquisitions or kids' achievements. There was just discussion and contemplation and work toward personal growth.

Kate went to Jack's rented studio in Westport the following Tuesday. She was both scared and excited to have time alone with him. She honestly didn't know if it would lead to an affair. She sensed that he liked her, and she had heard rumors about him being intimate with some of his students, but during that first session as well as the following few, Jack was extremely professional.

He quietly guided her through the poses, his direction allowing her to enjoy the full benefits of each one. Kate fell into it quickly, losing herself for the hour. The combination of dim lighting, a gentle hand, and the release that came from the strenuous poses made it feel closer to a spiritual experience than an hour of exercise. By shavasana, she was so relaxed that she fell asleep.

When Kate woke twenty minutes later, Jack was sitting in a chair, smiling at her, watching her. "I let you sleep," he said. "You looked so peaceful."

Kate left that session knowing she had a friend and maybe, hopefully, a lover.

13

As Abby pulled into the drop-off line at Cannondale Elementary, she looked in the rearview mirror and smiled when she saw her children, third-grader Quinn and first-grader Lily, contently staring out the windows. They were absorbed in a recording of Roald Dahl's *BFG*.

As they get closer to the unloading area, Lily started yelling: "Hannah! Hannah! Mom, there's my new friend, Hannah. Roll down the window. Quick! I want to say hi! Hannah!"

"Lily, settle down," Abby said. "You're about to get out. You can say hello to her then. Please make sure you have everything." Abby directed their car toward one of the nicer teachers, who helped the kids debark.

"Bye, Lily. Bye, Quinn," Abby said as they jumped out of the car one at a time, competing to see who could land the farthest out. "Have a good day."

"Bye, Mom," They both said in unison. "Love you," Lily added.

Abby's phone rang then, and she pulled into a parking spot. It was her voice mail service forwarding a message from her office phone. As she sat and listened, Abby watched Quinn and Lily head toward the entrance door. Lily had met up with Hannah, and they were holding hands and swinging their arms as they walked. Quinn and a boy Abby didn't recognize were throwing a tennis ball back and forth.

They adjusted so quickly, she thought. *This was a good move for them. They were definitely craving more space.*

Watching them enter the building smiling and laughing, one would never know that their father had killed himself under a year ago. *I wish I'd considered the move earlier,* Abby mused. *Maybe it would have taken some of the financial pressure off Colin.*

Abby was ready to pull out of the parking lot when she realized Lily had left her lunch in the car. Grabbing it, Abby walked to the school lobby. While waiting for a pass to gain access to Lily's classroom, she felt a tap on her shoulder.

Abby turned around to find Leigh Gilding standing there, smiling at her. "Leigh, what a surprise," she said, although it really wasn't. An image of Jack flashed in Abby's mind as she remembered her conversation with Elizabeth in Brioche.

"*Kate thinks a woman named Leigh Gilding is a client, but she isn't positive,*" Elizabeth had said. "*Petite, blonde, pretty, and can be a total bitch.*"

"Abby, I can't *believe* it's you," said Leigh. "It's been at least ten years. I didn't know you lived here. Did you just move?"

"Yes," responded Abby. "How about you? How long have you lived here? "

"We moved to Cannondale about a year ago—once our oldest was ready for kindergarten," said Leigh. "We sold our apartment and got out of Manhattan just before the crash."

"Lucky you," Abby responded.

"I'm sorry about what you've been going through lately," continued Leigh. "I saw it on the news. I meant to give you a call, but… You know how busy life can be."

Once striking with the wholesome beauty of a J. Crew model, Leigh had gained about fifteen pounds and cut her previously long blonde hair to chin length. She was still pretty but no longer in an intimidating way. The weight gain and time had robbed her of her once-effortless good looks. She was obviously trying to compensate by being impeccably dressed and accessorized even at this early hour.

"Thanks, Leigh," Abby said. "The kids and I are doing okay now."

"Of all places to move, what brings you to Cannondale?" Leigh asked.

"Work," said Abby. "I'm managing White's Realty. And my sister, Elizabeth Kelly, lives here with her family."

"Oh, our realtor works at White's, and I've met your sister through my kids' soccer league," she said. "Small world."

"Yes, it is," responded Abby. "Feels like it gets smaller every day."

"We love our realtor—Cecily Morgan," Leigh said, grinning. "She's a great agent and such a resource for local tradespeople."

"That's good to know," responded Abby. "Which house did you buy through her?"

"The castle in Kings Lord Manor," she said. "House number three."

"Oh, one of the new homes built on the old Sterling estate?" Abby said, surprise coloring her voice.

"Yes," Leigh responded. "Richie and I like new construction, so the development is perfect for us."

Although Abby hadn't seen any of the development's homes yet, she knew of them. White's Realty had handled the listing for the property's original seller, Richard Sterling III, and was subsequently handling the listing for the homes that Whole Development Construction Co. built on the property. At a time when few homes worth more than $2 million were moving in Fairfield County, the homes on the Sterling estate did, which was good for the firm. But the transactions were also a bit of a black eye for White's Realty—the town had been outraged when the original 1890s Stanford White-designed home and Fredrick Law Olmstead-designed landscaping were bulldozed to make room for the newer homes.

During a better economy, the Sterling estate would have been purchased before it even officially went on the market, but its upkeep and taxes made it a prohibitive buy. Cannondale residents tried raising money to turn it into a park but were unsuccessful. Other developers were initially interested, but despite the large lot, much of the property was wetlands and therefore unusable. In the end, the Sterling family donated twenty of the wetland acres to the town's local nature conservancy. The remaining sixteen acres were sold to Whole Development Construction Co.

Whole Development had a reputation for buying prime lots and ripping down perfectly situated, distinguished homes so it could build as many new, humongous homes as the property's zoning laws allowed.

Wedged together, its bulky McMansions made standard ones look quaint. The structures often had between three- and six-garage bays built at the front of the home, which awkwardly competed with the formal entrances. In Kings Lord Manor's case, the homes were grouped together in a half circle with the remaining property in the back. Abby had heard that the homes offered no privacy, which the developer thought would create a neighborhood feeling and be attractive to buyers.

When Whole Development named their projects, they favored cutesy, small-town Americana references, or for their high-end properties, as many imperial-related terms as possible—hence Kings Lord Manor.

With the exception of one home purchased by a local couple named Edward and Brianna Worth, the majority of houses listed in Kings Lord Manor were bought by out-of-towners, which apparently included the Gildings. Abby figured they either hadn't heard about the uproar in town or simply didn't care.

"Where are you living now and what did you do with your fabulous Park Avenue apartment?" Leigh asked Abby.

"We're renting a home on Millstone. I held onto the apartment and am renting it for now," she responded.

"Renting," said Leigh curiously. "Oh, of course. You can't afford to buy a home—Colin jumped because you were wiped out, and it was a suicide so you didn't receive any life insurance. He certainly left you in a bind, didn't he? How many kids do you have? Men can be such selfish assholes."

"Mrs. Powers," The school secretary—who'd overheard the exchange—interrupted and shot Leigh a nasty look. "Here's your pass. You can go in now."

"Bye, Leigh," said Abby as she started to walk away. *My God! She is still a bitch*, Abby thought. *A total fucking bitch.*

"Wait," said Leigh, running up alongside her. "If I recall correctly, you grew up around here, didn't you?"

"Yes," Abby snapped. "I grew up in Stamford, about thirty minutes from here."

"You must know a lot of people who live here," Leigh continued. "I've heard Fairfield County is a place people move back to as adults. Would you be willing to tell your friends and White's clients about my landscaping company? I can have you over so you can see my work."

"Okay… How is your landscaping business?" Abby asked, trying to figure out how serious Leigh was about working.

"I've been consistently busy," said Leigh. "And I need to be. I still have home and landscaping improvements planned, and Richie just told me I have to start paying for them. He said I've been spending too much money since we moved here, and aside from the basics and stuff for our kids, he basically cut me off."

As they parted, Leigh handed Abby a tall stack of thick, attractive—and ridiculous—cardstock business cards. "Would you place them in the lobby of White's?" she asked.

As Abby walked toward Lily's classroom, looking for the nearest trashcan to dump the cards into, she thought, *Leigh is a quick study. People in this town are easily impressed by anything expensive that conveys good taste.*

14

"Good morning everyone," Jack said to the women in the studio. "Given the rain, we will start a few minutes late today."

It was a school holiday, which generally meant the yoga studio would be full. For a number of mothers in the studio, this class would be their only personal time all day.

Jack slowly scanned the room and noted several women typing into their iPhones. "Ladies, let's put the devices away," he instructed with a playful grimace. "Unless it's an emergency, the studio is a phone-free zone.

"So how is everyone?" he continued.

"Good," a number of women muttered back.

Leigh, who was seated up front next to Jack, said, "I'd be better if the rain stopped."

"Yes, Leigh, I understand," Jack responded while reaching out and clasping her hand. "The rain can bring us down." He paused in reflection and then continued, "But we can't control it, can we? I always find it helpful to focus on the things we *can* control rather than the things we can't. When you feel down about something like rain, you have to train your mind to find another focus, because you can either be upset by it or not. It will still be raining outside.

"As a culture, we are losing the ability to look inside and develop coping mechanisms for the unpleasant aspects of life. Instead, we increasingly seek the stimulation offered in our privileged, wireless world, which really only functions as a distraction. Once that distraction is gone, negative feelings surface again. That is why your yoga practice is so important.

"For the next hour and a half, you can tune out the rest of the world and get back in touch with who you are and what's important to you. If uncomfortable feelings arise, you will be forced to sit with them. Sitting with them and thinking about them is the only way to work through them. It's one of the secrets to happiness. Isn't it cool to know that exists within you? No matter what happens in your life, if you can face the related feelings, you have the ultimate control."

Jack stood to lower the lights. Before sitting back down again, he stopped and chatted with Sylvia Dory, a local masseuse who was going through a difficult divorce. He gave her a heartfelt hug and then knelt behind her and massaged her shoulders. Moving back to the front of the studio, he settled in typical fashion on his mat and began to speak.

"Today, I want to discuss how yoga encourages daydreaming, and its importance in personal happiness," he said. "Studies show that positive, mindful daydreaming helps manage conflict and aids in conflict resolution, improves cognition, and boosts creativity and productivity.

"How many of you daydream regularly?" Jack asked the class.

A number of hands went up.

"Good," Jack said. "More of you do it than I anticipated. As I was saying earlier, it's less and less common in our busy, wireless world. The kundalini yoga workshop I will be running is designed to encourage daydreaming—specifically erotic daydreams, which are fuel for the kundalini energy. Given that society and our small communities can tamp us down, it's important for us to have a place, at least in our minds, where we feel uninhibited. Otherwise, all the restrictions and all the limitations can lead to aberrant behavior. Just like children who are told 'No!' one too many times, we react negatively when trying to fit into too narrow a view of acceptable behavior.

"My workshop starts a week from tomorrow. For those of you who want to take it and haven't signed up yet, please see me after class.

"I also want to announce that the entire catalogue of auction items from the upcoming Auntie Arts charity benefit at The Glass House is available for review and early bidding on my website. Some of the new items added to the catalogue are: $10,000 in Mandarin Oriental hotel credit; a spa week in Fiji at the exclusive Turtle Island; center orchestra tickets for *The Book of Mormon;* and a complete collection of signed books by the late Connecticut author, William Styron.

"The benefit will be held on November seventh. All proceeds will go to help a community in West Bengal, specifically the women and children who live there. I hope you will visit my website to review the offerings and, if you haven't already, consider attending the event. It's going to be a great night."

Jack stood up and began moving through the studio. As he walked through the room, his fingertips brushed across a few of the women's shoulders and he whispered, "Welcome."

"Today's practice is going to focus on the hips," he said. "The hips are huge depositories for physical and emotional tension. The poses we will do are meant to open up the pelvic region and release negative feelings and undesirable energy while activating kundalini. If the practice gets too intense, please take a break. Releasing the hips is often an emotional watershed experience, but don't be scared or embarrassed by your feelings. It's completely normal to have an emotional response. Students often weep during this class."

He moved to the front of the classroom to instruct and observe the women. "Let's start by sitting cross-legged with your left leg in front of your right. Place your hands on your knees. Take a deep breath in, and when you exhale, start moving your torso in wide circles. Make the circles as broad as you can while breathing deeply. Experience the entire range of motion in the hips and your lower back. When you are ready, change direction."

Jack walked through the room. Once he reached Leigh, he crouched behind her and puts his hands on her waist. While whispering instructions on how to breathe in her ear, he started to direct the pace and direction of her circular movements. Then he moved to Adair and repeated the process. When he whispered in Adair's ear, they both giggled.

For the next forty-five minutes, Jack instructed his students through a series of stretches to release the hips as well as the hamstrings and lower back. He ended the sequence with pigeon pose.

"This is one of my favorites," he explained. "Physically, it releases the intricate group of muscles, tendons, and ligaments that support the hips. Emotionally, it releases the lower two chakras, the root and the sacral, which guide our relationships and house our human need for survival, intimacy, and trust."

Jack ended the class with a longer-than-usual shavasana. "I'm giving you extra rest time today so that you have the opportunity to process the emotions you unlocked," he said, speaking in a soothing, quiet tone. "Relax. Allow your mind to follow its natural stream of thought. You have nowhere to go. You have nothing to do. This is your time. Feel. Process. Release."

When Abby and Elizabeth were rolling up their mats at the end of class, Leigh came over to them. "Hi again, Abby," she said. "So you've already discovered Yogi Jack. Wasn't that a great class? I've missed the last few and was so stiff."

"Yes," Abby murmured noncommittally. "Really amazing."

"When I have private sessions with Jack, he leads me through a version of the hip-opening sequence," Leigh volunteered. "If you can afford to, you should sign up for his private sessions. They *really* are amazing."

"I've already signed up," responded Abby, her interest piqued. "My first one is Friday morning."

"Oh, speaking of Friday—Abby, are you free for lunch after you meet with Jack?" Leigh asked. "I'd like to show you my property. Elizabeth, you're welcome to come, too. Brianna Worth is my neighbor, and she told me you're featuring her home in next month's issue of *Cannondale Cottages & Gardens.*"

She leaned in and continued in a stage-whisper, "If you ask me, our home is just as attractive as Brianna's but with much better landscaping. Olivia Blackwell is my decorator. I think you'll be impressed by it enough to want to feature it, too!"

The two sisters glanced at each other and grinned. "Yes," They said in unison. "What time?"

15

Two days later, Abby and Elizabeth were staring at an elaborate, black metal gate, waiting to be buzzed into Leigh's complex.

"Can you believe the size of that plaque?" Abby said to Elizabeth, referring to a slab of granite suspended from a massive stone pillar with KINGS LORD MANOR chiseled into it.

"I know," said Elizabeth. "It's ridiculous."

The gate slowly opened, revealing four gigantic homes built a stone's throw from each other. When dividing the sixteen acres into four-acre lots as zoning demanded, Whole Brothers Construction Co. sectioned the Sterling estate into a half circle of triangles and placed the homes at the tip of each lot—nearly on top of each other. A shared circular road accessed their driveways.

Unlike the former estate that stood on this property, there was no long, winding, tree-lined driveway to create anticipation. There was no mystery of what was to come. The moment the gate opened, there sat four really big, ugly homes.

The first home to the left of the property was Tudor-style, but it was oddly outfitted with protruding bay, oval, and circular windows. Next to it was one in Georgian Brick style but made out of white bricks with red brick coining and a peculiar double-height pyramid hip roof. Seemingly feet away was a classic clapboard

Colonial with a slate roof and oversize Victorian flourishes. The last home was a square-cut stone castle that looked like one kids might make at the beach—there were four turrets and also six giant cupolas. It was an odd collection of shapes and pieces completed with large, jutting Palladian windows. Most puzzling about its façade was that it was covered in ivy—so much so that the stone was barely recognizable.

"When did the ivy have time to grow?" Elizabeth asked as Abby directed her car toward Leigh's driveway.

"Let's start our tour in the garden," Leigh blurted out before Abby and Elizabeth had had a chance to close their car doors. Of the four homes, her castle had the most greenery on the property. "I did all the landscape design," she added. "When we bought the home, there was nothing but grass here. I'm trying to get the three neighbors as clients. Their properties are so barren."

During the tour, Abby and Elizabeth discovered that Leigh had planted twenty-eight mature trees at a cost of $10,000 each and added more than seventy-five large flowering bushes at $350 a pop over the last year. She had a large vegetable garden that was tended to daily. She'd added a terraced garden off the back patio that was filled with perennials. To the right of the terraced garden, she'd created a modern rock garden complete with a pool and fountain.

"It was expensive," said Leigh, as if all the other work she did wasn't. "I custom-picked each rock from a quarry in Massachusetts. They were trucked in. It cost about $80,000 to build."

"Did you use Miracle-Gro with the house's ivy?" Elizabeth asked.

"No," Leigh said. "Olivia thought the stone looked too new, so she had a team of gardeners here the week before we moved in.

They attached trellises of ivy to it. The ivy gives it a nice sense of age, don't you think?"

It did, but it also looked ridiculous in comparison to the neighboring homes. The oddity of the home's architecture and property lines made them all look brand new.

After touring the front yard's landscaping, the women moved inside. The home had been completely decorated by Olivia Blackwell—a local celebrity designer known for toning down the embarrassing glitz of new money and new construction. Leigh's house had all the trademarks of Blackwell's style: feather pillows, abstract art, and white modern furniture with cowhide rugs. The home was lovely in its simplicity and richness of materials. The artwork referenced Leigh's passion for landscape design—a tasteful choice. Elizabeth found it sad that so many beautiful things existed inside such an ugly castle.

Beautiful but sterile and museum-like, most of Olivia Blackwell-designed houses were a mix of formal and informal rooms, including a few spaces for kids. She was known for creating amazing play spaces similar to what you see in children's museums, such as pretend supermarkets and auto mechanic shops.

That was not the case in Leigh's house. Filling all the rooms in this 6,500-square-foot house with anything other than a playroom must have been a challenge for Leigh, but she'd succeeded. The house had his and her offices with adjoining libraries, a workout room with a separate yoga studio, a gift wrapping room, his and her circular cedar closets hidden behind secret doors in two of the turrets, and a wine cellar larger than a single car garage. There was a den off the kitchen outfitted with some of the finest fabrics Elizabeth had ever seen.

Do the kids ever have fun in that room? she wondered.

The children's domain appeared limited to the third floor, which was technically the attic. There was no playroom there, just three large, highly decorated bedrooms plus the nanny and housekeeper's barren, closet-like warrens. Oddly, there was a deadbolt on the outside of the door at the base of the stairs.

"What's with the lock?" Abby asked Leigh.

"Oh, you noticed," she said. "I was hoping you wouldn't. My kids suffer from nightmares. They wake up repeatedly at night. Richie and I can't stand it. We lock them up on the third floor so they can go into each other's rooms or into Mira or Lucille's. Richie and I need our sleep."

"What if there was an emergency and you and Richie couldn't reach the lock to let them out?" Elizabeth asked. "They would have to jump from the third floor."

"Oh, Elizabeth, what are the odds of that happening?" Leigh responded, waving a hand dismissively. "We'll take our chances if it means we get consistent good nights' sleep."

"Okay… We're working on a feature about kids' playrooms," Elizabeth said, changing the subject. "You must have one in this large of a house. Where do your kids play?"

"In their rooms," Leigh briskly responded. "To keep the mess down, we restrict their play to their rooms, the eat-in area of the kitchen, and the back staircase."

"Sounds like *Flowers in the Attic*," Abby joked.

"Very funny," Leigh said. "Oh, and they also have the play castle outside. How could I forget to mention it? That would be perfect for your magazine's feature, or even better—it probably deserves its own feature. Did you see it when we were walking behind the home? Look out the window toward the far corner of the property. It's a duplicate of the main house."

The sisters moved to the nearest window and looked out at the back of the property. The playhouse—also completely covered in ivy so it was nearly unrecognizable against the line of trees in the backyard—was the size of a small Ranch-style home.

"It has a kitchen, full bathroom, electricity, heat, and central air," boasted Leigh. "My kids could live in it." The mini-castle was located on the absolute edge of the property. It was placed as far away as possible from the main home.

"Your kids are still young," Abby said. "Why didn't you position it closer to the main house so it's easier for you to check in on them?"

"Are you kidding me?" Leigh started. "I hate the screaming that comes with free play. When I want them out of the house, I send Lucile with them. Last weekend we stocked the refrigerator, and Lucille and all three kids spent the entire weekend in it. Richie and I had the main house to ourselves. It was heaven!"

"After a quick tour of the playhouse, let's sit and have a latté," Leigh offered.

Abby and Elizabeth were ready. The highly detailed tour had been exhausting. Once they were back in the main house, Mira—one of Leigh's housekeepers—brought in skim lattés, macadamia nut cookies, and fresh fruit. As Abby heard Leigh give Mira instructions for putting down the tray, she remembered how rude Leigh used to be to people who waited on her in New York.

"Are you sure this is the skim I prefer for lattés and not the two percent milk you buy for the kids?" she asked Mira as she shoved a cookie in her mouth. "You know I'm on a diet."

Turning back to her guests, Leigh commented, "Did you know there's as much fat in a cup of two percent milk as in whole milk? What a waste of calories." Leigh started scanning the cookie plate, appearing to look for the cookie with the most nuts and chips in it.

Elizabeth responded by winking at Mira. She smiled at Elizabeth but quickly turned and exited the room.

The telephone rang then, and Mira told Leigh that "Mr. Gilding" was on the phone.

"Tell him I'm entertaining people who can help me get new landscaping clients," she said. "I'll call him back when they're gone. Don't unnecessarily interrupt me again." Abby and Elizabeth shot each other a look.

"Richie is furious with me," Leigh said. "I don't want to speak with him today. Last night he was going over our expenses and determined exactly how much I've spent since we moved into this house. He said I've spent nearly $2 million."

"Really?" Abby asked incredulously. "Did you build a hospital in Nigeria?"

"Of course not," Leigh said, laughing. "I spent most of the money on our home and property. I spent some on me, too, of course." Abby sensed another list of purchases coming and tried to think of a topic to distract her—something gossipy and cruel that would definitely grab her attention—but it was too late.

"Well, you know how expensive Livy's decorating services are," Leigh continued, unprompted. "I turned the entire house with the exception of the two servant rooms over to her. She helped us remodel the kitchen and all seven bathrooms. We added the pool, pool house, mini-castle—that alone was over $500,000—and an outdoor custom-built grill and fire pit. As you saw, I spent a small fortune landscaping the property. I don't think it's fair that Richie gets mad at me for the money I spend on the house and property. I do it for the family."

Oh yes, Elizabeth thought. *I'm sure Richie and your kids demanded the silk wallpaper in the dining room and that it be applied not just once, but twice because they were unhappy with the seams the first go-around. Yes, you chose the incredibly expensive paper for the betterment of your family. Your ego wasn't involved in that choice at all.*

"What else, what else did I spend money on?" Leigh said, looking around thoughtfully. "Oh, yes, our cars. We bought the Mercedes-Benz G class for me, a Porsche Cayenne for Richie, a convertible vintage Jaguar for Richie and me to share, and a Chrysler minivan for Lucille, our nanny, to drive the kids around in."

"Aside from your new cars, what about the 'me' part?" Abby asked, simply unable to resist. "What purchases have you made just for yourself?"

"That's right!" Leigh continued. "I can't forget about me. Well, just like you, I'm no spring chicken. We're getting older and have to stay on top of our beauty regimens." There were weekly facials, massages, and bi-monthly laser treatments to encourage collagen growth in her face, neck, and hands, Leigh explained as if this routine was a must for anyone over age thirty-five. She went for Botox and Restylane injections every three to eight months. Tired of shaving, Leigh had had all the hair on her legs, underarms, and bikini line removed by laser treatments—that took a year of treating small areas at a time.

"And you know how much I like nice clothes and accessories," she went on. "I'm a bit heavier than I was in New York, so I have to keep updating my wardrobe until I lose the weight and can fit into my old designer clothes that are still in vogue. By the way, I'm planning a shopping trip to Paris in August."

"Who's going with you?" Abby asked.

"Remember Mandy and Teresa from New York?" she said. "I'm

still in touch with them. And possibly my neighbor, Brianna. The economy is making it harder to shop in the way we're accustomed to. This year, Mandy, Teresa, and I had to ask our husbands for *permission* to go. In past years we informed them that we were going and only had to remember to extend our credit cards' credit. Well, it gives us an opportunity to be nicer to our husbands.

"You two should consider joining us," Leigh said, knowing Abby couldn't afford it. "Elizabeth, your wardrobe looks like it could use a few refresher pieces. Even though you're a suburban mom, you can update your classic look with trendy items.

"Hmm… What else did I buy?" Leigh continued as Abby shot a look at Elizabeth. "Oh, did I show you my purse collection yet? That's another big expense on my list. But I can't resist. I just received a new one yesterday." Leigh fancied alligator skins and was on several designer-handbag shopping lists, which required waiting for the bags to be available. "Purses are my fetish," Leigh said. "When I get a new one, I hide it from Richie for a few months," she explained. "Then I take it out and when he asks me if it's new, I tell him 'I've had it for a while.' That way I'm not lying to him."

The phone rang again, and after answering it, Mira walked into the room. "I told you to hold all calls, Mira," Leigh barked.

"But it's Jack Turner," said Mira. "You told me to always tell you when he calls."

"Oh, in that case, I'll take it," Leigh said without apologizing to Mira. "Excuse me, ladies. Don't eat all the cookies while I'm gone."

Abby and Elizabeth exchanged looks again, and Abby tapped her watch, indicating she wanted to go. Elizabeth nodded and excused herself to use the powder room. On her way there, she overheard Leigh on the phone. "Okay, Jack," she said. "I'll be at Le Beau

Château tomorrow at noon. The men better be attractive this time."

Wow! Abby thought. *She really is one of his sexcapade clients.*

When Leigh came back into the room, Abby and Elizabeth explained that they had to go. As they got up, Mira entered the room and asked if she could get Leigh anything else.

"We're fine, but you need to start lunch," Leigh said.

"What would you like today, Mrs. Gilding?" asked Mira.

"I want shrimp on a bed of bib lettuce with fresh blue-cheese vinaigrette dressing and herb-and-sour-cream scones. I'll have the dry white wine that we opened last night and Pellegrino with lime. Again, no cubes in the water glass. You should know by now that they dilute the sparking water."

"I'll have to drive to the farmer's market in Fairfield to get the scones and blue cheese," explained Mira.

"That's fine," said Leigh. "Get going. I want to eat no later than one o'clock today. Yesterday you didn't get lunch on the table until one fifteen."

"That's because the mussels you ordered arrived late," Mira responded.

"I don't want to hear your excuses," Leigh said. "Just go."

"Take note, ladies," Leigh said when Mira exited. "That's the way you keep your help in line."

To call the conversation tiring would've been an understatement, but both Abby and Elizabeth were accustomed to ones like it. Selling high-end properties and writing about them often forced the sisters to spend time with women just like Leigh. Having grown up extremely poor, Leigh had idolized wealthy lifestyles from afar. Once she got her hands on some money, she tried to imitate those affluent lifestyles but only succeeded at making her life into a caricature of one.

As Abby and Elizabeth walked to Abby's car, they saw Mira exit the home from the back service entrance. "Let's ask for the cookie recipe," Abby said. "Those were delicious." They approached her and thanked her for the homemade cookies. "Would you mind sharing the recipe with me?" asked Abby. "Those are my children's favorite cookies, and I find them difficult to make."

"Yes," Mira said as she smiled. "The secret is a quarter cup—"

"Don't try to steal Mira from me," Leigh shouted from the service exit with no hint of humor in her voice. "Mira, you signed a contract. You can't leave for another year." She had been watching them and was serious. For Leigh, the only reason anyone would speak to someone else's housekeeper was to steal them.

"Leigh, you're crazy," Abby responded as Mira scurried to the Chrysler. "The only thing I'm trying to steal is a cookie recipe."

16

Le Beau Château

Leigh Gilding

There will always have to be more than two men, Leigh thought.
*With the exception of Jack, I don't want to know them, and I don't
want the same men twice. Strangers. They must be strangers.*

*We meet once a month at Le Beau Château, the estate Jack cares
for. He sets it up. I don't know where he finds the men. They could
be his friends. They could be prostitutes. They could be day laborers
who were standing on a street corner a half hour earlier, thinking
their morning would be spent at a construction site—not on an
estate engaging in an organized, sanctioned gang bang.*

*Sometimes Jack watches, sometimes he participates. He's there
to make sure I'm safe, to make sure the play doesn't get too rough. I
like the men to take turns. One at a time.*

*During a private session that turned intimate, Jack asked me
about my fantasies. He wanted to know what I think about when
I masturbate. No one had ever asked me that before. No boyfriend,
no husband.*

*I fantasize that there's a line for me. That once one man has climaxed,
another one steps in. That the sex is long and varied and sating.*

Jack said he could make my fantasy a reality. That he does so for his private clients. He talked about the freedom that comes when you act out your sexual desires. He told me it would be liberating. That it would change my whole life. After three more private sessions with Jack—after he counseled me in kundalini—I agreed. He promised to protect me. To insist on condoms. I just had to show up. What did I have to lose?

Before the first meeting, I told the school that all emergency calls should go to Edward. I would not be interrupted by discoveries of head lice or low-grade fevers. I drove to the address Jack gave me. I had never been there before. It's a handsome property that's well-known in town—a large, private estate that represents a more genteel age. The kind of home I wish I'd grown up in.

The moment I turned off Old Farm Road and onto the property's long gravel driveway, I felt a lightness that the property's mani-cured—yet unspoiled—landscape encouraged. It was like being in a different place, in a different era. I felt like I was entering a zone where time would be suspended and the rules I allow to govern me wouldn't exist. My hyper-competitive mind could pause, and all the pretenses I wear could disappear. They had no place on that estate with those men. I could just be me.

Jack met me at the front door and brought me to the third-floor safe room where I would meet the men. We accessed it through a door in the master bedroom suite's massive walk-in closet. After punching a code into a secret keypad, we entered a stairwell that led to what felt like a separate third-floor apartment. So that I understood how safe the environment was where the sex would take place, Jack explained its six-inch-thick walls reinforced by rebar.

"It's like a vault," he assured me. "Its weight required extra support to be installed throughout the home."

Within the large safe room was a separate space dedicated to an extensive surveillance and alarm system. It was filled with screens that allowed monitoring of nearly every inch of the home and property. Jack explained how, during my sexcapade, he would travel between the bedroom I was in and the surveillance room to ensure no one had entered the estate uninvited.

"Does the video record, or is it just for surveillance purposes?" I asked. "I don't want to be recorded."

"It doesn't record unless it's programmed to tape," Jack assured me. "The purpose of all of these screens is so the person who secures herself in the safe room during a home invasion can watch the perpetrator's movements. According to the confidentiality agreement we both signed, there will be no recording of you during a sexcapade."

Jack led me to the bedroom where the sex would take place. It was as tastefully decorated as the rest of the home—in an elegant Swedish country style. I felt safe and at ease. I felt at home. Jack explained the rules he'd outlined to the men in advance. If I felt uncomfortable at any point, all I had to do was call out a "safe word" and Jack would intercede. I chose the word "cash."

Jack assured me he would be vigilant. "I want you to enjoy it, and I don't want you to feel scared in any way," he said. "This is about your pleasure. If you're scared, it will inhibit the kundalini's flow."

Shortly after, the men entered the room. There were five of them, clean but rough-looking, weather beaten and calloused. Men similar to the ones my mother told me to stay away from in the trailer parks of my youth. Very different from the men in Cannondale. There were no introductions. No small talk. We were all there for one thing. They disrobed and, one by one, joined me on the bed.

I got completely lost in the sex. I entered another dimension, a place of anonymity and impulses that was once limited to my imagination.

A place of strangers and erect cocks and sex without inhibitions. Sex exactly the way I wanted it.

And Jack was right. There is liberation in living out my fantasy, to rejecting, if just for one day, the rules that typically govern me. Is it kundalini-related as Jack insists, a release and movement of a libidinal energy that leads to a kind of divine wisdom? I don't know. Not yet. But what I experience in that room with those men is carnal and exciting and definitely freeing.

Am I happier now? I think so. I do the unthinkable and nothing bad happens. I'm not branded with a scarlet letter. I haven't been ostracized by the PTA crowd. My husband and kids will never know. I'm still the same person I was, but now I have a precious secret.

One day a month, I act in total abandon. One day a month, I'm nothing like the woman I must pretend to be. One day a month, I'm the woman who likes a good gangbang.

17

Pulling out of Leigh's driveway, Abby said to Elizabeth, "I'm so glad I didn't have to sit through that alone. Thanks for coming with me."

"It was worth it to see Leigh's home," responded Elizabeth. "I love Olivia Blackwell's style. The home would photograph nicely, and the kids' playhouse could be a spread in the front of the magazine. It's too special to lump in with the other playrooms we're planning to feature. It's totally excessive, which is exactly what the magazine's readership wants.

"So how exactly did you meet Leigh?" Elizabeth asked when Abby pulled over in the Kings Lord Manor's cul-de-sac so she could dig in her purse for her phone.

"We were dating brothers," Abby recalled. "Remember Bill Stein?"

"Vaguely," said Elizabeth.

"She was going out with his brother Jonathon. She hired me to help find her first apartment," said Abby, scrolling through her email messages.

"She hasn't changed," she continued, looking up from her phone to Leigh's house. "She just has more money now. But despite her bad behavior, I've always had a soft spot for her. She had a really rough upbringing."

Abby went on to explain what she had learned about Leigh's childhood from her former boyfriend. Leigh's father left the family when she was a toddler and never contacted her or her mother again. Leigh's mother was sweet but emotionally unstable. Leigh spent her high school years living like a vagabond in a Winnebago while her mother tried to get her act together in town after town. Leigh attended over ten schools between kindergarten and high school graduation.

"So she feels like she has a lot to catch up on and needs to win in every situation," said Abby.

"Too bad she isn't going for the happiness award," commented Elizabeth.

"Yes, it is sad," Abby agreed, "for everyone around her."

"That's the neighbor whose home we're featuring in next month's issue," Elizabeth said as she pointed to Brianna's home, Leigh's neighbor. "I've heard they're best friends."

"Is the interior of that house nice?" Abby asked incredulously. "The outside is so chaotic." As Abby looked at the house, she tried to make sense of it and the varied, pitched rooflines, its tacky overwrought gingerbread millwork, and its pink-and-mauve color scheme combined with classic Colonial massing, clapboard, and shutter windows.

"Today that style is what suburban developers call Victorian-inspired Colonial," said Elizabeth, watching as Abby plugged her phone into its car charger. "Pretty bad, isn't it? The interior was a standard box McMansion before the designer Meredith Fox got her hands on it. Now it's beautiful inside. It's decorated in an eclectic international style. You know Robert Couturier's work? It's not quite as polished as his spaces, but it's close. It's filled with a gorgeous collection of eclectic antiques and is paired with a novel color scheme and antique and modern accessories. It's really well done."

"What I still don't understand since moving here is why there hasn't been a universal backlash to what most developers build," stated Abby. "Their homes are huge and generic. You have to spend a fortune after you buy one to fill and personalize it."

"The developer homes look and feel so wrong because, in the interest of cutting costs, architects have been largely cut out of the suburban residential building process," responded Elizabeth. "Some developers buy architectural plans, but since they aren't formally trained, the homes look off when they adapt them. Once they're built, most people can't justify knocking down an entire home that's structurally sound, so if buyers are looking for an already built, newer home, they buy them and try to improve them."

"It's a totally backward system," Abby said.

"That's Brianna now," Elizabeth said, spying an attractive, middle-age women in heels and a blazer walk out of the front door. "Pull into her driveway. I'll introduce you."

"Hi, Elizabeth, how are you?" Brianna asked as Elizabeth waved and rolled down her window. "Visiting Leigh and her nursery?"

"Yes," said Elizabeth, laughing.

"Be careful with her," said Brianna. "Since she moved to town, she's become my closest friend—and I like to say my biggest rival. When she heard my house was going to be featured in the magazine you edit, her eyes flared. She's determined to get her home in it, too. If you do feature it, you better photograph the property soon. She has plans to do more landscaping. It's going to look like a jungle soon." She laughed. "I'm tempted to go over there in the night with a machete and hack some of it back."

"Leigh just showed us her surveillance system so, no matter how tempting, I wouldn't do that," said Elizabeth, teasingly. "Brianna, this is my sister, Abby. She's new to town."

"Nice to meet you," said Brianna. "And, Elizabeth, thank you for responding to my Easter party invitation. I'm so glad you can come. Abby, if you're free on April eleventh, I hope you'll join us. We hide eggs all over the yard for the kids, and I serve my famous colored deviled egg sandwiches."

"That sounds like fun," responded Abby.

"I'll get your address from Elizabeth and send you an invitation," said Brianna.

"Thank you," said Abby. "I hope I can make it."

"Where are you off to?" Elizabeth asked Brianna.

"I have to pick up an auction item for Jack Turner's benefit," said Brianna. "Words Bookstore is donating several art books."

"I heard you're helping with that?" said Elizabeth.

"Yes, Adair roped me in," said Brianna, "but I don't mind helping. Jack and I go way back. I better get going. I was supposed to be there a half hour ago. It was nice to meet you, Abby, and good-bye, Elizabeth. Hope to see you both soon."

"She seems nice," Abby commented as they pulled out of the complex.

"She means well and she is very generous," Elizabeth said. "Brianna is still trying to recover from a few embarrassing incidents that appeared in the police blotter a few years ago. I didn't live here yet, but from what I was told, she and her husband were regulars in the paper for about a month. After Brianna's second incident, she was court ordered to go through anger management treatment and is now an active anger management counselor in a Norwalk clinic."

"That woman?" asked Abby. "She seems so normal."

"I heard she's strongly medicated now and less prone to outbursts," said Elizabeth.

"My God, what happened?" Abby asked.

Elizabeth explained Brianna and her husband Edward's notorious past. While Edward was a known yeller, Brianna was violent. She was arrested twice in 2006. The first time was for attacking her mother-in-law in the couple's first home in Cannondale. The police blotter said that the mother-in-law had been admitted to the hospital for a gash on her arm that required fifteen stitches and a blow to the head that caused a slight concussion. No charges were filed. The fight was supposedly over Edward's mother's disapproval of Brianna's lavish spending habits.

After that episode, Edward was arrested. Someone dialed 9-1-1 from the couple's home but hung up, so that person was never identified. When the police arrived, there was a verbal argument in progress. Edward was drunk and in an absolute rage. He was belligerent with the police and arrested. Although Edward's mother was also in the home, given that the 9-1-1 call was a hang-up, everyone assumed Brianna set him up. He was the one who called 9-1-1 on her during the fight with his mother.

Brianna's second arrest was for spanking her son in Cannondale Nature Center's Rainbow Room minutes before his fourth birthday party started. Again, Brianna's attack was vicious enough to warrant a call to the police, but this time it came from the woman who ran the nature center's birthday parties. As the guests arrived—happy little boys and girls carrying brightly colored, wrapped boxes with dreams of catching butterflies and frogs—they watched Ward's mommy be escorted to a police car. The little boys were particularly interested and excited about the arrest, which only helped spread the embarrassing incident further around town.

In September, many of the boys remembered it as a summer highlight and detailed it in their "Back to Preschool" journals. "I went to Ward's party and his mommy got a ride in a police car," They told their teachers. The pictures they drew were of a woman with big tears on her cheeks looking out from a police car with Ward standing next to it and crying, too. Some added balloons and a cake. It was rumored that Edward was so disgusted with Brianna that he went ahead with the party and refused to bail her out for forty-eight hours.

The following week, the blotter reported that Edward's vintage Mercedes 230 SL convertible was vandalized in their locked garage. Paint stripper had been poured all over it. "I was told Edward loved that car," Elizabeth said. "Although they never found out who did it, everyone assumed it was Brianna."

"Wow," Abby responded. "Thank goodness for modern medicine."

18

Le Beau Château

Brianna Worth

Brianna was Jack's first sexcapade client. They met just after she finished her court-ordered anger management classes, when he was starting his study of kundalini. Jack connected kundalini with Freud's belief in the body's id versus superego internal struggle. Freud believed the need to conform to society and control the libido led to compulsive, negative behavior. Jack wondered: if people secretly indulged their sex fantasies in a safe and legal way, would it keep them from—in Brianna's case—being so angry, violent, and self-destructive?

Jack discussed what he called his "yogic hypothesis" with me, Brianna recalled. *And then he wanted to know my sexual fantasies. I had many, of course, but there was one recurring one that had often brought me to climax over the years, and it seemed like an easy one to try as my first.*

When I have sex, I imagine a man in the room watching me. In my fantasy, he sits in a corner, silently observing.

That sexcapade was easy enough for Jack to set up. We met in his studio apartment the first time. As Jack and I had sex, a man in his fifties sat on a chair in the corner. After a few sessions of acting out that fantasy, it lost its appeal. The guy, who favored wing tips and fedoras, actually started to creep me out. Jack called it my 'rated-G fantasy.'

"What about other ones?" he asked me. "Or at least let the guy participate." That's when I told him about my stripper fantasy.

When I was in college, there was a strip club called Foxy Lady not far from our campus. After a night out at the bars, most of the boys at our school who hadn't hooked up went there. Curious about the scene, my roommate and I went once with our boyfriends.

Perched on the side of a highway entrance ramp and behind a liquor store, it was about as seedy a place as you would imagine: a large, one-story, dark wood-paneled structure with the trademark scripted neon sign. Broken beer bottles, drug paraphernalia, and used condoms littered the poorly lit parking lot. Inside was a large, cavernous space populated entirely by local men and college boys. The main room had two stages surrounded by U-shaped bars and four-top tables. Private parties and lap dances were conducted in a series of small rooms that split off the building.

The hostess brought us to a square table in the main room close to one of the stages. She knew our boyfriends by name, which should have upset us, but we were too curious about the place to care. We ordered a round of beers, and as our boyfriends lightly groped us beneath the table, we watched the dancers. Of the two, I preferred watching the younger one, a beautiful Hispanic girl. She looked to be about our age and was naturally voluptuous. She was wearing a black camisole with a veiled midsection and tap shorts. Every time she spun, her long, wavy hair fanned, adding to the beauty of her movements.

During her routine, which involved a lot of teasing and then the *removal of all her clothing down to a hot-pink thong, she avoided eye contact with everyone in the room. She looked blankly out into the space, showing no emotion. The men around the stage were memorized with her, their eyes quelling with controlled lust.*

It must be intoxicating to have so many men want you at once, *I'd thought.* She has all the power in the room right now.

At the end of her show, she walked onto the bar that radiated around her stage and accepted money from the men. She pulled bills as high as fifty dollars from their hands, which was clearly a lot of money for the local crowd. As she sauntered by, the men held onto their money tightly, hoping the exchange would allow them to engage her or at the very least force her to be close to them for a moment longer. After she collected her tips, the woman disappeared behind a curtain, and I didn't see her again for the rest of the night.

"You still have your figure," *Jack had coaxed, trying to get me to move beyond my rated-G fantasy.* "You're still as hot as a college girl." *Given my breast implants, my tummy tuck post-pregnancy, and my daily two-hour workouts, I'm actually in much better shape than I was in college, although, I know my body looks very different. Gone are the natural curves and supple skin. They've been replaced by a harder, albeit still attractive, muscled form.*

"I can set it up for you in the carriage barn at Le Beau Château," *Jack suggested.*

"But who would be in the audience?" *I asked.* "I need a good-size audience."

"That's the least of your concerns," *he replied.* "I'll bring a crowd of strangers."

Two months later—post training, lingerie shopping, spray tan, hair weave, and a Brazilian wax—I'm peeking through a curtain into an audience of men. It's a motley crew, and I wonder if Jack rounded up the guys at a soup kitchen. *With baseball hats covering dirty hair, smiles arranged to hide missing teeth, and grass-stained jeans, I worry that they could work for my landscaper.*

Did a few install trees in my yard? *I wonder. I try to banish that thought from my mind. Jack would know to get men who live far out of town, wouldn't he? Before I can get too good a look at the crowd, a spotlight is directed at me, blinding my view. And that's just fine. Today is about me, not them. I just need an audience.*

I had practiced. I had hired a pole-dancing expert, Lola Bell, and I even rented a pole that came on a weighted, wheeled stage. Edward thinks it's my latest exercise craze and even bought me a copy of Demi Moore's Striptease, *which I think he secretly masturbates to. He likes watching me practice with Lola. It's one of the few things that seem to make him happy lately. There is no complaint from him about this expense. He thinks I'm learning how to use the pole to arouse him. He would be furious if he knew I was performing outside of the home.*

But here I am. And I'm dancing and slowly shedding my teddy while deciding if I'll take everything off today. The fewer clothes I have on, the easier it is to work the pole. You need friction, you need exposed skin. The attention is intoxicating. I'm glad I had a ponytail weaved into my hair. I love watching women's hair swing when they twirl. I think it adds so much to the show. I feel like I'm a dancer at the Foxy Lady. I haven't practiced with a live audience yet, but I contemplate collecting tips with parts of my body other than my hands.

19

Several weeks later, Andrew and Elizabeth were at Kings Lord Manor with their daughters in their Easter finery. Elizabeth was excited to see Andrew's reaction to the new development. He grew up in Cannondale and was heartbroken by the way the landscape kept changing. Andrew sometimes felt so defeated by it that he threatened to move the family to Litchfield County, which had retained a more rural, natural charm. When they drove by new developments, Andrew always had a story about the field or the farm or the antique home that used to occupy the space.

Being the youngest in his family by many years, he'd often been on his own after school and during the summers. As was customary in the late 1970s in suburban America, he and his pals rode bikes all over town. They were always in search of a new fishing hole, a creek to wade in, or an awesome tree to climb. The Kings Lord Manor development was especially poignant for him. The house he grew up in abutted the Sterling estate's property, and he used to play there with the Sterling boys.

"They had a huge old barn that we made into our fort," he'd told Elizabeth when he was reading about the sale of the property to Whole Brothers Construction Co. "We met there every day for a few summers. It was before we were old enough to get jobs other than part-time caddying at the country club. I knew every inch of that property—where its streams were located, the apple orchard, the best swimming holes…"

"Be prepared," Elizabeth whispered when the black gate swung open that Easter weekend. "The change will be heartbreaking for you, but remember, the girls will repeat anything you say."

"Are you kidding?" Andrew said in astonishment as he surveyed the transformation. Then he whispered to Elizabeth, "I feel like I'm looking at a really bad movie set. These homes are the worst McMansions I have ever seen." His eyes moved to Leigh's ivy-covered castle. "And why does one property have all the trees?"

"That's a landscape designer's home," Elizabeth whispered back. "She actually spent a ton of money putting back the trees that Whole Development ripped up. The neighbors haven't gotten around to it yet."

"Of course she did," muttered Andrew. "Well, girls, today is like a trip to Disney. There are several very different kinds of manor homes to see. Keep an eye out for your favorite princesses and princes. I've heard a few live here."

Andrew handed the car keys to the valet hired for the party.

This party is much bigger than I anticipated, Elizabeth thought as the family of four approached the Worth's front yard. Alexis and Alice noted a ribboned, sectioned-off area sprinkled with blue dots.

"Why are all the eggs blue?" asked Alexis.

"I'm not sure, girls, but it looks like a robin has been very busy," Elizabeth responded.

"Hello!" Trilled Brianna as she hurried over to greet them. She was wearing a 1950s-style silk blue dress with matching bonnet. The hat had giant blue plumes coming out of the brim. She couldn't look more genteel. "Welcome, welcome!" she said as she reached for the flower arrangement of stargazer lilies, roses, and eucalyptus leaves that the Kellys had brought. "How lovely. Edward never buys me flowers anymore. He thinks they're a waste of money."

"We're admiring all the blue," Elizabeth said." It's Alexis's favorite color."

"Oh, sweetie," Brianna cooed as she pet Alexis's hair. "Thank you. Since you all are new to this party, let me explain. I was VP at Tiffany's for years and the classic Tiffany Blue is my favorite color. I have our kids make all our Easter eggs in my favorite blue each year. Isn't it lovely?"

Elizabeth imagined Brianna's children's boredom with coloring well over two hundred eggs the same color. No experimenting with dyes. No accidently creating brown ones from too much color mixing and egg dipping. Her kids probably colored a few and then escaped to the backyard while she and her housekeeper made the rest. Elizabeth smiled at Brianna and moved on to meet Edward, who'd walked up behind his wife. He was handsome in a classic way, although he wasn't aging well. He was in his late forties but looked well into his fifties.

"Hi, Elizabeth," he said, gesturing with the iced drink he held in one hand. "It's nice to meet you. Sorry I couldn't be home on the day of the *Cannondale Cottages & Gardens* photoshoot. Work has been insanely busy lately."

"No need to apologize," Elizabeth said. "Given it's typically wives who want their homes featured in design magazines, most husbands usually aren't around the day of the shoot."

"Brianna is definitely the one driving our home's publication," he said. "It was in her mind with every purchase she made. I think we spent an extra $300,000 on antiques just to ensure our home would make it into one of the design magazines. She really wanted *Architectural Digest* to feature it, but after its editor rejected us, she set her sights on the magazine you edit."

"Well, at least she and Meredith Fox did a nice job decorating your home," Elizabeth said. "It's lovely."

"Yes, and as a result, filled with expensive stuff we have to tiptoe around," he responded. "It's a good thing I was able to get another job this year."

"Where do you work?" Elizabeth asked.

"I work for a boutique firm called Standard Bearer out of Westport," he said. "I'm a commodities trader."

"Where were you before?" asked Elizabeth, who vaguely remembered someone gossiping about the family and Edward being out of work for a period of time.

"I had been at AIG in Cannondale for ten years but lost that job in late 2008 when the firm was bailed out by the government."

American International Group, Elizabeth thought. The credit derivatives department in the Cannondale office was blamed for bringing down the entire multi-billion dollar company and helping to create the current financial crisis. When it happened, picketers stood outside the AIG executives' homes daily. It appeared on national news. *Maybe that's why the family moved to a gated community?* she wondered.

"I'm sorry to hear that," Elizabeth said. "Andrew was out of work in 2007. It was very stressful for everyone in the family."

"It wasn't stressful for Brianna," responded Edward. "She was in complete denial about our financial situation and continues to be so. She hasn't adjusted her spending habits, and she is exhaustively positive. I keep telling her we need to cut back, especially since we bought and decorated this house, but she completely ignores me. People are still losing jobs in finance. And look at this party. It's ridiculously over the top. Kids don't need all this. On a nice day like this, they just want to play outside and collect a few eggs."

Edward wearily surveyed the party scene: expensively dressed children racing from bouncy castles to pony rides to arts-and-crafts stations. "Want a drink?" Edward offered Elizabeth. "I'm drinking mojitos today." Edward took a long, last chug of his spiced rum-and-mint drink. The ice crashed against his mouth and part of the drink dribbled down his cheeks and chin. He smiled as he wiped the liquid away, his teeth littered with bits of wet mint leaves. He looked around the party again. "Time for another," he said, forgetting he'd offered her one.

Elizabeth looked over and saw that Andrew was still speaking with Brianna. She scanned the crowd. *No sign of Abby and her kids yet,* she thought.

"Hi, Elizabeth," called Adair Burns, who was on her way over, trailed by her four young children. Adair's husband, Hugh, went to college with Andrew, and they now worked at the same Manhattan-based hedge fund. The association brought the two families together a lot. Elizabeth liked Adair. She was a perfectionist, but she had a sense of humor about it. And she was very nice—ultimately, she just wanted everyone to like her. "I'm a hopeless people pleaser," she would say when she caught herself volunteering for something no one else would do, such as make four dozen tea sandwiches for a teacher luncheon or drive home kids whose parents forgot to pick them up after a Daisy troop meeting.

"Hi, Adair," Elizabeth said. "How are you?"

"I'm great," Adair enthusiastically said. It was her usual response.

She was never "fine" or "okay." She was always upbeat and positive, ready for whatever the day might bring.

"Don't my kids look adorable in their matching Easter outfits?" she said, forcing Elizabeth to note their perfectly ironed and miraculously still-clean outfits.

"Matching Burberry," Elizabeth noted. "Yes, very cute and matchy. You won't lose them at this party."

Adair's two girls were wearing jumpers made out of the trademark Burberry tan plaid with matching wide headbands. The boys were in "John John" suits also made out of tan plaid with matching plaid sneakers. The girls looked okay, but the boys, who were eight and seven, looked ridiculous. They were much too old for the suits, and the matching sneakers were comical.

Adair always took things like this too far. It was as if she'd watched too many Kennedy home movies and wanted to recreate Jackie O's stylistic charm. Her kids were always matching. Not just on holidays or other special occasions, but every single day. If the girls were wearing navy-blue dresses with colorful striped tights and coordinating headbands, the boys wore matching striped colored shirts with navy-blue khakis and baseball caps.

I hope her boys aren't being teased today, Elizabeth thought. She'd seen them bullied at the country club for their outfits by some older kids once.

Adair's home was meticulously ordered in a similar way. If she could control something and make it fit her desire for a more perfect world, she did. "I just can't fall asleep when things aren't in order," she once confessed. "I don't feel settled and safe otherwise."

"I know what I'm getting you for your next birthday," Elizabeth joked. "Six 'Team Burns' shirts."

"Oh, that would be so cute," she said. "I love that idea, although Hugh wouldn't wear it. He thinks it's ridiculous how much time I spend coordinating our kids' outfits."

"Were you able to get Hugh to play along with the Burberry today?" Elizabeth asked.

"I tried to," she said, rolling her eyes. "I bought him a pair of plaid Burberry pants, but he flat-out refused," she said. "The closest he would come was to wear a Burberry white oxford. You can't even tell it's made by Burberry."

Elizabeth looked over at Hugh. He wasn't paying attention to where Adair and his kids were at the party. *He always ignores her*, Elizabeth thought. Based on Hugh's gesticulations, it looked like he was talking about fly-fishing with some of the men near him. He was casting with two hands and then pulling an invisible line back with one. He was drinking a bottled Heineken and had a second one full and uncapped waiting for him on the table.

Abby had arrived and was walking her kids over to Elizabeth's, who were in line to have a go at an enormous bunny-shaped piñata. The kids embraced and then appeared to discuss the best strategy for breaking open the piñata.

"This is some party," Abby said as she approached her sister. "So far I've seen three horse-drawn carriages taking the kids on tours of the neighboring conservation land, a petting zoo, countless costumed bunnies, and three egg-coloring and face-painting stations. I feel like I'm at a country fair."

Adair smiled sweetly at Abby, and Elizabeth introduced them. After hellos, Adair brought up Jack's upcoming benefit. "Jack told me you would be willing to help with the final planning and execution of the benefit," she said to Abby.

"Did he?" Abby said, smiling.

"Yes, he said you agreed to help during a private session," said Adair. "When did you start taking private sessions with him?"

"A few weeks ago," Abby responded.

"He seems to be offering them to everyone now," Adair said with a hint of annoyance.

"I guess I did agree," Abby said, choosing to ignore her comment, "although I could claim that the agreement was made under duress. I was at the end of shavasana when he asked."

"Elizabeth, will you help, too?" Adair asked. "I'm feeling completely overwhelmed. Many of the women who volunteered have turned out to be halfheartedly involved and haven't followed through on what they promised. Brianna is the only volunteer who has been a real help to me. Jack's assistant Leaha is helping, but she also assists him with his yoga business and the clothing aspect of the charity. I'm scrambling to get things done. It would be great if you two could help me."

"Aside from reading to my kids' classes, I don't volunteer for much, but since White's a sponsor, I can ask my secretaries to help," Abby said.

"That works," Adair enthused. "We'll have a planning meeting shortly. I'll email you the details. We always meet at Pound Ridge's Mon Petite Café. Have you been there? It's staffed by absolutely beautiful young French men. Do you think you can come?"

"Yes," They both responded.

"Thank you," said Adair. "I know I can trust you to follow through. You have no idea how much weight you just took off my shoulders."

The children were soon called to the front yard, and the ribboned area was opened for egg hunting. The older children ran wildly through the yard, grabbing as many eggs as possible. The toddlers' adorably picked up one at a time, staring at them and then shaking them, hoping to hear candy inside. Once all the blue dots disappeared from the Worth's front yard, Brianna awarded large, stuffed Steiff bunnies to the kids who'd collected the most eggs. The children were then asked to congregate near a series of white picnic tables. They were served a sit-down lunch provided by Kate Musto's catering company, Katherine's. Neighboring the area, a secondary station of more sophisticated offerings—prepared gourmet sandwiches and salads—were brought out for the adults. Some of the food was dyed the trademark Tiffany Blue.

"Tiffany Blue deviled eggs and Tiffany Blue egg salad sandwiches are on!" Brianna called out.

"Disgusting!" rang out in the distance.

"That sounded like Edward's voice," Elizabeth whispered to Abby.

After lunch, the catering staff brought out platters of dessert and placed them on the children's and adults' tables. They were filled with individual cakes, each one expensively made to look like a Faberge egg. Some of the partygoers admired the eggs and ate them, but most people did nothing more than pick at them. The children not being watched by their parents—who were in the majority since alcohol was being served—started sticking the tables' Easter decorations into the cakes. That led to throwing them.

"Want to play egg toss?" said one mischievous boy to another before chucking a chocolate ganache egg at his head.

At the end of the party, Brianna was in the front yard saying good-bye while Edward was nowhere to be found. Andrew offered to find him to say thank you for all of them. He had seen Edward walk into the conservation land behind the home. That's where

Andrew found him, but upon seeing the state Edward was in, Andrew chose not to disturb him.

Edward was standing alone with a pitcher of mojitos, a tall glass half full, and a basket of eggs. One by one, he picked up colored eggs and whipped them at a large oak tree. As the eggs smashed against the bark, Tiffany Blue pieces flew into the air.

20

Brianna Worth (Mobile):

Call me when you're free. Real estate question.

Abigail Davis-Powers (Mobile):

I will in twenty minutes.

Abby and the rest of town had already heard about the Worth's most recent misfortune. Just weeks after the Worth's Easter party, the hedge fund Edward worked for—Standard Bearer—was being investigated for securities fraud. It was front-page news in *The Cannondale Bulletin*, *The Cannondale Villager*, several online sources—*The Daily Cannondale*, *Breaking News: Cannondale*, *Neighborly News*—and was even mentioned in the back pages of *The Wall Street Journal's* "Greater New York" section.

SECURITIES FRAUD AND CONSPIRACY CHARGES
RAILED AGAINST STANDARD BEARER

STANDARD BEARER'S PROFITS CALLED INTO QUESTION

QUESTIONABLE STANDARDS AT STANDARD BEARER

Several top executives were accused of trading on information from company insiders at computer and chemical companies, reaping a combined $12 million in illegal profits. Three had been arrested and more arrests were anticipated.

"Standard Bearer is riddled with criminal conduct," said the federal prosecutor. Edward had been questioned but not arrested. He swore to Brianna that the misconduct had occurred before he started his job six months ago. Brianna wanted to believe him, but when *Neighborly News* ran an article titled HOW DID WORTH REALLY GAIN HIS WORTH?, she started to question Edward's culpability, too.

Brianna and Edward first met at the University of Michigan while in business school; she'd known right away that he would be successful. She was attracted to his smarts and savvy. Post-graduation, Edward was the youngest managing director in the Chicago office of Merrill Lynch. His career had been on an upward trajectory...until the AIG meltdown. And now this.

It's just a career challenge, she told herself. *Edward will get us through.*

After all, he was still employed. Standard Bearer hadn't gone under yet. The firm was being investigated and a few of its top players were arrested, but no one had been convicted yet. Without a conviction, clients couldn't pull funding before their agreement dates were up. It was contractual.

As long as Edward wasn't arrested, Brianna knew he, along with the remaining executives, could make Standard Bearer profitable, which would keep their clients' money with the fund. She believed in him, and her feel-good meds bolstered her conviction.

Edward wasn't feeling as confident. He worried that he had peaked as a twenty-eight-year-old managing director at Merrill Lynch, which seemed like eons ago. The AIG firing had rocked him, and now this.

We lost so much money when I left AIG, he often thought. *All those stock options that were part of my bonuses...*

At Standard Bearer, he *hadn't* traded on insider information, but he was afraid he would be taken down with the others. Everyone at work was panicked, and it didn't help that he came home at the end of every day to Brianna's Xanax-laced pep talks.

I liked her better when she lived her days in a rage, he thought. Before her counseling, before her anger management/life-coaching skills, before her daily yoga routines, before her meds. Their kitchen was now littered with positive affirmations: "Anger is a short madness" and "For every minute you are angry, you lose sixty seconds of happiness." He wanted to rip them from the walls.

Edward knew Brianna, and he knew that, even with the meds, it was just a matter of time before she cracked. That was why he continued to allow her to throw lavish parties and spend money carelessly. He loved her, and doing those things buoyed her, helped her function. But the financial pressure was starting to kill him, and he felt increasingly isolated. He didn't know when it would happen, but he knew he was going to break in his own way, too.

Now, weeks after the initial bad publicity, Abby was calling Brianna back after receiving her real estate-related text.

"Hi, Brianna," said Abby as she reviewed the Worths' current and previous listings. She noted the couple's long working relationship with realtor Skippy Travis. "How are you?"

"Not great," Brianna responded, "but okay. Edward's firm will survive. We just have to wait. With that said, Edward wants to sell the house. He's in total panic mode again. You'd think we have no savings with the way he's reacting."

"Speaking as someone who has been through something similar, I do understand why he is worried, Brianna," Abby said. "Don't you?"

"Of course, and I'm worried, too, but he can be so overly dramatic," she responded.

"How can I help?" asked Abby.

"We need a good agent," she said. "Since moving to the area we've used Skippy, but Edward wasn't happy with how he negotiated on this house. Edward was wondering if you can represent us. If not, he wants to interview two or three of White's top agents."

"My firm doesn't allow managers to have listings," Abby responded. "White's sees it as a conflict of interest given that I'm supposed to be mentoring and should not be in direct competition with the agents that work for the firm. But I can suggest several agents for you and Edward to interview. What are you looking for in an agent?"

"They have to be the firm's highest producers," Brianna responded.

"Okay," Abby said, "will do. And how are you and your kids doing?"

"The kids are okay. I keep Edward from them when he gets into one of his moods," she said. She felt she could speak with Abby about her personal life given Colin's suicide. "When Edward took the job at Standard Bearer, we hoped things would finally settle down, including him. But he hasn't, and he's drinking way too much, which doesn't help anything. I never know what to expect when he walks in the door. I have my own history of mood swings, too, so I understand what he goes through, but that doesn't make it easier when he's freaking out. *I* got help and medication. *I* started practicing yoga regularly, and I meet with Jack weekly for private sessions. All of it keeps me level. Edward won't even go to a shrink."

"Sounds like you are doing as well as can be expected," said Abby. "It's harder for men to admit they need outside help. I hope he figures it out soon."

"Have you considered private sessions with Jack?" Brianna asked. "He could guide you through your grieving process. He has been instrumental in helping me."

"I appreciate the suggestion, Brianna, very much," said Abby sincerely. "I did start sessions with him, and they are helping."

21

APowers@WhitesRealty.com writes:

Dear Cecily,

I hope your open houses over the weekend went well.

Our appointment with the Worths is tomorrow at noon. Let's drive over together. I'll meet you at the office at 11:30 a.m. Also, when previewing the home we can't forget to see the spa in the basement. It's supposed to be amazing. I think it's the only one in Fairfield County, so we won't have a comparable to determine the value, but you and I should be able to assign one after seeing it.

Fondly,

  Abby

Abigail Davis-Powers
White's Realty
Managing Director

As Abby and Cecily approached the Worth home, Abby mar-veled at how a manufacturer could create a single door with so much crap on it. As she reached for the doorbell, the Victorian-inspired, elaborately carved, two-toned, mauve-painted door with etched glass panels slowly opened.

"Hi, Abby and Cecily," said a subdued Brianna. "I'll warn you now that Edward isn't having a good day."

The colleagues exchanged glances. "We can come back another time," offered Abby.

"No, he wants to meet with you," she said. "He wants to move forward with what he refers to as 'unloading this albatross.' I have to keep reminding him that he wanted to buy this home a year ago. It's not all my fault."

Filled with a combination of art deco and French empire antiques coupled with modern artwork and accessories against a surprising all-white background, the home was breathtakingly beautiful.

"It's stunning," Cecily said. "Absolutely stunning."

Brianna took them on a tour but purposely avoided Edward's office. "We'll wait and deal with him later," she said.

As they entered the kitchen, Brianna said, "First I'll show you what my decorator Meredith refers to as her 'tour de force.' Follow me."

Adair led the women to a basement door. They descended an illuminated, black stairwell to a single door. There was a warm bathhouse feel.

"You must have a pool down here," Cecily stated.

"Yes," Brianna said with a grin.

Brianna opened the door to a walled area of the large basement that was tunneled after the home was built. It was composed of fieldstone walls with two small pools, a large glassed-in shower stall with steam, a sauna, and a reclining area filled with chaise lounges and covered by striped tenting. The pools, shower, and sauna were lined with various shades of blue-and-gray glass tiles.

It was a classic Turkish bath—a hammam—and steam room. The ultimate escape. Another door opened into a yoga studio and gym.

"Have you ever been to L'Hotel in Paris?" Abby asked, remembering it and the long weekend she and Colin spent there several years ago. It was so similar: the bright, updated dungeon look, the pool and glass shower with blue mosaic tiles, the tented rest area.

"Yes, we have stayed there several times," Brianna said. "For me, that hotel is the ultimate in luxury: it's intimate, it's beautifully designed, and it has a cool literary history. Did you know Oscar Wilde died there? The public rooms are filled with fine art and each hotel room has a different, garish style. And then you descend into a space least expected: a hammam room. Stone walls, glass tile… It's the perfect combination of ancient and modern. It's so lux and secret. I had to try to recreate it."

"Is that a stripper pole?" Cecily blurted out as they entered the adjoining yoga studio and gym. The pole was supported by a six-by-six-foot base festooned with a royal blue-and-red tasseled swag. The actual pole was brass and resembled the ones kids cling to when riding on a merry-go-round. "If it is, once the house officially goes on the market, I recommend you put it in storage."

"Yes, it is a stripper's pole," Brianna said. "It's an amazing form of exercise. Want me to give you a demonstration? I've gotten really good."

"No, thank you," Abby blurted out. "Another time. We have an office meeting after this appointment."

"Well, then it's time to face Edward," Brianna said. "I'll warn you in advance, Cecily. He's going to grill you on your market knowledge, negotiation skills, and past sales."

"As to be expected," Cecily responded.

The meeting with Edward went as Abby and Cecily anticipated. Given the price points of the houses they sold, they were accustomed to dealing with master-of-the-universe-type personalities—whether real or self-inflated. Homeowners moving by choice or trading up were generally more pleasant during the initial meeting but not necessarily easier to work with over the course of the sale. The ones who had fallen on hard times were, understandably, another story.

During the meeting, Edward sat behind his desk alternating between tense and relaxed poses. *He's like a simmering teapot,* Abby thought. *At any second, he could blow.* The women were relieved when it was time to go.

The following day, after Abby spoke with Edward again and ensured him that she would be intricately involved throughout the selling process of their home, he decided to use Cecily as their agent.

"Congratulations. You got the Worth listing," Abby said over the phone to Cecily.

"That's good news, I think," Cecily responded with a laugh.

"It'll be fine," Abby said, "and if they become difficult, I'll help you."

"He's the one I'm most worried about," said Cecily. "There is so much tension between the two of them, and he's so quick to anger."

"I know," Abby replied, sighing. "He's a bit of a ticking time bomb. Let's hope they get multiple offers the first weekend and then you can be rid of them quickly. Who do you want to shoot the property?"

"I think Neil Landino would be best," Cecily said.

"I agree," responded Abby. "He's great. Set it up and you and I can go there beforehand to scout and plan the best shots."

Two days later, Abby was ensconced in Cecily's pristine convertible Mercedes-Benz CLK550. After a morning of touring Cannondale's open house offerings together, they pulled into Kings Lord Manor. "Did you let them know we're coming by today?" Abby asked.

"No, but I texted Brianna while were at the last house to say we just need to stop by quickly and survey the property. I already know what's going to photograph best inside the home."

"Okay," Abby said. "Let's hope they aren't home." As the women pulled in, Abby noted a large, dated Winnebago parked in Leigh's driveway.

"How funny," she said.

"Hope that eyesore is out of here before the open house," Cecily said.

"Don't worry, Leigh won't let something like that sit in her driveway for long," Abby responded. "It's probably a relative's."

"They have a cousin Eddie, too?" Cecily joked, referencing Chevy Chase's movie *Christmas Vacation*.

"At least one," Abby responded.

Cecily and Abby parked and, after surveying the front of the home, walked around to the back patio. It was large enough to fit four furniture groupings and had the requisite Fairfield County fire pit, outdoor kitchen, and pergola. The colleagues discussed staging items.

"Edward said he doesn't want to spend another penny on this home, but we do need a few bowls of fruit and a number of those large colorful ceramic pots filled with ferns and mums," Cecily suggested. "I'll call their decorator; I'm sure she'll lend a few."

"Now what about the backyard?" Abby asked. "It's all grass."

"I wish the houses weren't so close together," Cecily continued. "Neil is going to have to come in so close on certain angles to keep the neighboring homes out of the shot. And then you have this huge, empty triangular expanse in the backyard."

"Since Leigh and Brianna are very close," said Cecily, "maybe Leigh would be willing to get them a few Rhododendron and ivy bushes at cost. I'll pay for them. It would definitely help sell the house. Otherwise, potential buyers will be calculating all the money they'll need to spend landscaping the backyard. We don't want its barrenness to be so striking.

"What's that structure in the way, way backyard of the Gildings' property?" Cecily asked. "It wasn't there when I sold them the house. It looks like a mini-castle covered in ivy?"

"That's the kids' playhouse," Abby said with amusement. "It's a replica of the home."

"Are you kidding me?" Cecily said, giggling. "That's as big as the house I grew up in!" Then they saw two people exit Leigh's mini-castle. It was initially difficult to tell who it was.

"Maybe it's Mira and a workman," Abby offered. "She makes the best macadamia nut cookies."

As the figures got closer, the women realized it was Leigh and Edward walking side by side. Leigh was wearing a long white terrycloth bathrobe tied at the waist. Edward was dressed casually. They were chatting and smiling.

"Do they have a hot tub back there?" Cecily wondered aloud.

Then Leigh reached out to Edward and tugged at his untucked shirttail. She stopped walking. He turned his head to say something to her but kept moving toward his house. She crossed her arms and pouted.

"Uh-oh," said Cecily. "This looks odd."

"Before we see more, maybe we should call out to them and wave," Abby suggested.

But they said nothing and instead moved behind two fieldstone masonry pillars as Edward continued walking toward his house. Leigh called him again. This time he turned around, and she dropped her bathrobe. She was naked, posing with one knee bent.

"Oh my God," escaped Cecily's mouth. "We have to get out of here."

Edward quickly glanced around their two adjoining yards, wearing a childlike, mischievous look, but he didn't see Cecily and Abby. He turned and moved toward Leigh. She grabbed her bathrobe and started running to the mini-castle. Within moments, they were both inside.

"Holy shit," Cecily said.

"Let's get out of here," Abby responded.

"I don't particularly like Brianna," Cecily said as they pulled out of the driveway, "but I do feel sorry for her. Leigh and Brianna are really close friends, or at least Brianna thinks they are."

"I know," Abby responded. "I wouldn't have put Leigh and Edward together or guessed that the mini-castle had dual purposes: a high-end jail for the kids and a love shack for Leigh."

22

Abby looked over at Jack. *Is he asleep?* she wondered. *I can't believe we finally slept together.*

Given that this had been their fifth private session, Abby had started to wonder if it would ever happen. All of the sessions had been intimate—extremely so—but Jack had remained professional.

God, it was killing me, she thought. *It must be one of his tactics. The sex has got to be better if he makes his private clients wait, building our desire to a boiling point.*

And the sex was good—really good, Abby thought, *but he is such a tease.* Jack had brought Abby within seconds of climaxing several times only to pull back and prolong it. Knowing he was playing her and not wanting to give him the satisfaction, she had refrained from begging.

I would have begged if he didn't make me wait until the fifth private session, Abby thought.

Once she and Colin got to know each other well, they used to play a similar game. But it was good-natured, Abby recalled. *It was fun,* she thought, *not manipulative. At some point, we stopped doing it. I don't even remember when. We just did. He just did. Was it after Quinn was born? When we made less time for sex?*

Abby guiltily started to wonder how she had curtailed their sex life, too. How her beautiful collection of silk teddies and nighties languished in her dresser when she started to favor sleepwear that would avoid raising questions from their children.

"Mommy, aren't you cold wearing that?" Quinn asked her the first evening he wandered into their bedroom half asleep. After that night, it became a habit Colin and Abby tried to break but weren't successful with until he turned five. And by that point, Lily had also started the nightly migration.

"For God's sake, when did our bed turn into the family bed?" Colin had whispered to Abby when he heard the *pitter-patter* of little feet entering their room during sex. A lack of time and privacy had been their enemy. *How sad*, Abby thought. *Does that happen to all married couples?*

Abby looked back over at Jack. *He's definitely asleep*, she thought. She had no doubt he'd been impressed by her. It wasn't in Abby's DNA to question her abilities, especially not with sex. Before getting married, she'd had a lot of experience with both men and women. It had been a while since those trysts, and she'd never cheated on Colin, but she knew she was good when she wanted to be.

And now I'm single again, she thought, happy to have finally slept with someone since Colin's death. *I need to start acting like I'm single again*, she thought.

∼∽∼∽

"Abby, I want to talk to you about something," Jack said after he emerged from her bathroom showered and dressed. "It's a private matter, but I feel I can trust you with the information even if we don't end up working together on it. I think you'll be interested because of the potential financial benefits."

"Okay," said Abby. "Go ahead. I promise to keep whatever you tell me between us."

"You can't even tell your sister," he said.

"Okay," she lied, knowing Elizabeth would be the first person she called after he left.

"I offer a service to my private clients where I fulfill their sexual fantasies, a type of sexcapades," Jack began. "I want to know if you'll broker for me by feeding me clients. For each client you send to me—they have to start out as private-session clients so that I can vet them, I don't want any crazies—I will give you an agreed-upon fee. If they sign up for my sexcapades service, then you'll get a cut from each tryst."

"That sounds interesting," said Abby, "and potentially lucrative."

"Yes, it would be," said Jack. "I'm asking you to broker for several reasons. The first day you were in my yoga class, I recognized a shrewdness to you that I don't see in most of the Cannondale women. Secondly, given that you are the manager of a top real estate firm, you know and will come to know many women in town. I've found the best time to get women to sign up for private sessions is when they first move to Cannondale. Most of the husbands who live in town commute to Manhattan. The women are left alone for long stretches of time. They're new, so haven't found a clique yet. Basically, they're lonely and a bit lost. That's what makes you the ideal broker for me. Also, you'll have gotten the lowdown on them from your agents and can begin the vetting process for me."

"I'm interested," Abby responded, "but I need to test the service before I recommend it. Also, I want a contract specifically detailing how and what I will be paid as well as legal assurance that I will never be tied to your service. Lastly, there has to be a guarantee that none of the women I send to you will be in any kind of physical danger."

"That's fair," said Jack. "Now, what's your fantasy? If you need to think about it, you can get back to me. Most women need to think about it a bit."

"I know mine," said Abby, not missing a beat. "I'd like to start by having sex with several firemen in a firehouse. There's a small, secondary one near the border of Ridgefield. It shouldn't be too hard for you to set up given their rotations and that only a few of them spend the night in the firehouse. Next, I want to be with a few policemen. It doesn't have to happen in the station. I know there's only one in town, and it's fully manned around the clock."

Jack laughed.

Did I answer too quickly? Abby worried. *I wasn't supposed to know about this service.* Abby knew that the only reason she had an answer thought out was because of the conversation she'd had with Elizabeth.

"I should have known you would instantly know what to ask for," Jack said. "That's part of why I like you so much, and why I know you'll be perfect as my broker."

23

Le Beau Château

Abby Davis-Powers

It wasn't until Abby was waiting in the tiny room in the firehouse a few weeks after her conversation with Jack that she began to remember. The familiar scratchiness of the fire department-issued blanket underneath her hands and its faint mildew smell instantly took her back to the night of Colin's death.

He was tall, and he had large brown eyes, she recalled. *He was the one who stopped me as I ran from the club toward the tarp, the garish blue tarp that was positioned half on the sidewalk and half in the street covering Colin. He stopped me and, as I initially struggled to break free, held me tightly. Someone walked up behind me and placed a blanket on my shoulders. The fireman wrapped it securely around me, holding me in what felt like a hug. At some point, I stopped resisting his grip and collapsed against his chest, against his rough Nomex jacket. He held me like that for what must have been several minutes before two female police officers arrived and, shielding my eyes from the tarp, took me to a waiting ambulance.*

The moment I deduced that Colin had jumped—that he had taken his own life while I was inside at a party, sipping champagne—I had to go to him. *There had been a number of sirens, but that's common enough in New York. And then an officious-looking man who turned out to be the club manager appeared in the dining room with two security guards and brought the lights up. He spoke gravely with the Brownings and pointed to the roof. Following the Brownings' lead, many in the room walked to the windows that look out onto Fifth Avenue and stared down in shock. The band was instructed to stop playing. I scanned the room.*

No Colin, *I thought.* How long has he been gone? *And then the manager and security guards were on their way over to me. I panicked. I knew, and I knew I would never get to Colin if they got to me first.*

What if he's near death and struggling? *I wondered. I ran to the fire exit, down seven flights of stairs, and out into the lobby. It was clear. Everyone in it had moved to the windows—everyone but an ancient doorman, but he was easy enough to dodge. And then I was on the entrance steps and on the 54ᵗʰ Street sidewalk. As I rounded the corner of the club, the bright-blue tarp directed me to him.*

I was about ten feet away when the fireman stepped in my path. He couldn't have known that I was the victim's wife, but he must have understood it on some level. Later, as the police officers gently pulled me from him, I looked at his face for the first time. I saw his eyes—his kind, big brown eyes.

I should have been smart enough to know that my fantasy had nothing to do with sex. Jack had asked me all the tacky stereotype questions in advance: do you want them to wear their uniforms? Do you want to have sex in the cab of the fire truck? Does the fire pole need to be involved?

Then, of all things, he warned me that they wouldn't run the siren at that time of night. What am I? Five years old? *All I could* do was laugh. *It sounded like such a dumb idea when imagined through those questions. So cheap. So desperate.*

I told him that I had no interest in seeing them in their firemen uniforms, that there was no need for them to wear their black boots. I didn't need to see the truck or the pole. I certainly didn't want a siren. He was surprised when I told him that all I wanted was to be with them in their private quarters. He warned me that the accommodations weren't much better than a prison cell, but I didn't care. There was a part of me that knew I wanted to be in that room, that I needed to be there to remember the only comfort I felt the night Colin died.

Elizabeth knew. She said it: I feel safe with civil servants now. Since Colin's death, I'm vulnerable in ways I have never been before. I've changed, and I need help. Lots of help. Will sex with a few firemen in that room help me? I don't know. Can I trust Jack? I hope so. Can his faith in kundalini make a believer out of me?

Abby shifted on the cot and decided to get underneath the blanket and top sheet while she was waited for the firemen. *That blanket really was scratchy*, she thought.

There were footsteps in the hallway. The door to the room opened.

Wow, they're young, she thought. *Oh God, why are they wearing their helmets? This is embarrassingly bad. What could they possibly think of me? But they are cute...very cute. And fit. And eager. Extremely eager. Maybe twenty-five years old? If they lose the helmets, I might be able to do this. I definitely can do this. But, you know, Jack was right. This room is very basic. How are all three of us going to fit on this cot? I certainly don't want them to push two of these together and attempt it. I'd end up on the linoleum floor.*

Jack was right. This room is like a prison cell. Maybe sex in the cab of the fire truck would be better? It certainly would be different, more fantasy-like. Better to stir up the kundalini energy.

When we're done, when I've exhausted myself, maybe I'll take home one of their blankets as a keepsake.

24

Le Beau Château

Stacy Blake

"Yes, Jack," Abby said into her phone. "Extreme bondage."

"Yes, that's what she said," Abby continued.

"No, I don't know if she's done it before. I really didn't want to get into it with her. I figured you could ask her during your vetting process. She's into yoga and looking forward to the private sessions leading up to the sexcapade. I'll text you her information. And you better treat her well. She's buying a $6 million house on the water in Southport through us. We have both the seller and buyer sides of the deal. All cash. The house closes in a month… Bye for now."

~~~

Jack spent two private sessions with Stacy Blake before he broached the subject of bondage. He felt that he had to tread carefully—if she didn't have past familiarity with extreme bondage, then the experience might frighten her. Despite the confidentiality contract every client had to sign, a really bad sexcapade could lead a participant to go public about the service. He couldn't have that. He had to make sure that each client was happy and discreet. And in Stacy's case, he also didn't want to screw up the house sale for Abby. He needed her to keep feeding him clients—to date, their partnership had been very fruitful.

But after discussing the sexcapade with Stacy, Jack realized she knew exactly what she was asking for. No doubt about it. Stacy wanted B&D—bondage and discipline—which was basically torture. She wanted the role of "madam," which meant she would be totally in charge. The men—she wanted six of them, not five or seven, but exactly six—were to be bound with leather straps, chains, and cuffs, including thumb cuffs or monogloves, as well as blind folded and gagged. She wanted a few to have cloth bags over their heads. "They have to be rendered completely helpless," she insisted.

For the torture part, she requested leather whips, rattan canes, metal knuckle rings, and hot wax in black, red, blue, and burgundy.

Holy shit, Jack thought as he listened to her cavalierly rattling off her list. He was actually kind of scared by the request. This was the first sexcapade where he would have to worry about the men's safety instead of the woman's.

After planning the details with an underground B&D group, Jack hired three off-duty cops to keep an eye on Stacy and a nurse to perform "aftercare" on any of the men who needed it post-session.

Stacy insisted her first sexcapade take place at night with the room lit only by candlelight. Jack had six men positioned around the room waiting for her, each tied in complex leather bindings. She entered the room wearing a dominatrix outfit: leather thigh-high boots, a black leather corseted bustier, and a coordinating thong.

Stacy proceeded to beat the hell out of the men and then demanded Jack set them free one at a time. She ordered the free man to lay prone on the floor or the bed. She covered their chests in hot wax, creating a wild, splattered Jackson Pollock-like design as they writhed in pain—but at the same time, they appeared to enjoy every hot drip.

This is sick, Jack thought as he watched. *What the hell happened to these people for them to enjoy this so much?* Then she had sex with each man, riding each one hard, totally in control. Once a man climaxed, she demanded he leave the room. Each one went to a bedroom just down the hall to meet with the nurse for cold compresses and bandages.

What is she going to request as her next sexcapade? Jack worried. When driving home, he reflected: *do sex acts as brutal as this one encourage kundalini's movement or stop it dead in its tracks? Does brutality lead to enlightenment?* He wasn't sure.

25

As Abby sat in Duff's Pub waiting for her lunch date with the police chief, Kevin Knight, she had to stop herself from asking the waitress to wipe down the seemingly-clean-but-probably-germ-ridden tabletop. She reviewed the menu: French onion soup, a soup of the day, burgers, more burgers, a chicken breast on bun, chicken wings in almost every flavor imaginable, and garden and Caesar salads.

I bet the salads in this place are terrible, she thought. *They'll be a few hunks of iceberg lettuce and thickly sliced vegetables with a glob of fat-saturated dressing on top.*

Regardless, Abby was impressed with herself for suggesting this spot over a more refined selection. *This is probably where police officers like to eat lunch*, she thought. Abby had never let a chicken wing touch her lips, but she told herself that if Kevin ordered some, she would try one—despite knowing that each wing had something like twenty grams of fat.

This would be the third date for the couple since they met during a sexcapade at Le Beau Château. After her experience at the firehouse, Jack had Abby meet him at the estate for a romp with police officers. Once there, Jack had walked her to a secluded part of the property where a police car and three policemen, one being the captain, were waiting. Somehow, despite the scenario and all the sex, she and Kevin connected.

Although names weren't shared, Kevin had seen her profile in *Neighborly News* when she joined White's. A week after the session, he called her and explained that he wanted to take her out. After her initial alarm, she agreed. There was something about him that she liked.

On their first date, he took her to Compo Beach for a long walk with his two rescue dogs and a picnic that he made himself. During their walk, he told her about his years of working as a detective in Manhattan and how his current job was a change he made to get away from crime in a large city. He spoke of his wife and how she had died from ALS two years before. His sharing made Abby comfortable enough to speak freely about Colin and his suicide. Kevin remembered the story well. Kevin was smart, quiet, and observant. He was empathic in the way that good cops were.

During their second date, Abby asked how he knew Jack. "We met when Georgette Ark was installing the safe room," he explained. "She called me in as a consultant, and Jack was overseeing the work. We became friends."

"Are you involved with a lot of his sexcapades?" Abby asked, afraid of his answer and what it would mean for her burgeoning hopes of a relationship with him.

"You were the first one to ask for a cop," he said with a smile. "You were my first entry into that world. To be honest, once it started, I wasn't into the foursome part of it at all. The minute I saw you, the minute I touched you, I wanted to have you all to myself. I didn't like having to share you."

Abby blushed and unconsciously raised a hand to her cheek.

"I felt the same way," she admitted, making Kevin smile broadly. "I just wanted to be with you."

"Most of the time, I think sexual fantasies are better as fantasies rather than as reality," he added. "A foursome sounds fun, but I didn't enjoy watching the other guys have sex with you. I thought I would, but it was too coarse for me."

Abby now felt embarrassed to have been the cause of it.

"Yes, most fantasies probably are better than their enactment," she responded.

"Anyway, I'm not really a part of his sexcapades, but I've known about Jack's service for a while," Kevin continued. "Jack hires some of my officers for them. They just aren't presented as officers like they were with you. The guys like the sex. It keeps them happy. It's not exactly legal because money changes hands, but everyone is of age and no one gets hurt, so I'm okay with it. And I help Jack by keeping Le Beau Château secure when a sexcapade is in process. I send a patrol car to the neighborhood and have them stay in the area until it's over. Sometimes I station a car at the base of the driveway."

Kevin had wanted to ask Abby about the extent of her involvement in the sexcapades service, but he was hesitant. He couldn't believe he was on a date with a woman like her. When Jack first discussed Abby with Kevin, he told him that Abby was going to broker for him and was testing the service by meeting with police officers. "You and your men are going to have to perform," Jack had said. "She's no babe in the woods." Kevin hoped she was done testing and using the service.

After waiting for a few minutes, Abby saw Kevin enter the pub for their third date. He greeted her with a huge hug. "I love this place," he beamed. "They have the best buffalo wings."

She smiled. She was genuinely happy.

26

Only three more hours until Jack arrives, Adair mused as she sipped her morning latté and gazed out her kitchen window. *I wish I were his only private client. Why can't I be his only private client? I told him I would pay him a salary equal to what he gets from all his private-client work. I don't want to share him. I want him all to myself.*

It was Monday morning—Adair's favorite day of the week. She'd been up for hours. She always felt restless on this day, too excited to sleep in. She wished it were ten o'clock already.

Adair heard movement on the second floor of her home. *It's Trevor heading to the bathroom*, she thought.

Of her four children, all age eight and under, Trevor always woke first. She heard the bang of the toilet seat crashing against its tank. She heard a flush followed by the start of the shower. Shortly after, she heard the *pitter-patter* of six additional feet on their way to find her.

Adair looked at her phone again and saw it was 7:22 a.m. Their nanny, Sheila, and housekeeper, Betty, wouldn't be there for thirty-eight more minutes. Her husband, Hugh, had been gone for over an hour. He commuted to Manhattan, leaving at six o'clock in the morning and returning after seven o'clock in the evening.

He's always gone for this morning routine, Adair thought, sighing.

It was now 7:24 a.m. Her three youngest, Tristan, Penny, and Tatum, with their hair in tangles and rubbing their eyes, padded into the kitchen. Adair put on the best smile she could muster at 7:24 a.m. and, as she opened her arms wide to collectively hug them, asked, "What would my sweets like for breakfast this morning?"

Monday was the day that Jack spent two uninterrupted hours with Adair in the bamboo-paneled yoga studio she built on her stately Georgian Colonial house specifically for this purpose. Citing a full schedule, Jack only allotted Adair one private session per week.

It killed her. She wanted more time with him. She angled for it whenever she could. In order to see Jack more, Adair went to his yoga classes religiously. She volunteered for his charity, Auntie Arts, accepting whatever task he asked of her.

By nine o'clock on Mondays, Adair's kids were fed, washed and dressed. Depending on their age, they would soon be in or on their way to preschool, school, or with nanny Sheila at the Stepping Stones Museum for Children. Housekeeper Betty, who also did all the grocery shopping, would be off to the Village Market, Garelick & Herbs, Pagano's Seafood, and Trader Joe's with an impossibly long list of groceries. The landscapers—with the exception of the foreman, Manuel, Adair always seemed to forget their names—were instructed to stay off the property until one p.m. Deliverymen were told to leave packages at the front gate.

By nine thirty on Mondays, Adair was always showered with her long blonde hair blown dry and straightened, her entire body moisturized with the cream that Jack once told her smelled "delicious," and her face covered in a light application of makeup. She dressed for yoga in an Under Armour black sports bra, matching fitted Capris, and a loose, translucent tank top. Fuzzy UGG slippers were on her feet.

On this particular Monday, Adair went to her yoga studio after surveying her perfectly maintained thirty-eight-year-old body in her large dressing room's three-way mirror. Once there she waited, prone with eyes closed, lying on her stomach as Jack requested. The lights were low. The iTunes playlist Jack made for her played quietly. She breathed and expelled deep, long breaths.

Knowing Jack would be with her shortly, she started to calm down. She started to feel hopeful. She felt desire. She started to get to wet.

Jack let himself in and walked through the fashionably decorated and immaculately clean and orderly home to the basement studio. He removed his shoes and lay down next to Adair on a mat.

Once he was settled, Adair heard his breathing, imagining the rise and fall of his chest. Soon their breathing synced, becoming one. Shortly after, Jack reached for her hand and intertwined their fingers. Several more minutes passed, and then Jack, as he slowly stood and released their hands, moved over Adair's body and straddled her. He placed his hands under her hip bones and then slowly moved them to her breasts, cupping them while whispering "Good morning, Adair" in her ear in a way that made her feel faint. Lingering in that position, massaging her breasts, Jack instructed her to breathe deeply.

From that point—the routine varied every week—Jack slowly moved his hands along her arms, taking her wrists and pulling her upper body toward him in a series of gentle, long stretches. Then, laying Adair flat again, he massaged her back while tenderly grinding his hips against hers. On cue, she rolled over and, with Jack at her side, her legs were moved through a sequence of slow, long stretches. They moved into a partner forward fold, their legs and arms in a V-shape with their toes and hands touching. Rhythmically, he rocked Adair back and forth. Then he knelt in front of her, moving her legs into a wide-angle posture with his hands on either side of her outstretched arms.

Minutes passed. She waited in anticipation for his next touch. Jack was teasing her. Adair's desire built.

He slowly lowered and kissed her. His eyes were open and kind, desiring her, only her.

Jack's hands moved under her back, and he pulled her chest toward his. The kisses and pace quickened. Instinct took over, and they fought free of their clothes. Their foreplay was done. Jack's initial thrust momentarily stopped her breath. It always did. She had been longing for this feeling all week. She had wanted him inside her all week, because only then was there no denying the real connection between them.

Afterward, they showered in silence. Adair washed him the way she once washed her toddlers, with tender and thoughtful hands, noting the errant freckle, the patch of uneven skin. Jack's hands were equally kind, gently and slowly running a washcloth over her body and deeply massaging her scalp. Adair enjoyed this time together, too, for she craved physical proximity, the warmth of a kindred spirit, the lack of tension in their silence.

As Jack stepped out of the shower to dress, he tenderly kissed her cheek. She'd recall the smile he left her with later that night when falling asleep next to Hugh. Hugh's distance, first attributed to a burgeoning career and now just a painful reality, had been heartbreaking.

Why doesn't he want me more? she often wondered. *What am I lacking?* He *is the reason I cheat. It's all his fault.*

After Jack left, Adair remained in the shower. The housekeeper returning with the groceries at noon marked the official end of her Monday respite. She once again had to engage, remembering that she was a wife and a mother. She alone carried the responsibilities that came with those roles.

Without Jack, Adair didn't know if she could have come back to her family. It scared her to think how lost she would be without him.

27

Mon Petite Café opened in the former Kandy Kitchen next to the Pound Ridge Theatre Company. Completely staffed by attractive young French men, it drew a large female-only lunch crowd. Making reservations had become such a problem that the restaurant changed its policy to first come, first served. There were women who ate up a good portion of their day by going directly from their morning workouts to the restaurant—they had to ensure that a table would be available for themselves and their friends at lunchtime.

Adair was one of those women who would go very early to get a table and who always tipped generously to ensure they remembered her. Today, she had asked Abby, Elizabeth, and Kate to join her. After ordering two plates of mussels in a garlic butter sauce, two plates of escargot, a loaf of French bread, a large cut of Saint-André cheese, and a bottle of crisp white wine, the ladies began to talk.

"I heard a juicy story about Jack recently," said Abby. "You know that Marcel Breuer glass house on Meadow Street that was on the market recently? It's typically not visible to its neighbors, but the property lost a number of trees in the last hurricane. As a result, you can see right into some of its rooms at night. The current renter is a mother of two going through a divorce, and apparently she's been seen having private partner yoga sessions with Jack *and* her best friend. I was told that, with the three of them, it looks like a game of erotic Twister. After the sessions, the lights are dimmed. He leaves an hour or so later."

"Who told you that?" asked Elizabeth.

"I can't say, but it comes from a reliable source," said Abby smugly. "She swore me to secrecy."

"Wow," said Elizabeth. "He's one busy man."

"Sounds like a rumor," Adair said sharply. "I've been hearing a lot of rumors about him lately. Since I work so closely with him, women feel the need to share stories about him with me. I know he only takes on most of his private clients to supplement his income. He doesn't make that much from his classes and workshops."

"I take private sessions with him and he's always very professional," added Kate. "I think he only has sex with a select group of his clients."

"I'm sure it's very few," insisted Adair. "He's the kind of guy that needs to have a connection with a woman to sleep with her."

"Yes, Adair, I'm sure you're right," Abby responded, smirking at Elizabeth.

"If you ladies don't mind," Adair continued, "I'd like to discuss what's left to do for the benefit. I can't thank you enough for offering to help. The event is getting close, and I'm feeling overwhelmed. I've never planned an event this big. I didn't even plan my own wedding—I had a wedding planner who worked with my mother. I realize now that I should have co-chaired this position with someone who knows what she's doing. Brianna has been a big help to me, but she only has so much time to give. I'm starting to feel so out of control as the event gets closer. All the details are spinning like a movie reel in my head."

"That doesn't sound pleasant," said Abby, who had little patience for women who took on too much volunteer work and then lived their days in a panic, like Adair had. "How can we help?"

Adair pulled out several colored folders and handed one to each of the women at the table. Outlined on elaborate Excel spreadsheets were the details of their duties as well as a master list of everything that had to be done to pull off the event.

"Well, you're highly organized," Abby commented, reaching for the folders. "Why don't you give me a few more of these? Remember I said I would ask White's secretaries to help?"

"Oh, that would be wonderful," beamed Adair, whose mood was instantly buoyed.

"Do you just plan parties for him, or are you involved with his charity in other ways?" Abby inquired.

"This is his first large benefit," Adair said. "I've known Jack for over five years. We met around the time he started Auntie Arts. I generally handle his charity's PR. Jack has one full-time assistant, Leaha Kitzmann, who helps him with his yoga practice and the charity. She's great but increasingly overwhelmed with work. Jack keeps expanding the retail aspect of the charity, and now he wants to crack the European market. His goal is to double the number of garments he sells next year."

"Given the number of people in his classes, I'm surprised you weren't able to get more volunteers to help with this benefit," Abby said. "This town is filled with women who don't work outside the home."

"I had a bunch of volunteers start the work I assigned them, but they never finished," she explained. "Do you know Whitney Johnson and Christine Bellow? Or Helen Michaels? Or Anastasia Barlow and Dalisay Ward? Well, that's a few of them. Initially, they wanted to come to the planning meetings because they knew Jack would be at them. But Jack only came to the first three meetings, and when he stopped coming, so did they. Since it's volunteer work, I have no recourse."

"I'm sorry, Adair," said Elizabeth. "That's happened to me in the past. I now only volunteer for things where I'm completely in charge of one small task, like teacher appreciation gifts. Coordinating with volunteers can be incredibly frustrating."

As the ladies exited the restaurant after lunch, Elizabeth walked Adair to her car. "You should have asked me to help you sooner," she said. "You know I'll always help, don't you?"

"Of course," Adair said. "I consider you a good friend, but I also know you have a full-time job and are busy."

"I'm not *that* busy," Elizabeth responded, reaching out and embracing Adair.

"I'm embarrassed to say this, but I've grown so panicked that I won't get everything done in time that I asked my shrink to increase my Xanax prescription," Adair admitted. "But the higher dosage doesn't seem to be helping me. There's so much to do, and I can't disappoint Jack. There are moments that I feel like I'm losing my mind."

28

The following week, Elizabeth called Adair with a few questions about the benefit. She had been put in charge of tabletop décor: linens, floral arrangements, place cards, and candles. "Do you mind if we meet quickly to go over what I've collected?" Elizabeth asked at the end of their conversation. "It will be easier for me to show you."

"Can you text me photos?" Adair asked.

"I could, but it's definitely better if you see them in person," Elizabeth asserted. "I'll come by when it's convenient for you, but we have to meet soon. The linen company needs the order by Friday."

"Okay. But only if you promise to keep a secret," Adair insisted.

"A secret?" echoed Elizabeth. "I should be able to do that."

Several moments later, Adair said, "Okay. Are you free tomorrow? Visiting hours are 10:00 a.m. to noon and 4:00 p.m. to 6:00 p.m."

"Visiting hours?" Elizabeth exclaimed. "Where are you?"

"That's the secret." Adair paused conspiratorially before continuing. "Sunny Meadows."

Sunny Meadows was situated in one of Connecticut's lovely valleys. A river ran through its center, surrounded by buildings that were a mix of 1930s classic residential architecture and newer, tasteful additions. Sunny Meadows was the place for the rich and, occasionally, the famous. Once inside the building's walls, most of the property felt more "luxury bed-and-breakfast" Than "institutional ward," but it was impossible to hide the fact that it was a mental hospital.

"Sunny Meadows?" Elizabeth blurted out. "The mental institution? But why?"

"I needed a few days to myself," Adair sighed. "When I'm home, I'm pulled in too many directions, and I need to focus on the benefit. Here I can concentrate on one thing."

"Jack's charity event?" Elizabeth asked incredulously. "Why don't you just quit? Your peace of mind is more important than a party."

"I can't disappoint Jack," she said, "and he only trusts me to run the event."

"Jack is resourceful," Elizabeth assured. "He'll figure it out or postpone it for a few weeks."

"But it has to be hosted during peak foliage season," Adair insisted. "If we wait, the property will look barren. And, to be honest, this isn't my first time here. I actually check in here about twice a year. It's my version of a spa weekend."

"Oh," said Elizabeth, thinking of the cost of a stay at Sunny Meadows. "Wouldn't you rather escape to a nice hotel somewhere?"

"I guess I could, but I like it here," Adair reasoned. "I've been told that there are a number of women in the area who come to Sunny Meadows to rest. They have a special ward for the 'R&Rs'— that's what the staff calls us short-term visitors. It's so peaceful here, and the group therapy is very helpful. Did you know Jack volunteers here? He teaches a weekly class. This is where I first met him."

"No, I didn't know that," said Elizabeth, anger coloring her voice, thinking it a prime place for him to find new students. "I can meet you at Sunny Meadows tomorrow at four. And why don't you think about additional responsibilities to give me for the event? I knew you were overwhelmed, but I didn't realize how overwhelmed you felt. I'll ask the women I work with to help, too."

"I'm here to see Adair Burns," Elizabeth said the following day to the Sunny Meadows receptionist. "My name is Elizabeth Kelly."

"Is she expecting you?" she asked.

"Yes, we scheduled a visit," Elizabeth responded.

"Please have a seat, and I'll contact Mrs. Burns," she said, adding, "Don't you just adore Adair? She is such a happy, positive soul."

"Yes, she is a very kind person," Elizabeth said, thinking it unusual for the receptionist to comment on one of the patients. *If she's so happy and positive, why is she here?* Elizabeth wondered. *Why would Adair want to check into this place several times a year?* She took in the patients and visitors meandering through the room. *I'm completely depressed and I've only been here ten minutes.*

The attendant led Elizabeth into what was called the Game Room. It was the hospital's group den and one of the areas outside of the sleeping quarters where guests were allowed for visits. It was a comfortable room with dark wood floors, sea grass wallpaper, woven wood blinds, and generous upholstered furniture. There was a large TV, a pool table, and several card tables with inlaid chessboards. "Mrs. Burns will be in shortly," said the attendant. "Please help yourself to the refreshments."

"Thank you," said Elizabeth. "I will."

She walked to the refreshment station and perused the seemingly endless variety of expensive, imported teas. She noted eight types of sweetener and four creamer options, a plate of bakery cookies, four sliced fruit breads, and a tray of chocolate truffles. Elizabeth picked an exotic-sounding green tea, placed it in a large Williams-Sonoma mug with steaming water and sat down on an upholstered tweed chair to wait for Adair.

After a few minutes, Adair entered the room looking more serene than she had a few days ago.

"Hi, Elizabeth," she said, settling down across from her. "Thanks for coming here with the linen samples and other things. I can't wait to see what you collected. I bet they're lovely."

"No big deal," Elizabeth assured. "You look rested."

"I'm getting there," she responded.

"So when did you figure out that this place is more restorative for you than a spa?" Elizabeth asked.

"The first time I came here, I really needed to be here," she admitted, "and now I come back for shorter stays for a mental tune-up." She shifted into the chair's plush cushions before adding, "I guess word of my crack-up never really got out."

"I didn't hear about it," said Elizabeth.

"It was several years ago when my kids were very young," Adair started explaining, but Elizabeth stopped her.

"You don't need to go into it with me," she said, sincerely not wanting to know. "More people should seek help than those who do."

"Do you ever get overwhelmed by being a parent?" Adair asked.

"Just about every day," Elizabeth admitted.

"Me, too," she responded, "and one day it was so bad I...abandoned my kids."

"Oh... I'm sorry," said Elizabeth, concealing her astonishment of Adair's admission. "I know how much you love your kids, so that must have been awful for you."

"I still feel guilty about it," she said, "although Hugh convinced me that they don't know it happened. Fortunately, they were very young. We were at Stepping Stones Museum when I had a massive panic attack, and I took off, leaving the kids with Sheila. At least I didn't leave them alone, thank goodness. That night I called Hugh and told him I needed some time. He understood, but he insisted I come and stay here for a period of time after I came back."

"I'm really sorry," said Elizabeth, uncrossing her legs and leaning closer to Adair. "I didn't know. If Hugh told Andrew, then Andrew kept it a secret from me. And I don't think anyone else knows, either. You know how women love to gossip in Cannondale. In fact, most people say you're the most dedicated, best mother in town."

"I certainly try," she said. "My doctor said I try too hard to be the perfect wife and mom and that's the root of my problem. That's what made me snap that day. It was so weird, because nothing major triggered it. The kids were in the Toddler Room playing on the slide and in the pretend kitchen. They were moving in circles, like a cycle: up the stairs, then thirty seconds of opening and slamming shut the oven and refrigerator doors, then down the slide, and then back to the stairs. Again and again and again with a few trips and face-plants in between. I was still breastfeeding Tatum, although that had become really hard to do while trying to take care of the other kids. I knew my milk production was starting to dwindle and, I don't know, maybe it was that second cup of espresso I don't normally have, but my mind started reeling.

"All the potential illnesses doctors say children who aren't breast-fed are susceptible to crept into my head: lung infections, allergies, heart disease, and cancer. I pictured Tatum sitting on the sidelines during recess because of allergies. I saw her, middle-aged and hairless due to chemo. I saw her old and hooked up to a wheeled breathing machine. Would her little immune system be harmed by my not breastfeeding her for at least a full year? I wondered.

"And then my mind jumped to how unfair I was being to her by not breastfeeding her as long as I did the other three kids. I started to consider buying breast milk, but as I'm sure you know, it's not a regulated industry. I wondered how I would determine which breast milk provider to trust. Onlythebreast.com has posts from thousands of women hoping to make money by selling breast milk, but God only knows what they put into their bodies.

"I started getting totally grossed out—imagine milk coming from someone whose online profile says 'Healthy Texas Farm Girl With Abundant Flowing Breasts' when in fact she's a meth addict holed up in a desolate one-room motel room in desperate need of some cash. And even if you *do* find a normal mom who really just wants to share her extra breast milk, I've read that a lot of that transported milk arrives contaminated because of issues with storage and shipping.

"The other option is to hire a wet nurse who comes to your home and breastfeeds your kids, but again, you can't know what they're ingesting like you do yourself. So I mentally ruled out those options and told myself that I'd go home that night, hook up to a pump, and keep at it until my milk production came back up again. I didn't know if it would work or not. In my experience, those pumps kind of suck, but the thought calmed me down a bit. Sadly, it didn't last very long.

"I started to fixate on all the ways I'd already accidently hurt my kids: how I unintentionally didn't eat as much salmon and spinach when pregnant with Penny as I did with Trevor. How I forgot to test the bath water once and put one of them into a scalding tub. How I used non-BPA-free plastic before I knew the dangers of plastics' chemicals. The times I got out of the shower and found one of them post-squirm with their head jammed into the corner of the bassinet. Realizing after I pulled into the driveway that I forgot to buckle the car seat into its harness. How I would turn on a *Baby Einstein* video so I could have a cup of tea in peace even though I know it's advised that no videos or TV be watched before age two.

"My mind was whirling. My heart was racing. I started to perspire profusely. Sheila asked me what was wrong, and I couldn't give her an answer—she is such a calm person. I was so embarrassed. I excused myself, and before I realized it, I was walking out of the room. I was hyperventilating, and my legs were on autopilot, bringing me out for air. As I walked by the gift shop, my mind started churning in a totally different direction. It reminded me of all my kids' toys and art supplies and how disorganized they had become despite my best efforts: blocks, cars, trucks, balls, magnetic tiles, wooden puzzles, dolls, stuffed animals, dress-up costumes, bath toys, crayons, glue, finger paints, and on and on. It all turned into one large, colorful jumble in my head. I could see the pieces scattered in various rooms in our house, thrown into a myriad of toy bins in their bedrooms, playroom, secondary playroom, den, guest room, and the exterior playhouse.

"I thought of the Play-Doh whose tops weren't put on securely hardening in their plastic containers and how I needed to buy more before the next playdate; the Color Wonder and Dry-Erase and Glow Explosion pads whose coordinating pens had been wrongly organized in the marker bin; their out-of-order bookshelves: David

Carter Pop-Ups mixed with Sandra Boynton board books, and Richard Scarry's with Dr. Seuss; their once-organized-by-type learning videos thrown on the top of the TV cabinet, hastily put up there by me after Trevor pulled them all out of the cabinet and onto the floor."

"I'm so sorry, Adair," interrupted Elizabeth. "And I'm so sorry to hear you've been struggling for so long. Maybe you need more help at home? How about hiring a personal organizer to come over once a week? Lots of women have them. They help determine what's no longer needed and tidy up what remains. They even take what you no longer want to donation centers or the dump. Its might help you feel less overwhelmed?"

"I *have* a personal organizer—Wendy Luce. She'd been there just two weeks before my breakdown and had put everything back in its place, but it was all mixed up again. It only takes one playdate with a few active, curious children to destroy the order. So even with a housekeeper, even with visits from Wendy, I'm not able to keep up.

"I must have looked like a basket case as I stood there hyperventilating, because the Stepping Stones manager, Martha Banks, was approaching me with concern in her eyes. She woke me up in the 'Tummy & Tumble Time' area of the age three-and-under section one time—Tristan was five months old, I think, and I was exhausted. I literally fell asleep next to him on a mat. After she woke me and determined that I wasn't drunk or high, she kindly told me I wasn't the first tired mom to fall asleep on the floor in the museum. Ever since then, Martha and I say hello and generally have a good laugh together, but on the day of my breakdown, I couldn't even muster a smile for her. I left the building and speed-walked to the museum's community garden.

I tried more breathing exercises while staring into its koi pond.

"Then my mind flooded with the kind of questions that always pop up, but usually not in such rapid succession: should we become a gluten-free home? How about vegetarian? Should I buy new, improved car seats for the kids? Did Penny develop a rash from my switching laundry detergent? Is she going to be one of those kids who's allergic to everything? Should I be preemptive and bring her to an allergist now? What if she's deathly allergic to something we just don't know about yet?

"What type of elementary school should we be focused on getting them into: private, public, Catholic, Montessori? Do I have the patience to homeschool? How much is too much time on the computer? Will it be okay if the boys play football, or is it too dangerous of a sport? What about ice hockey?

"How many after-school activities can I sign them up for? One or two a day? There is so much for them to do, to try in childhood. If we don't try it all, we may never discover their special talent, but how are we going to fit it all in for all four of our kids in just eighteen years? Skiing, skating, paddle-boarding, swimming, sailing, crew, fencing, rock climbing, fly fishing, karate, soccer, tennis, paddle tennis, ballet, tap, ballroom dance, etiquette, theatre class, vocal lessons, piano, violin, electric guitar, chess, art, Spanish, French, Mandarin, cooking, baking, religion, charity work, Boy Scouts, Girl Scouts, Children of the American Revolution…

"When should we first introduce Europe to the kids? Since they're taking Spanish, maybe we should limit the trips to Spain and South America to encourage their foreign language skills. How old should a child be when she gets her first pair of Uggs? Should she save up for them? Should Santa bring them?

"I Googled it right then and there. I posted to the Cannondale

Mom's Group. I visited the *Fairfield County Today: Parent Alert* chat room. But then, as a few teenagers flew through the parking lot in a Mercedes convertible, the thought that no mom's group or chat room can really help me hit home. My darling, albeit accident-prone and unwieldy children will one day become adolescents and want nothing to do with me. That stage will be even more difficult than the just-keep-them-alive early stages or the adjusting to school and sports and peers stages that occur before their tweens. After all I've done for them, once they're adolescents I will experience the ultimate rejection while they rebel and likely put themselves in harm's way. They will do dumb things like getting into the class clown's convertible and traveling ninety miles an hour on the highway. I will feel so alone and helpless and terrified during those years.

"Why do we do this? rang through my head. Why do we become parents? So I walked to my car in the Stepping Stones Museum parking lot and drove away. I didn't think of it at the time, but I left Sheila and the kids without a car. They were stranded at Stepping Stones. I drove straight to The Carlyle and checked in."

"Oh," said Elizabeth as she processed the epic rant given by the woman who was considered the most dedicated and loving mother in town. Elizabeth understood what Adair was struggling with. Parenting was hard, but she didn't think Adair was one of those women who allowed herself to fully understand the complexities of it. Many women in town distracted themselves with things like compulsive shopping and excessive exercise. It was easier for them that way. Adair, on the other hand, totally got motherhood and actually hated many aspects of it, but threw herself into it every day and walked around beaming.

"Parenthood isn't how I imagined it would be," Adair continued.

"It's such a big adjustment, and I'm one of those women who always wanted to be a mom. I thought that the more kids you have, then the more love you have in your life, and the more satisfied and happier you will feel. But from the moment I had children, I have felt completely overwhelmed and inadequate every single day. I've dreamed of going back to work where I could at least do the job assigned to me; I could accomplish something small and check it off my to-do list forever. I just can't get it right as a mom. I'm not the mom I wanted myself to be.

"I always fall short of my expectations and, to be honest, the expectations of the other mothers in our town. It's like one big competition with them. They're always trying to determine if they fall above or below you with everything: whose kids got into the better preschool? Whose kids know all their colors by eighteen months? Who is a better cook or *has* a better cook? Who is a better hostess? Who is a member of the better country club? Who is a better tennis player? Who takes the best vacations? Whose husband got a bigger bonus? Who bought a new car? Who is remodeling? Whose property has the best landscaping? Who is adding a pool? Who donated more money to the private school? Who's doing better than me and who am I doing better than?

"It's fucking exhausting. And tied into it all are my guilty feelings about how much I really hate planning meals each day, keeping up on the laundry and cleaning and organization, and the playdates and the carpooling and preschool activities and on and on. I'm so tired of trying to be a perfect mom and have a perfect family. I'm so tired of the perfect moms in town. They are so judgmental and condescending. Being a suburban mom in Cannondale is all so overwhelming and boring at the same time. There's got to be some sort of release from it."

29

"I see you made it," Jack said as he opened the door to his studio apartment.

Leigh was breathless from running from her car. "Yes, I did," she said triumphantly.

"You aren't in yoga clothes," noted Jack, giving her a once over.

"I don't need to be," Leigh said coyly, trying to compose herself after the short run.

"We generally spend part of our private sessions doing yoga," Jack said, closing the front door. "Not today?"

"No, not today," Leigh chirped, trying to look girlish while smoothing her hair and smiling. "Thanks for fitting me in. I couldn't wait until Thursday to see you." Jack took her hand and they walked to his bed.

"Do you want a drink first?" Jack offered. "I have a nice Pinot open."

"No," Leigh quipped.

"You really are in that much of a rush?" Jack said.

"Well, my kids are in my car in the garage," Leigh explained.

"Which garage?" Jack asked.

"Yours," Leigh said. "Here."

"You're three-, four-, and six-year-old are in your car downstairs right now?" Jack asked incredulously. "I'm not a parent, but even I know not to do that."

"They're fine," she said flippantly. "I left a movie on for them. No one would be dumb enough to kidnap three kids at once. Who would want to take that on?"

"So your car is running?" Jack said.

"Yes, but it's a new car; I can leave it running without a key in the ignition. It can't be driven. They'll be fine. The doors are locked and they know not to open them to anyone. I've missed you. I wanted to see you, and my nanny called in sick again."

"I have free time tomorrow," he said. "You can come back."

"Your bangs are getting long. I like the unruly look on you," Leigh purred, ignoring his suggestion. She leaned her forehead against his lips.

Jack stared down at her, quizzical.

She moved her hands inside his shirt and up his back. "I'm here now," she coaxed. "We can make it quick. There are days I just can't get you out of my head. Today is one of them."

"Really?" he said. As she looked up at him, he altered his expression into a smile.

"You make me do reckless things," Leigh went on. "Completely reckless things."

Knowing Leigh's affinity for rough sex, Jack turned her sharply so that she was facing away from him. "So we need to be quick," he said a bit too harshly, annoyed by her brashness today. *What kind of mother leaves little kids in a parking lot so she can have sex?* he thought. *Some of these women are unbelievable.*

Holding her tightly by the waist, his other hand dove into her skirt. His fingers clawed into her as Leigh called out his name and her body collapsed against him. Soon she was facedown on the bed. Soon he was on top of her. Soon he would cum and tell her to leave.

Twenty minutes later, Leigh was on the elevator pressing the B button. She was a bit disheveled. *Jack was really rough today,* she thought. *And I feel like I was just hustled out of a dorm room.*

Once Leigh arrived on the lower level, she walked to her car. She saw the garage security man she drove by on the way in peering into her car and waving at the kids. He pulled out a phone and started dialing a number. Her heart raced. *Oh no,* she thought. Leigh started running toward him.

"Hi," she yelled out in a rushed tone. "I'm back now. I just had to run into the building for a few minutes. Sorry if I caused you any trouble. It hasn't been but a minute since I left the car."

"It's been more like thirty minutes, ma'am," he countered. "I realized there were kids in the car when one of them popped his head out of the sunroof. Do you realize that leaving three children of such young age in a car is illegal in Connecticut? You endangered the safety of minors."

"I didn't mean to take so long, and I figured they were safe in the car given the security in this building," Leigh said. "My friend, Jack Turner—he lives in the building and said it's the best. It's part of why he bought his unit here. Thanks for watching them. I have to get going now."

"You're one of Jack's visitors," The security agent said with a broad smile. "Makes sense. They generally stay under an hour. I'll let you go this time, but I don't want to see three unsupervised kids in your car again or I will contact the police."

30

Elizabeth was staring into her closet when Abby came upstairs.

"What are you wearing to Leigh's birthday party tonight?" Elizabeth asked her sister, hoping it would help with her own indecision.

"A black Armani silk baby doll dress and a pair of Burberry black boots that have a streamlined biker edge to them," said Abby.

"Sounds like a great outfit," Elizabeth responded. "I need to go shopping with you."

"From the looks of this closet, yes, you do," Abby said teasingly. "But I do like your Diane von Furstenberg wrap dresses, and I love your Tocca silk dresses. You should wear one of those and mate them with these snakeskin Delmar shoes, or if you don't want to wear heels, your brown Ralph Lauren riding boots."

Abby, who should have become a fashion designer as she originally planned, had always had better clothes and related accessories than Elizabeth. In fact, when they were children, as soon as Elizabeth fit into Abby's clothes, she started raiding her closet. Abby went ballistic every time she realized something of hers had been worn without permission, but that never stopped Elizabeth, whose school bus came after Abby's. Her taste in clothing had only improved as she got older, and Abby spared no expense when filling her closet.

"I like those, too," Elizabeth said. "But just watch—tonight, no matter what I wear, Leigh will make a snide comment. Every time I see her, she says at least one nasty thing about what I'm wearing. Remember what she said about updating my 'classic look' at her house? Does she do that to you, too?"

"She did a few times when I was first getting to know her." Abby responded. "That's her nature. She's like a dog, always testing those around her and trying to determine the pack order. But I started saying meaner things back, so she eventually stopped."

"Of course you did," said Elizabeth, laughing.

"The last person you should be thinking about during your dress selection is Leigh," said Abby. "She has absolutely no taste. Every time I see her, she's covered in designer logos and looks ridiculous. You could buy a ratty dress and stick a Missoni label in it and she would wear it."

"Did I tell you what she said to me last week, the day after the Richards' party?" Elizabeth asked. "I had just gone running and stopped in the market to pick up a few groceries. She walks up to me and literally said, 'You look as bad as I feel. I way overdid it with the chocolate martinis at the party last night. With all the sugar and alcohol in my system, I barely slept. Looks like you didn't, either.'"

"She is unbelievable," said Abby. "You would think her desire to appear in *Cannondale Cottages & Gardens* would curb her bad behavior. She just can't seem to help herself. I'd tell her off for you but I have to watch myself given my new job. You just need to get better at retaliating—which you've never been good at, by the way. That would eventually shut her up.

"So who do you think is going to be at this party besides her potentially volatile neighbor, Brianna?" Abby asked, flipping through a few clothing items in Elizabeth's closet.

"Well, she's also friendly with Anastasia Barlow and Dalisay Ward," Elizabeth said. "Have you met them yet?"

"No," responded Abby.

"You're well traveled, so you'll find lots to discuss with them," Elizabeth said before plopping down on her bed. "Conversations with them are limited to their latest trips and foreign shopping sprees. Most annoyingly, they're always literally *wearing* their trip. *'Oh, I bought this at CÉLINE in Paris when I was there last month'* or *'Thank you, I bought it while on holiday in Meghalaya this past fall. I searched for days until I finally found a lovely shop that sells silk tunics that don't look too ethnic India, if you know what I mean'*. If I ever saw them in jeans and a plain white shirt, I'd have no idea what to speak with them about."

"How about just not speaking with them at all?" Abby offered. "You're not a real estate company manager who has to ensure she's liked. The women in this town want you to like them because they want their homes featured in the magazine you edit."

"Now you sound like Andrew," Elizabeth responded, annoyed. "I just stick with being polite. As you well know, I'm forced to spend time with the same women again and again and again because of the kids."

"So who else will be there?" Abby asked, changing the subject.

"Well, my boss and his wife Monica will be there," she said.

"You've said she's nice and not a snob," Abby replied.

"No, she isn't a snob and is pleasant enough," Elizabeth said. "But she has a myopic focus on her children. After she goes on about their dance and soccer and lacrosse for what feels like hours, she always finally says, 'And what about your kids? You have two girls, don't you? You haven't said a word about them!' As if I had an opportunity."

"Maybe Betsy and her husband Tom from my office?" Abby offered. "She isn't Leigh's agent, but I know they know each other from their children's preschool."

"Oh, I doubt Betsy will be there," Elizabeth said. "I saw her at Balducci's a few weeks ago and Leigh's name came up. She had an amusing story about her. Shortly after Leigh first moved to town, they were placed together on a preschool committee that welcomes incoming families to the school. According to Betsy, Leigh insisted that she divvy up the list. When Betsy saw both lists, which included addresses, she realized that Leigh had picked the families on her list based on their addresses. All the homes on Leigh's list were worth $3 million and up! When Betsy called her out on it, she said Leigh giggled and admitted that she signed up for the committee to troll for landscape clients."

"That's definitely a Leigh move," sighed Abby, noting the time. "So what are you going to wear tonight? I have to pick up Quinn in twenty minutes."

"My navy wrap dress with the brown riding boots," responded Elizabeth. "Pretty and comfortable and perfect for a long dinner party. Thanks for helping."

"Anytime, little sis," Abby said.

"Oh, are you sure you don't want Andrew and I to pick you up?" Elizabeth asked.

"No, I'll drive myself," Abby replied. "I like to have a car at parties in case I want to leave early."

"See you there, then," said Elizabeth.

31

Two hours later, Andrew and Elizabeth pulled into the parking lot of the latest fabulous restaurant to open in Cannondale. It was called From Farm to Table and boasted an all-organic, locally grown menu, which included the chef, who was raised in neighboring Weston. It was relatively small and designed in a rustic, chic way. Elizabeth carried a Scully & Scully box containing a Limoges porcelain figurine for Leigh. She hoped Leigh didn't have one already given that she did have pricey jewel-like Limoges boxes scattered all over her home.

"Elizabeth and Andrew," greeted Richie when they walked in the door. "It's so good of you to come. Please let the doorman take your coats. What can I order for you to drink?"

"Pinot Grigio for Elizabeth and an Arnold Palmer for me," said Andrew.

"Nothing stronger for you, Andrew?" said Richie. "I need some-one to celebrate my wife getting older with me. Sagging skin and graying hair. We have so much to look forward to."

"I'll get a drink on the next round," said Andrew. "Where's that aging beauty of yours anyway?"

"She is on her way," said Richie. "Wardrobe malfunction. She's waiting on Saks to deliver a new dress. The store sent the wrong one this afternoon."

"Oh, she must be upset," Elizabeth said, amused, imagining the scene that must have unfolded in Leigh's home when the wrong dress arrived. "I pity the delivery person. He's probably looking for new work."

"Yes, and probably in a different country," said Richie. "Once Leigh opened the box, she threw a fit. When she got her Saks personal shopper on the phone, she threatened to call immigration because the delivery person could barely speak English and obviously couldn't read. He'd mixed up two deliveries. Leigh got the box with a size sixteen blue 'muumuu,' as she called it, not the size six petite Hugo Boss fitted dress. She was screaming 'I'm not that fat yet' at the deliveryman. Evidently, it was intended for someone else in town today. To spare the kids the full scene, I grabbed them and we went to the country club."

"Well, I hope she doesn't allow a dress to make her very late for her own party," said Andrew.

"She better not be too late," said Richie. "She demanded I throw her a big party with everyone we know in town. Since she's always going out, I suggested a trip or quiet family dinner, but Leigh wouldn't have it. 'I can always celebrate with you and the kids,' she said. 'It's not special enough for turning thirty-five.' You would think she's turning seventy-five. What's wrong with women anyway, Andrew?"

Fortunately, before the Kellys had to hear more, their drinks arrived along with two more guests. They politely excused themselves from Richie and went to mingle.

The party was larger than Elizabeth imagined it could be for the space, and she was happily surprised by the range of guests.

That said, the invitees clearly demonstrated Leigh's cunning ways. She'd used her birthday to network to the hilt.

Among those in the room were: Candace Murphy, the owner of the trendiest dress shop in town, Svelte, along with her partner, Hayley Wellgood; Olivia Blackwell and her husband, Mitchell; Cannondale Country Day School's headmaster Ron McCabe and his wife, Barbara; the Protestant minster Betty Jefferson and her husband, Robert; the mayor, Richard Ferguson and his wife Ramona; the most obnoxious realtor in town, Skippy Travis, and his long suffering wife, Alyssa; the owner of the local Porsche dealership, Joseph Albano, with a date Elizabeth didn't recognize; Brianna and Edward Worth; Anastasia Barlow and Dalisay Ward—their husbands were out of town; one of the town's few excellent developers, Bo Uznaka, and his wife Bozena; Sharon Lity, the town's best dermatologist and go-to doctor for Botox, fillers, and other anti-aging procedures; and Yogi Jack, who brought Michael Kat, the hedge fund manager who provided the funding for Jack's yoga studio.

Michael Kat was a recently divorced man-about-town type. Elizabeth saw Abby and Michael chatting. *They might make a good match.* Elizabeth thought. Not wanting to interrupt them, Elizabeth decided to wait before going over to Abby.

About forty-five minutes into cocktails, Leigh arrived. As if her tardiness were part of the planning, Richie told the crowd to yell surprise when she walked in. Leigh smiled politely to the cheering crowd, but it was obvious she wasn't really amused. She was still mad about the dress mishap.

"Saks delivered the wrong dress to me today," she loudly announced once everyone stopped clapping. "You should have seen the first dress that arrived. It looked like something a gospel singer would wear: bright blue with no waistline. Absolutely humongous. Who wears those kinds of dresses?"

As Leigh continued to talk, thinking she was amusing, all eyes fell on Skippy Travis's wife, Alyssa. A plus-size woman, she wore the exact dress Leigh described.

Fortunately, Leigh took note of the darting eyes and glanced at Alyssa. "Well, it was a bit stressful to have it happen on this day of all days," she said in closing. "I'd love a glass of champagne. Richie, it's my birthday. Where are you with my champagne?"

Cocktails lasted for another hour because of her late arrival. There were no name cards on the tables or at a central table so Elizabeth assumed there would be no seating arrangements. She greeted Abby. "Having fun?" she asked.

"Yes, so far," Abby responded. "Michael Kat is funny, and I got to meet Livy, Leigh's decorator. She seems cool."

Just then, From Farm to Table's maître d' made an announcement: "As per Leigh's request, tonight your seating will be determined by the luck of the draw," he said. "As you walk toward the tables, please pick a card from one of the hurricane lamps. Then look for that same number on one of the seats."

"I hate these dinner party seating games," Elizabeth whispered to Abby. "The older we get, the more common they are. It's a middle-age attempt to inject fun and spontaneity into gatherings."

"Why wouldn't Leigh want to sit next to her husband tonight?" Abby responded. "More importantly, who am I going to be sandwiched between?"

"No trading!" Leigh chirped as she went over and drew the first card. Andrew, Abby, and Elizabeth got in line. Andrew picked a fourteen, Abby a seven, and Elizabeth a three.

"See you after dessert," Andrew said to Elizabeth and Abby

with a smirk. "Enjoy your dinner companions."

Elizabeth walked to her table and surveyed it. Skippy Travis and Candace Murphy were already seated. She moved to the opposite side of the round table and sat down. Joseph Albano sat on one side of her. *He'll try to sell me a car about thirty minutes in,* Elizabeth thought.

As Elizabeth started to note who had already sat at the other tables in the room, Barbara McCabe sat on the other side of her. *She's nice, and a dinner conversation with her would be pleasant enough,* she thought. *At this party, her job is to not offend.*

At table seven, Yogi Jack pulled out a chair next to Abby. Michael was already sitting on the other side of her. *I bet Jack and Michael didn't pick numbers,* Elizabeth thought. *They just want to sit next to Abby. She's the prettiest single woman here.*

Elizabeth looked over at Andrew. He could get through any dinner arrangement, but Elizabeth was amused to see him slotted between Betty and Robert Jefferson. Having avoided church since Alice's baptism, they would surely attempt to make him feel very guilty for not being an active part of Betty's congregation.

After a delicious dinner of squab, beluga lentils, hedgehog mushrooms, and braised leeks along with a petite salad of greens, candied pecans, and goat cheese, Richie was officially drunk. He was increasingly loud and rude to the wait staff, too. It was awkward. Elizabeth was relieved when she saw dessert trays set on stands appear next to the tables.

Dessert was a chocolate soufflé with a vanilla bean gelato served with champagne. It was prime time for a toast, but Richie seemed to be completely oblivious. From a neighboring table, Brianna's husband Edward started tapping his glass with a spoon. Everyone looked toward Richie, who was in conversation with Bo Uznaka. Bo took note and nudged him while gesticulating raising a glass.

At that point, a few of the husbands ribbed Richie for his cluelessness. At first he looked embarrassed, but then his expression turned to anger when his eyes fell on his wife, who was glaring at him. Richie stood up, downed the remaining champagne, and ordered the waiter to bring him more. Once his glass was full again, Richie surveyed the room.

"I hope you all are having a good time on my dime," he ungraciously started. "It's time to praise our guest of honor. I'm hoping Leigh scripted me a toast because I didn't write one." Richie started patting down his pockets as if looking for a piece of paper.

"Nada," he said with a wicked smile. "Leigh planned every other detail of this party. Why not my toast, too, honey?" he said as he looked in Leigh's direction with raised eyebrows.

Her steely expression remained unchanged.

"Leigh told me where to have this party, who to invite, what to serve, and even tried to control what I wore tonight. You see, none of my ideas were big or clever enough. A celebration with just our family was, in her estimation, too dull. How do you think our kids felt when they overheard her say that?"

He paused and looked around the room again. He chugged his champagne and the waiter, who had smartly sensed to be right next to him, filled up his glass again.

"Well, Leigh, maybe you're right about me. I'm really not a good planner because I haven't thought of what to say about you tonight. I'll have to wing it.

"Happy thirty-fifth birthday, darling. You've hit the age where everything starts to decay. Better keep up that gym membership and, if you haven't already, find a good dermatologist and plastic surgeon. But I know you will. You always take care of yourself, and you will have no problem spending the thousands upon thousands of dollars it will cost to keep you looking thirty-five. You, Leigh, are a wonderful spender. It's really is your best attribute. So cheers to that and cheers to you!"

32

The following day, while Abby was working at White's in-town office, she walked to Lemongrass, a caterer with a storefront for gourmet takeout, to get lunch. While crossing the street, she spied the Winnebago she had seen in Leigh's driveway wedging into a parking spot in front of Dunkin' Donuts and the neighboring Svelte. *My God, Cannondale residents are now trying to fit Winnebagos into these small parking spots?* Abby thought. The Winnebago's name, *The Rolling Stone*, which was painted on its side in large curved letters, was impossible to forget. It looked hulking even between two large SUVs. Its license plate was from Pennsylvania.

As she got closer, a tall woman with long, gray hair emerged. She stomped out a cigarette and lit another. It was rare to see anyone other than a teenager smoking in Cannondale. Abby couldn't help but notice that the woman looked like a taller and older version of Leigh.

That's got to be Leigh's mother, Abby thought. She contemplated introducing herself as she approached.

"Excuse me," The woman said to Abby. "I'm looking for a store that sells newspapers. Is there one nearby?" Abby told her that she was headed toward one and that the woman was welcome to walk with her.

"You look like a friend of mine," Abby said. "Are you related to Leigh Gilding?"

"Yes," she responded. "I'm shocked you can still see a resemblance; I've gotten so old. I'm her mother, Claudine Mead."

"My name is Abby Davis-Powers," she said. "I know your daughter from New York."

"Oh," she said. "I just arrived in town. It's very pretty here. Another world, really."

"Yes, it can seem a bit unreal at times," Abby added.

"Leigh recently moved here, so I came to surprise her and see my grandchildren," Claudine started out excitedly, but then her voice started to trail off. "But she told me to come back once I find a place to keep my Winnebago. It's too large for her driveway. Do they even have trailer parks in Fairfield County?"

"I'm relatively new to this area, too, but I've driven by a trailer park in Norwalk that is about twenty minutes from here," Abby said. "I don't know the name of it, but it's on Boston Post Road near the border of Westport, across from a large movie theatre and Bed Bath & Beyond. I manage a real estate company. If you want to come back with me to my office after you get your newspaper, we can look it up together. I'd be happy to call for you and see if there are any open spots."

"That would be great," Claudine said. "Thank you!"

As they walked to the store—Abby picked up lunch for both of them at Lemongrass—the women talked. *If what she's saying is true, she seems to have her life together now,* Abby thought. *She went back to school and got her high school diploma, and then an associate's degree in childhood art development. She's been a preschool art teacher for a number of years.*

"I pulled myself together later in life," Claudine admitted. "I wish I had the capacity to do it before I became a mother, but that wasn't in the cards for me. I wasn't the greatest mother to Leigh, but I did my best. And my motto now is to look forward and not backward. I can't change the past."

Back in the office, Abby was able to quickly arrange for Claudine to have a spot in the trailer park.

"I don't know what you're used to," Abby said, "but it appears to be very clean and safe. According to the website, the park is forty-five-years old and still run by the same family. It's on a busy main road, but they can give you a spot in the back, next to two long-term tenants. The trailer park is in a good location—close to the highways and three towns, including Cannondale."

"I can't thank you enough," Claudine said. "Leigh told me that I probably wouldn't be able to find anywhere to put my Winnebago locally unless I was willing to pay for a spot at one of those car storage spaces, which she said are really expensive. She said she thought the closest I would be is an hour or so from here."

"No, just twenty minutes," Abby said, smiling.

"What do I owe you?" Claudine asked.

"Nothing," Abby said. "This took no time at all. Glad I was able to help you." The comment escaped Abby's mouth before she realized it.

Am I becoming a nicer person? Abby wondered. A year ago in Manhattan, she wouldn't have spoken to a woman walking down the street who looked like Claudine. Ever. She probably would have stepped right over Claudine if she had fallen down in front of her, assuming she was drunk.

I am *becoming a nicer person*, she thought. *Yes, but only to those who deserve nice behavior. That's the distinction. Claudine appears to be genuine and sweet. She is nothing like her daughter.*

33

A few weeks later Abby was going to Norwalk's Education Barn to buy a few birthday presents for the kids' friends when she remembered that Leigh's mom, Claudine, was living in the neighboring trailer park. She looked through the sea of Winnebagos for her unforgettable *Rolling Stone*. There were twenty or so parked in a grid-like pattern. Situated on an asphalt lot behind a chain link fence hundreds of yards from Route 1, the so-called "park" was devoid of grass and trees. It wasn't pretty, but it appeared orderly and safe. Claudine's Winnebago turned out to be easy to find. It was clean while most of the others were in desperate need of a power wash. Their exteriors were tainted by various dulling shades of rust—they reminded Abby of middle school science projects.

The Rolling Stone was parked on the edge of the lot in between two others. The thirty-by-ten-foot retro vehicle had tinted windows and was decorated with a rainbow array of gradually thinning blue stripes. The pattern was broken only by the name written in a sharply slanted italic next to its door. The large front windshield glowed—a silver cushioned sun breaker had been pulled across it.

Claudine sat under a mesh pop-out tent that reminded Abby of the one she had on her 1970s-era Barbie Country Camper.

That camper, similar to the Scooby Doo Mystery Machine, was orange, yellow, and decorated with a rainbow and cloud design. Its interior was hot pink and orange with faux wood paneling and two pop-outs: one a tent, and the other a table for dining. Advertised as "the swinginest camper on wheels!", it personified cool to the preteen set. To Abby, the idea of taking home with her when she traveled and eating s'mores for dessert every night was ideal. Living in a home without wheels certainly didn't offer such a carefree lifestyle.

Of course, Claudine's *Rolling Stone* parked in an asphalt parking lot looked nothing like Abby's fantasy of life with Barbie, Ken, and a few equally gorgeous friends. But she did look settled. Claudine had set up a small living area under the mesh canopy with an outdoor green grass rug, folding furniture, and flowering plants. It was modest, especially in comparison to her daughter's excessive outdoor design, but still tidy and attractive. She was sipping what appeared to be lemonade and reading the *New York Post*.

Abby looked at the time and saw that she had an hour before she needed to be back in Cannondale for elementary school pick-up, so she walked toward Claudine. There was a metal chain link fence separating the trailer park from the local stores' parking lot. Abby saw no gate so she called to Claudine from behind it. Looking up from her paper suspiciously, Claudine eyeballed her before recognition hit. Once she realized it was Abby, a huge smile spread across her face.

"Oh, Abby!" she said. "I was hoping to see you again. Thanks for getting me into this place. If it wasn't for you, I think I'd be back in Pennsylvania."

"I'm so glad," Abby said. "You look settled already. Are you enjoying living in this area?"

"Oh, it's just great!" she said. "Got a minute? Want some lemonade? The entrance gate is next to the manager's trailer. It's about forty feet that way. Hard to see from here. Ring the bell and he will let you in."

Abby found the gate and joined Claudine under the tent. As she poured Abby a glass of lemonade, Claudine continued, "This is the safest trailer park. The management screens the people they let in. The day you sent me over here, I was interviewed and the manager ran a background check on me. I like that. And I love my neighbors. Frank is a retired mechanic—he lives in the sage-green camper on my right. He's a local guy. Fran and Bob live on the other side of me in the mustard-yellow camper. They're both retired schoolteachers from Indiana. The gal in front of me has lived here for fifteen years. Sally. She was a nurse. Haven't met everyone else, but like who I have met so far."

"Oh, that's great," Abby said. "Do you remember the Barbie Country Campers? You're reminding me of Barbie."

"I do remember those," she said. "It was one of Leigh's favorites,"

"Have Leigh and your grandkids been here to visit yet?" Abby asked.

"I wish I saw my grandkids more," said Claudine, frowning. "Leigh has made that impossible. She even stopped returning my calls. I think she wants me to disappear. When she told me to go find a mobile home park, she had no idea this one was so close. She actually shrieked when I told her where I parked it and that I found a job at Cannondale's FIT, where she exercises."

Abby stifled a smile and asked, "What work are you doing there?"

"I'm a night cleaner," Claudine said. "It's not my ideal job, but it's a job for now. I want to get back to teaching art to kids, but in this economy that's one of the first things schools, preschools, and families cut back on.

"But I have other exciting news," she added. "Believe it or not, I already have a beau in town. His name is Eddie Silvio, and he owns the Getty on Route 23 in Cannondale. I met him the day I met you, when I was filling up *The Rolling Stone's* tank. It's a small gas station, but I explained I was almost out of gas so I had to buy it there. He directed me to the side of the station and brought out a long hose and filled up the tank for me. He told me I was the first mobile home at his station. Then he asked me if he could show me the local sights. We're going out tonight on his motor boat."

"I'm really happy for you," Abby said. "Sounds like everything is coming together. I think you should contemplate changing the name of your camper."

"Why?" she asked.

"Well, you are settling down," Abby said. "Making roots. 'Gathering moss,' as they say. You're not on the go."

"Oh," she said. "I guess not. It feels good to be settled. I haven't always been. As I told you, I wasn't the best mom when Leigh was little."

"Well," Abby said, "as a parent now, Leigh should understand the difficulties that come with raising kids, especially under your circumstances. Maybe she'll come around. If nothing else, she should appreciate the attention and love you can share with her kids."

"I hope so," she said. "If you see her, will you tell her we spoke?"

"If the opportunity arises," Abby said, doubting she would ever have a heart-to-heart with Leigh.

"Do you know anything about the Education Barn?" asked Claudine.

"Yes—actually, I was just headed there," Abby said. "It's an arts supply store for kids as well as an educational toy store. Teachers buy supplies there. If you want to teach kids art, it might be a good source for you. You might be able to find work through the owner or start offering classes in one of its back rooms? Since we moved here, I've been in there a lot buying birthday party presents. I know the manager. Want to come with me and meet her?"

"That'd be great," Claudine said.

As they walked to Abby's car, Claudine asked about local used car lots.

"I really need to buy a car," she said. "Right now I have to travel by camper, which eats gas and means I can only partially set up home here. If *The Rolling Stone* was stationary, I could add window boxes and potted trees to make it look landscaped. And I know my driving it in Leigh's nice town embarrasses her. I was pulling into FIT for my shift and saw her zoom out of the parking lot. I know she takes an evening spin class there on Thursdays, but when she saw me, she turned the car around and left. I don't want to be an embarrassment to her."

"Well, I know you have access to your grandkids to consider, but it sounds to me like everything else is working in your favor," Abby said. "I hope that part of your life resolves itself soon for you and your grandkids."

34

Elizabeth@CannondaleC&G.com writes:

Hello Leigh,

I need you to do a favor for me. Adair is completely over her head with the benefit, and I'm doling out tasks that still need to be done. Since I'm putting a rush on your home's magazine feature and getting it in the March issue, I'm hoping you will return the favor. We are meeting at 10 a.m. tomorrow at Brioche. Can you make it? If not, let's connect at another point this week.

Best wishes,

   Elizabeth

Elizabeth Kelly
Cannondale Cottages & Gardens
Managing Editor

Leigh@GildingLandscaping.net writes:

Hi Elizabeth,

I'm a bit up to my eyeballs with my new client. Did I tell you I hooked up with the developer Mitch Tallwall? I'm going to landscape his spec houses. He's almost done building a home on Chipmunk Lane. The two-acre lot was all trees abutting the town's conservation land. To make room for the house, a pool, and a tennis court, he bulldozed the property, so there is a lot of work to do to make it blend in with the surrounding forest-look. I love the way most of these local developers work! LOL!

I don't mind taking on one very small task. I'll see you tomorrow after my spray tan appointment.

Hugs,

Leigh

Leigh Gilding
Gilding Landscaping

The following day, Leigh entered Brioche with her typical flourish. Most days she was overdressed and looked like a walking billboard for *Vogue's* priciest front ads. Today, however, she was dressed down—although she still exuded the same expensive look she always aimed for. Her outfit was a tight, black, terry workout suit with a pale-pink tank top and black Prada sneakers. She was carrying a teal-green Hermès purse. Despite looking like she was headed to the gym, she wore two-carat antique diamond earring studs and a striking band of emerald-cut one-carat-each diamonds.

Her makeup was appropriately light for daytime, her hair bounced in a high ponytail, and her nails were perfectly manicured in nude.

"Hi, ladies," said Leigh as she sat and dumped her Hermès purse on the floor next to her. "Did you see the size of the carrot muffins? They look fab. Who wants to share one with me?"

"They are," said Abby. "We just had one."

"I'm getting my own then," said Leigh. "I'll skip lunch.

"I wish they weren't so busy here," huffed Leigh as she sat back down with a giant muffin and a generous side of whipped butter. "Their customer service sucks. I'm starting to go through caffeine withdrawal from my morning coffee. I might as well just add sweetener and cream to the twelve-cup coffee carafe and drink it directly from there. I just ordered an extra grande latte. Given the backup at the barista bar, the waitress is going to bring it over to me. Oh, did either of you want another coffee? I didn't think to ask before."

"No, thanks," Abby said.

"I'm still working on my tea," Elizabeth added.

"So what volunteer work for Jack's benefit are you going to saddle me with?" Leigh asked, smiling.

"Adair thinks it would be nice to bring in fall perennials, like sedum," said Elizabeth. "Do you know a good source where we can buy them? After the event, Adair wants to leave them on the property as a thank-you to the association that runs The Glass House for cutting the estate rental price for the charity event."

"Yes," said Leigh. "There's a great place in Bethel that's, like, half the price of the source I used in Brooklyn. Classically designed ones would offer an interesting contrast to the modern buildings. Let me know how many and where they have to go. I'll make sure it gets done."

"Sounds perfect," said Elizabeth. "Concerning payment—let me know if the company needs to be paid in advance or if it will invoice us. Adair gave me access to her account on Jack's server, so if payment is needed in advance, I can authorize it through the charity's bank account."

"Okay," said Leigh, standing. "I'll be right back. Have to use the lavatory."

"Do you have access to Jack's calendar, too?" Abby asked in astonishment once Leigh was out of earshot.

"I don't know," said Elizabeth. "I haven't gone onto the server yet. It would be fun to see how many private client appointments he has and get a sense of his stamina."

"But *I'm* one of his private clients," Abby whispered, looking around at neighboring tables to make sure no one else was listening. "I didn't know Adair had access to his computer files."

"She might only has access to the charity-related files," Elizabeth offered. "Given the different aspects of his business, he probably has separate passwords."

"Let me know when you go on?" Abby insisted. "It makes me nervous. I'm going to ask him about it. Does he know you have access to these files, to his charity's bank account?"

"I have no idea," Elizabeth said. "Adair is in desperate need of help, so she gave me access. I also think she knows I'm not the type to do anything inappropriate with the funds or whatever else I can find."

"Abby, what are you wearing to the benefit?" Leigh asked as she sat back down at the table. "Since moving here, you have officially become the best-dressed woman in town."

"I'm not sure yet," said Abby. "Maybe my long, billowy, black Trina Turk dress with a tribal-type necklace or a similar style of dress in gold. I'm not strictly abiding by the Indian theme."

Leigh looked contemplative, borderline angry. The sisters exchanged a glance. "What are you going to wear, Leigh?" Abby asked.

"I have my personal shopper scouring Manhattan for a tasteful adaptation of the sari," she sighed. "I haven't liked anything she's found yet. She's sent me about fifteen photos of dresses. Maybe the problem isn't her… Maybe it's the Indian theme. That country's clothing is so damn colorful and exuberant and littered with golden threads and jeweled beads. Between you and me, I think it's absurdly lurid. If you're not going with the theme, maybe I'll drop it, too. Otherwise I'm going to have to have something made."

After that comment, all the appreciation Elizabeth felt for Leigh helping with the benefit evaporated. *How absurd! What is she paying her personal shopper to find the dress?* Elizabeth wondered. *And what will the final selection cost? There are definitely better ways to spend thousands of dollars.*

"That sounds like a *real* dilemma for you, Leigh," Abby responded. "Personally, I like traditional Indian clothing. It's colorful and gauzy and sensual. I'm not rejecting it, just choosing to wear my own interpretation of it."

"Good for you," Leigh shot back. "I don't."

As the women continued to talk, Leigh cut her muffin into four and slathered butter on a piece. Elizabeth and Abby were facing the window. Seemingly out of nowhere, *The Rolling Stone* appeared and then went into reverse. Claudine was trying to parallel park her camper on Main Street in front of Brioche. She was aiming for a spot right in front of their table. The timing couldn't have been worse—or perhaps better, depending on how you looked at it.

As Leigh shoved the entire quarter piece of muffin into her

mouth, she looked around for the waitress with her latte—and saw *The Rolling Stone* out of the corner of her eye. Leigh snapped her head toward it, but being the pro that she was, her face only slightly registered something amiss. Leigh scooted her chair so that the window was just barely in her line of sight and, while chewing, started to rapidly add an excessive amount of butter to her second piece of muffin.

"Oh, look," Abby said. "There's Claudine Mead. She is so nice. Have both of you met her? She works at FIT."

"You know her?" Leigh barked.

"Yes," she said, and waved to Claudine, who was looking in the window. A giant smile took over Claudine's face and she began to furiously wave at the women.

Leigh shifted her chair again, this time completely turning away from the window.

Claudine's smile dropped. Abby gave her one last wave and turned back to Leigh.

"I met Claudine in town one day when she was looking for a trailer park," Abby said. "I told her about the one near the Education Barn. You must know her, too. I saw her Winnebago parked in your driveway a while before I met her."

Leigh looked incensed. "You told her about the trailer park?" she hissed. "*You!?*"

"Yes, me," Abby said. "I *am* in the real estate business."

After much frantic chewing dissolved the third hunk of muffin, Leigh finally said, "I do know her. In fact, she is my mother, and I will admit that to you if you promise not to tell anyone. *Claudine,* as you call her, showed up at my new home in that piece of crap she has been driving for years saying she wants a relationship with Richie and me and our kids. I think the timing is interesting given that I now have a home with enough space for her to live, too. Our Manhattan apartment was too small. I'm not interested in having a roommate or any kind of relationship with her."

Abby looked back at the camper. Claudine was nowhere in sight.

"Is she gone?" Leigh asked.

"I don't see her," Abby said.

"I told her to go find somewhere else to park that white trash mobile and then maybe we could talk," Leigh explained. "I didn't expect her to find a trailer park. I thought she would go away. Thanks for giving her the tip. Now, I see her in that lumbering tin can all over town. I've had to switch the times I go to the gym around her work schedule and pray she isn't telling people she meets there that we're related."

"Oh," Abby said. "I don't know her motivations, but I've had a few conversations with her and she seems to have her act together now. She teaches art to children. That's kind of great."

"Yes, she pulled herself together after I was all grown up," Leigh said angrily. "Great timing, Mom."

"Well, bad parents often make good grandparents," Elizabeth offered. "Did you ever read *The Prince of Tides?*"

"I know, and I'd probably let her spend time with my kids if she wasn't so damn embarrassing," Leigh said in an exhausted tone. "She is so worn-looking. I don't think she has ever had a facial. And her hair! At least a foot needs to be chopped off that brittle mane. I absolutely hate the way she whips it into a bun with a knitting needle. She drives that Winnebago with *The Rolling Stone* proudly painted on it in a rainbow of blue. Do you think I enjoyed living in that hunk of tin when I was in high school? The Winnebago allowed her to move us on a whim. She would lose a job or break up with a boyfriend and we'd be on the move again. Can you imagine what that was like? For me to have to start over in a new school again and again and again? And today, well, she is hands-down the most embarrassing person I know. How can I possibly be perceived as a high-end landscape designer with a mother like that? I've been mortified by her my entire life, and I have the right to decide the type and extent of relationship I have with her now."

"I know the players in your industry well and many of the best ones come from humble backgrounds," countered Elizabeth. "Most people—actually the ones you should want to work with—will judge you for your talent. They don't care about your mother."

"I think they do judge you by your background," Leigh responded. "I don't know a lot of people around here whose mothers are such opposites of them. It's striking."

"It means you had to struggle," Elizabeth said. "Have you ever considered how that might be an admirable trait?"

"If I was a doctor or a teacher or a charity worker then maybe having a white-trash super-depressed mother when I was a kid would be okay," said Leigh. "People could say 'look at what she overcame.' But I'm in the appearance business. I'm in the beauty and refinement business. I think that the people who are most trusted in those kinds of businesses didn't grow up in a dump with, like, no property surrounding their home. They grew up surrounded by beauty on large, perfectly manicured plots of land. They tended to their land, created gardens as children, and learned from it. They were exposed to and toured great properties here and abroad. In essence, the trade is built into their DNA. My mother makes me look like a fake."

"We all have baggage from our upbringings, Leigh," Abby offered. "If you could just accept your mom for who she is and move on, you would be a lot happier."

"Yes, let's hear the psychobabble speech," Leigh angrily responded. "'*Leigh, your real problem isn't your mother, it's you. It's you feeling that you're a fake, as fake as the plastic grass your mother rolled out in front of the camper. Maybe that's why everything you do has to be perfect. Why everything you buy has to be the best.*' Blah blah blah..."

"Well, you did bring a $15,000 purse to morning coffee and then just dumped it on the ground as if it was worthless," Abby pointed out.

"This purse cost $20,000," Leigh corrected her as she picked the purse up and hurled it onto the vacant chair next to her.

"That's even worse," Abby said.

"So what, I carry a nice purse during the day!" Leigh said. "What does that have to do with anything?"

"It's that you *have* to carry a purse like that or you would be mortified," Abby said. "*And* your need to beat everyone else around you all the time."

"I'm finding you really tiring right now," said Leigh.

"Well then leave!" Abby said. "Your mom's vehicle is right outside. Why don't you go find her?"

"You can be a real bitch, Abby," Leigh snapped. "What I need is for my mother to go away. To permanently disappear. I'm thinking of giving her money to go away. Short of destroying her trailer or buying her a home somewhere else, I don't know what else to do."

She sat for a minute, looking out at *The Rolling Stone*.

"Do you want the last piece of my muffin?" Leigh asked the sisters. "It really is too big."

"No," They said.

35

He shouldn't have canceled on me, Adair thought as she drove wildly toward Le Beau Château on Monday morning. She had already stopped by Jack's Westport apartment, his Cannondale yoga studio, and the charity office. *How could he cancel on me two weeks in a row so close to our benefit? We have things to discuss; details that need to be worked out. And I miss him. Doesn't he miss me? He didn't even give me an explanation. "Can't meet today. Sorry. -J.T." was the extent of it. He didn't even respond to my return text. For all I do for him, the least he can do is keep our private sessions.*

Once the gate opened, Adair whirled her hunter-green Volvo V50 Sport station wagon into the estate's gravel driveway, kicking up more stones than a municipal snowplow. Once her car was close to the home, Adair noted several cars parked in its courtyard.

So Jack is *here,* she thought, spying his white Toyota Prius. Having finally found him, she began to calm down. *Whose car is next to his?* she wondered. *Is that Kate Musto's car? Looks like it, but there are so many black BMW M5s in this town. Why would they be here together? He told me he doesn't hold private sessions here. Maybe they're going over the final details of the dinner menu? If so, I should be involved.* Adair parked and stormed toward the home.

Entering the double-height foyer, Adair was halted by its elegance. *They rarely design homes like this anymore,* she thought. *Everything is in proper proportion; its details are all congruous.*

The lavish mansion was decorated in a Swedish country style common in original French château homes. The paneled walls were custom-tinted an ethereal, pale bluish-gray. Cream limestone lined the floor and ran up the stately staircase, which, along with its hand-wrought bronze banister, gently curved toward the second floor. A large, antique bronze lantern hung in the hall's center above a round French country antique table, and a series of gilt-framed abstract landscapes in subtle hues of blue, gray, and lavender lined the walls. Just being in the space relaxed her, as classically designed homes often did.

Adair had never been in Le Beau Château before. Jack had never invited her. He had never told her about his sexcapades, understanding that, despite her dedication to him, she wouldn't approve. Even if she was a full believer in kundalini, sexcapades fell too far out of her model of good behavior. It would be righteous and hypocritical of her—she was a married woman sleeping with her yoga instructor after all—but Adair had always found ways to justify what she called her "guilty pleasures." With Jack, it was Hugh's fault. There was no intimacy left in their marriage. His only interest in their life together was what directly involved their children.

Adair walked through the impressive foyer's large coffered arches in search of the kitchen.

If they're planning the menu, they'll be in the kitchen, right? she thought. Adair found it. It was the original scullery kitchen and butler's pantry, filled with industrial-style appliances, zinc countertops, and handsome custom cabinetry complete with hand-wrought pewter knobs. It was just like the ones in period homes she had toured. *This is so much more attractive than the showcase kitchens of today,* she thought.

But it was empty, so she searched the informal and formal dining rooms but didn't find Jack or Kate or even a housekeeper. She walked out onto the expansive slated patio. She saw no one but a few men working in a far-off garden.

Could Jack be upstairs? Adair wondered. *Maybe hosting a private session?* Adair knew Kate was one of his clients. What had Kate said during their lunch at Mon Petite Café?

"I take private sessions with him and he's always very professional. I think he only has sex with a select group of his clients."

Remembering Kate's comment reassured Adair, and she walked to the staircase.

As she climbed the stairs, Adair ran her hand along the cool metal banister and looked into the driveway's courtyard, again wondering who owned the black BMW.

That can't be the landscapers', she thought.

The upstairs consisted of a long hall with rooms branching off of it. The walls were the same airy, light blue-gray tint of the first floor, and the whitewashed flooring was lined with a pale-gray Stark runner. With the exception of a few linen closets, all the hallway's doors were open. Adair peered inside each of them, noting large, secondary bedrooms decorated beautifully but with no personal touches.

No one has ever made one of these rooms their own, she observed.

At the end of the hall was a closed door. She heard the ethereal, meditative sound of Enya floating into the hallway.

Finally, she thought. *Jack must be in this room.*

⌒∼⌣⌣⌐

When Jack had called Kate the night before to confirm her sex-capade with Carly, he had discussed, once again, the importance of her learning to trust men.

"You've been abused, Kate, by your husband and when you were raped at the gas station as a young girl, but not all men will abuse you," Jack said. "It's important for you to learn to trust men again for your personal growth, for your personal happiness. It's important for the advancement of kundalini's movement through your chakras."

Kate was slowly falling in love with Jack. His kindness, his empathy was winning her over. *He doesn't realize it, but I am learning to trust men again through my relationship with him,* she thought.

And as much as she enjoyed the tenderness of being with Carly, she recognized that she wasn't a lesbian. *I'm just not as turned on with her as I have been with men in the past,* she'd thought during their last two sessions.

So while they were talking on the phone, she invited Jack to join her and Carly the following day to not only watch, but to participate. She wanted it to happen in the estate's master bedroom. For all the luxury of the safe room, a part of her was always aware of the security aspects of the space: the room of monitors, the alarm panels not far from the bedroom, and the tinted windows. For Kate, it was inhibiting in a locked-down kind of way. She wanted to be in the master bedroom that she had walked through each time they went to the safe room. Its bed was luxurious and there was more natural light in the space.

Jack agreed. He gave the housekeeper the day off, had the

property's landscape staff work on areas far from the home, and asked Kevin to have a patrol officer in the area. *No one ever just shows up to the house,* he convinced himself. *If this is what she needs to include me, we can do it.*

Despite his best efforts, Jack had fallen in love with Kate, too. There was so much to like about her. She was beautiful and smart and kind. Equally appealing to him was that she needed to be saved.

~~~

I'm finally going to see a human being, Adair thought as she opened the door to the master bedroom and was greeted by a lovely formal sitting room. Enya was radiating from an adjoining room. *He's never put Enya on* our *private session playlist,* she thought. *And he's never invited me here.*

Adair started to think twice about walking farther into the master suite. *If Jack's in a private session and I barge in, he will be furious with me,* she thought. *He's warned me about my impulsivity in the past. But, if that is in fact Kate's car, then he did cancel on me for her. But what if it's not her car? Who did he cancel on me for? I have to find out.*

Adair tiptoed down a short arched hallway toward the bedroom. As she walked, her hand ran along the wall. *This is Venetian plaster,* she thought. *This home is so refined.*

Expecting to see two yoga mats and two clothed bodies, Adair was shocked to peek around the corner and instead find Kate and a woman naked in bed together. As Adair stepped a bit closer, she saw Jack seated cross-legged in a club chair to the right of the bed, watching them, encouraging them.

He's dressed, she thought, oddly relieved.

Jack told Kate to "give Carly lip." Kate stopped kissing the other woman and, after giving Jack a coy smile, proceeded to go down on her.

What is she, a puppet? Adair angrily thought. *He's into lesbians? He never told me that.*

Next, Jack stood and walked toward the women. Kate's long hair blocked his full view. He gently combed her hair back with his fingers and held it in a loose ponytail at the base of her neck. He laid his hand on Carly's undulating stomach.

Adair wanted to lunge into the room and strangle him. *You canceled our private session—an appointment that's been on your calendar for five years—for this? For the cheap thrill of seeing two women fool around? I signed on with you when you had so few clients, before your yoga studio, before your following. When you barely had enough money to eat!*

Forbidden by her parents to naturally express her anger, Adair had always been afraid of it. It would rise and she would instantly try to quell it, transferring it into a racing heart and trembling hands. Even if what upset her wasn't her fault, what followed was self-blame.

I don't own him, she thought standing in the hallway. *I don't have a right to think that I do. I'm married, after all.* It had always been easier for Adair to blame everything on herself. When she turned her anger inward, no one would hit her, no one threatened abandonment or disownment. Her parents were the only ones allowed to get angry in her home.

This is my fault, she thought. *I shouldn't have tried to find Jack today. I don't own him. I share him.*

Jack pulled Kate from Carly and started to passionately kiss her before laying her vertically on the bed. He placed his hands near her head and hovered over her, his thighs pushing into her.

"You're so beautiful," he told her while staring into her eyes. "You are absolutely beautiful."

As if on cue, Carly stood and walked toward the master bath. The movement frightened Adair. She didn't want to be seen, especially not by Jack, not in this state. She felt completely out of control.

Adair quietly took two steps back. She realized that nearly ten minutes had passed since she first saw them. She heard the bathwater pulse through the home's original plumbing. It gave her the confidence to peer forward one more time. Jack and Kate's eyes were locked, and he was in the process of removing his shirt.

I have to get out of here, she thought. *I can't see any more.*

Adair turned and ran down the hall, away from that room, away from that magnificent home. As she pulled her car out of the courtyard as quietly as possible, she thought, *Jack is in love with Kate. Not me.*

36

The parking lot was brimming. Immaculate Porsches, Ferraris, Maseratis, Range Rovers, Mercedes, BMWs, Cadillacs, and Teslas, as well as vintage models—Austin Martins, Bentleys, and MGs—filled the field to the left of the estate's showpiece structure: the late architect Philip Johnson's iconic Glass House. Built in the mid-1950s, the glass and steel building was Johnson's expression of minimal structure, which allowed ultimate transparency and broke down the barriers between inside and out.

After the guests had their cars valeted on the cool November night, they were directed to the sculpture gallery, one of The Glass House's satellite buildings on the rolling, gently manicured, nearly fifty-acre lot. The property was aglow in rich autumnal colors. A wooden walkway had been laid and illuminated by bronze oil lamps, allowing the guests to easily traverse over the properties narrow gravel pathways. "I don't want to hear about ruined Manolo Blahnik and Jimmy Choo shoes the day after," Jack had said to Adair.

Classic Indian music called to the guests from the gallery—which Johnson designed to house a large-scale sculpture created by modernists, including Andrew Lord, Robert Morris, and John Chamberlain. It was a brick-paved building with a multi-tiered stucco exterior and exposed interior staircases. Its ceiling was largely glass, supported by tubular steel. After sunset, the lights were lowered, which allowed for an expansive view of the night sky.

Inside, an eight-piece orchestra of sitars, santoors, and violins accompanied by fluted veenas played while handsome waiters and waitresses of Indian descent dressed in Indian garb passed around colorful vodka-based cocktails: "Instant Karma," "Indian Summer," and "Sex in Mumbai."

The guests who played along with the Indian theme were dressed in largely custom-designed jewel-toned saris and kurtas. As a result, the room was a riot of color: royal blue, ruby red, teal green, sunflower yellow, and sparking gold. Excited to be at a theme party in such an incredible setting, the partygoers' moods were equally exuberant.

"This is such a unique party theme," said one guest. "And look at those waiters. I didn't know Indian men could be so attractive."

"I know," responded another. "When I think of attractive, medium-toned men, I think of Hispanic Enrique Iglesias-types. These men are beautiful."

"Where is India anyway?" a third woman in the group asked. "And what's up with the women's forehead dots? I've always wondered about that."

"Those are called bindis," The first one said. "They're the 'third eye.'"

"Third eye? That's really gross," she responded.

The conversation going on in the next group was similarly condescending: "I feel like I'm in Mumbai without having to deal with the beggars and gastroenteritis," said one hedge fund manager to an entrepreneur.

For many of the guests, this party was the closest they would ever get to India, not because of the trip's one-way, fourteen-plus-hour flight, but because of a wish to avoid exposure to extreme poverty, which would depress them temporarily.

"I've heard there's a lack of toilet paper among the lower caste members, so they wipe themselves with their left hands," said the hedge fund manager.

"Oh," The entrepreneur responded. "Is that why it's considered offensive to extend your left hand for a handshake in India?"

"Yes, exactly!" The hedge fund manager exclaimed. "And guess what? The lower castes work in the restaurant kitchens."

"Even in the five star hotels and restaurants?" The entrepreneur responded.

"Yes, I've heard even there. They work there but live in slums."

Jack was at the center of the gallery near the orchestra dressed in a sozni-embroidered indigo-blue kurta, which resembled a long silken tunic, paired with baggy pants. To complete his traditional Indian outfit, he wore burgundy slippers. His party was off to a great start. He was beaming, moving from one silk-swathed group of people to the next.

After the guests had their fill of cocktails, they were encouraged to explore the property and experience the different offerings in the satellite buildings. Many people were curious about the hookah lounge and went directly there. Those intent on winning the silent auction items headed to the painting gallery and library to review the bidding sheets, which had started online the night before.

The hookah lounge was in the property's guesthouse, a one-story structure that acted as folly to the transparency of the Glass House. The windowless building was made entirely of brick and capped with a flat steel roof. The cave-like space was the perfect place for a smoky, sultry hookah lounge, where people gathered around and smoked tobacco from large shared pipes with disposable mouthpieces. The space had been transformed into a tented space with draped, crimson, silk fabric. Celestial-shaped metal lanterns hung from the ceiling and votive candles were sprinkled throughout. Its two rooms had been emptied of their typical contents and filled with low sectional seating, poufs, and round mosaic tables that supported the hookahs. Artwork themselves, the tall, ornamented pipes supported communal gathering and were used throughout India and in the Middle East.

At Jack's party, a few of the guests traded the pipes' tobacco for potent, engineered marijuana buds, and those unaccustomed to getting stoned got ridiculously high.

Some of those women visited the henna station and showed up at the next venue with the natural-based temporary tattooing in places on the body that wouldn't be easy to conceal until it faded a week later: a delicate pattern on their necks with the flowery design crawling up onto their cheeks or earlobes, a similar pattern covering each digit on their hands. Some of the women whose saris exposed their midriffs had elaborate patterning encircling their belly buttons.

From the hookah lounge, the partygoers stumbled to the painting gallery and library. The gallery, which was built like a bunker hidden in a hill, was entered through a long concrete pathway that sloped into the earth. The space was filled with fine artwork by modern masters such as Andy Warhol, Julian Schnabel, and Frank Stella, including a Warhol pop art piece of Johnson done in the Campbell Soup style. Just as in the sculpture gallery, there were a number of stern-looking security guards keeping watch.

The library, which resembled an interpretive castle and was covered in stucco, was a solid cave-like structure lined with wood bookcases filled with the late architect's expansive literary collection.

In those two spaces, trays and trays of Indian hors d'oeuvres were passed, including the traditional *tandori*, samosa, and *seekh* kebab. To quench thirsts, imported Indian beer and wine was available: Tadi—palm wine—Kingfisher lager, and handia rice beer in addition to the themed cocktails. For those more interested in a solid vodka tonic or grapefruit martini, the bars were stocked to please.

Once the majority of guests had amassed in the Glass House for a dessert of maharani cupcakes, *kaju katli*, and coconut *laddu*, it was time for Jack to give his toast. Images of impoverished Indian women and children printed on poster board-size canvases were stationed on easels throughout the room.

Jack moved to the center of the room and asked everyone to close their eyes and take a moment of silence. "Think of the community in India that you are helping tonight. Think of the needy women and children who, without your generosity, would have no other hope of better lives. Imagine them and feel happy. Feel good about yourselves and your selflessness." Most of the men in the room looked at him like he was crazy but played along and closed their eyes, swaying a bit from too many "Sex in Mumbai" cocktails. A minute passed, and Jack began his toast.

"I'd like to thank you all for coming tonight. I'm so glad so many of you dressed in theme. You all look ravishing in your jewel tones. I know many of you are all anxious to know who has won the items in the silent auction, but we are waiting to tally the auction item results until tomorrow morning so that the event's organizers can enjoy tonight as much as the rest of us. We will call the lucky winners, and for those interested, the results will be posted on my website.

"That said, given Rod Jenson's incredibly generous bid of $62,000 for a week-long stay at Fiji's exclusive Turtle Island, I will announce

THE ADJUSTMENTS

that he and his wife Whitney are the winners! Apologies to Michael
Kat, who missed out by just $2,000 after a good-natured battle
with his friend and squash rival, Rod."

There was laughter and clapping in the room. Rod and Michael
shook hands. Once it quieted down, Jack continued: "The owner
is a personal friend of mine and will ensure your stay is as ideal as
possible. Given the funds Rod's donation brought in, I'm going
to request that you be picked up in Hawaii by private jet. I'm sure
he'll oblige. I can't wait to speak with you and Whitney upon your
return." There was clapping throughout the room and a few men
heartily slapped Rod's back. Women gathered around Whitney,
smiling brightly.

"I'd also like to thank Adair Burns for her tireless efforts to
make this party such a success. Adair, I would be lost without
you. Thank you so much."

The crowd turned to look at Adair and gazed on her with
admiration. She was drunk and supported herself by leaning
against one of the home's few interior walls. She smiled. Jack
waited a few moments to see if she was going to say a few words
to the group as they had planned, but instead her head dipped a
bit before recovering. Jack quickly resumed his speech.

"Lastly, I want to speak about the people you are helping by
being here. Given the ticket sales and after reviewing some of the
highest bids on the silent auction items, I can proudly say that
we have raised over $500,000 tonight." The crowd broke out in
applause. "That money will be used to build a large factory-like
structure that will allow the women to work together in groups
and which will also house a preschool and school for their children.
Any money left over will be used in their communities.

"This charity, Auntie Arts, has completely transformed the

lives of more than 250 women and children. All profits from the sale of the garments the artisans create go directly back to them. This charity has raised their stature in the community and in their families. For an area of extreme poverty where women are treated poorly, this charity is changing their lives and offering a better future for their children. With your help, my goal is to continue to expand Auntie Arts' reach, one village at a time. Now, if you would please indulge me, I'd like to show a short video of the women at work and their community."

A screen lowered and displayed images of women and children in colorful, worn-looking saris and kurtas posing in their ramshackle, mud-floor huts. The pictures depicted the group amassed outside their meager dwellings, women sitting in the dirt making the tunics and shawls, and children playing in the countryside with roaming, starved stray dogs. Later images showed the Indian women holding up their completed work and then the products on display in high-end boutiques. In the final images, Adair, Anastasia Barlow, and Dalisay Ward modeled a few of the tunics and shawls. The latter images earned the most applause, whereas the earlier ones produced looks of feigned concern and even gasps.

At the end of the slideshow, Jack closed with: "After seeing those images, if anyone would like to donate more to Auntie Arts, my assistant, Leaha Kitzmann, will be walking around with a clipboard to take your pledges. Thank you again and enjoy the rest of the evening!"

At this point in the night, many of the partygoers were wasted. Adair made her way over to Kate Musto's husband Lorenzo after he returned from checking on his Maserati. It was his prized possession, and he hated handing over its keys to a valet. Lorenzo had a good buzz going but wasn't anywhere near Adair's state.

"Did you ever think you would be sporting an outfit like that?" she said in jest as she surveyed his cream-colored kurta.

"Never," he responded, "but I must say it's very comfortable, much more so than the tuxes we usually have to wear to events like this. Kate begged me to wear this given that her company catered the party, and since my friends are wearing the same getups, I agreed."

"Well, out of all the men here, you and Jack look the best in the silk pajamas," she said.

Lorenzo stared at her. He had never considered her before. She was pretty in the typical Fairfield County way—blonde, blue-eyed, and wholesome-looking—but there was nothing outstanding about her in a town where most of the women were attractive. Around here, the wives' beauty went hand in hand with the success of their husbands. Most of them were pretty. In order to stand out, they had to be model-level beautiful, like Kate. Lorenzo knew that when he picked her. He wanted to be the guy married to the showpiece.

Tonight Adair was wearing a pale-pink sari banded with a woven hot-pink-and-gold ribbon. Her long blonde hair had been arranged in an *I Dream of Jeannie* style that required hair extensions.

She's pretty enough, he thought. *I'd fuck her.*

"Where's Kate?" Adair asked as she took two steps closer to him, slightly wobbling as she stood. "Oh, let me guess, off with Jack somewhere. You should keep an eye on her when she's around him."

"What does that mean?" Lorenzo asked. He never considered that Kate would be unfaithful to him. Not once.

"It's just a friendly warning," Adair responded. "There is a lot that goes on in this town while the men are at work."

Lorenzo looked at her quizzically, trying to determine why she would say that: because she was hitting on him, because she was clearly drunk, or…was she giving him an honest warning?

"Do you want to go to the hookah lounge with me?" Adair asked. "Given how crowded the room is, Kate won't even know you're gone."

"No," said Lorenzo, deciding that she was hitting on him. He pushed her aside and walked away. "I think you'd better go find Hugh."

Adair did walk away, slowly weaving through people who were trying to congratulate her for the successful party. She realized that she needed to use the lavatory. *How much did I have to drink tonight?* Adair wondered, reviewing the two "Indian Summer" drinks she consumed within the first half hour of the party followed by one or two "Instant Karmas" and a tasting of several of the palm wines. *Have I eaten much?* she questioned. She could still taste the cilantro from a *tandori* chicken hors d' oeuvre and vaguely remembered eating a few others.

The Glass House's bathroom was one of the private areas in the otherwise transparent home. It was located in a large cylinder in the structure's center. Its door was locked, so Adair swayed outside, waiting. It opened and Kate appeared, looking stunning in a billowy teal sari with exposed midriff. She wore her hair in a bun ornamented with gold and teal beads. She greeted Adair happily and reached to give her a large hug in congratulations.

"This party is such a success," Kate said. "You should be so proud of yourself."

Adair looked at her angrily, remembering what she'd seen in Le Beau Château, but then stumbled and giggled to herself. Kate realized Adair was wasted.

"Do you want me to help you into the bathroom?" Kate innocently asked as she looked around the space to see if Hugh was nearby.

"No," Adair said. "I don't want help from you, you *lesbian*. You'll probably hit on me in the bathroom." Kate looked at her in shock. "I *saw* you. I saw you and some woman and Jack at Le Beau Château. He was with *you* instead of me that day. That is the day and time when I meet with him. *Not you*."

Kate grabbed Adair and pulled her into the bathroom.

"Adair, please," Kate said. "Not here. If you want to talk to me about this, lets meet tomorrow, but please don't go into this here. Not at this party."

"I saw you. I snuck into the house and saw you and Jack." Adair continued. "Lorenzo makes you fuck him every night, so I would think you get enough sex, but no, you still need more. You *lied* to me. You told me Jack was always professional with you."

"Adair, please stop." Kate begged. "We are friends, remember? Please don't do this to me tonight. I didn't know I took your appointment. I had no idea."

"Then stay away from Jack," Adair said. "He's *mine*, not yours."

Trying to calm Adair, Kate agreed, but Adair's drunken state made her beyond reason.

"That's *our* private session time. Not yours!" she continued, slurring.

For the party, the bathroom had been outfitted with Indian-themed powder room-related accessories that Jack was considering adding to the Auntie Arts product line: jeweled hand mirrors, combs, and brushes. In her drunken rage, Adair picked up one of the jeweled hand mirrors and threw it at Kate, who ducked. It smashed into a massive modernist mirror behind her, which shattered and then fell to the ground, causing mirror splinters to spray across the room. Given the chatter in the Glass House and the insulation of the core, the crashing noise was not heard outside of the bathroom.

"Adair, are you insane?" Kate said shakily. She pulled a fragment of mirror from the side of her wrist. She could feel a few splinters in her ankles. She was completely shocked by Adair's actions. "I think once you get over tomorrow's hangover, you better check into Sunny Meadows again. It's obvious that your last stay there didn't help enough."

"How do you know about that?" Adair calmly asked, having grown eerily tranquil after the mirror shattered. She was eying a large broken shard and was contemplating picking it up to wield at Kate.

"Jack and I do more than have sex together," Kate said vindictively. "He tells me all about you and your neediness. He's only nice to you so that you'll run his charity!"

As Adair reached for the glass, Kate turned and quickly exited the bathroom. Adair slumped down on a vanity stool. She realized her foot was bleeding.

Kate wanted to leave the party immediately. She looked for Lorenzo and saw him speaking with Jack. *Oh shit*, she thought. Kate approached them, but saw that Jack looked scared. He was backed up against one of the glass walls with Lorenzo towering over him. Kate stood just behind Lorenzo to listen.

"I heard you fuck a lot of the women in town," he said. "If I find out that you're fucking my wife, I will kill you. I will break your boney, pathetic little limber body into two. And then I'll kill her."

Kate touched Lorenzo on the back. He turned around sharply. "Sweetie, I'm ready to go now," she said as sweetly as she could muster, holding a bundle of napkins over her wrist and under her clutch to hide the wound. "Please, let's go home. I'm tired."

Lorenzo looked back at Jack once and then agreed. As they walked away, it took every muscle in Kate's body not to turn around and make eye contact with Jack.

37

"Adair told me something tonight," Lorenzo said as they were getting undressed in their massive his and her walk-in closets.

Panic began to rise in Kate.

"She insinuated that you and Jack are fucking," he said as he walked up behind her, towering over her. She continued to remove the sari's layers in a calm fashion before turning to face him.

"Adair was very drunk tonight," she said, "and she has a thing for Jack. She is very possessive over him. I'm not sleeping with him. I'm not sleeping with anyone but you."

"That's good. Because if I ever find out that you *are* sleeping with someone other than me, I'll kill both of you," Lorenzo said with a straight face.

"I don't doubt it, Lorenzo," Kate responded, hoping this would be the end of it. After parties, he was typically too tired to have sex.

"I'd rather our kids grow up with no mother than one that can't be faithful to her husband," Lorenzo said before grabbing her by the neck and pushing her against the wall.

"Please, not tonight," Kate said as he tightened his grip on her. "We had a nice time at the party. Please don't ruin the night for me." His grip became so tight that she couldn't speak. Lorenzo had learned how to cut off her oxygen without leaving a mark, and the pressure made Kate's bandaged wrist throb. He held her there for a few moments until she started to gasp, then let go of her neck, but he didn't let go of her.

Instead, he picked her up and carried her to stand in front of the large full-length mirror. She knew what would happen next. She knew how much he enjoyed watching himself during sex. He would bend her over and, as he violently pounded into her, note his physique in the mirror.

He loved that his stomach was still a washboard at age fifty-three. He loved the hard-earned and impressive bulges in his biceps, his triceps, his deltoids, and his quadriceps. He turned sideways and noted his perfect profile, his tight gluteus maximus muscles.

He climaxed with a series of grunts, a sound that both revolted and relieved Kate, for it signaled that he was finally done. The climax was sharply followed by his releasing her, which, after the force of his thrusts, generally forced Kate to collapse. She had grown so accustomed to this routine that she knew when to put her hands out in front of her to buffer her fall.

When they were in bed later, Kate would turn away from him to face the wall, and Lorenzo would recount the parts of his body that he thought needed more work at the gym. How he thought he was getting a bit flabby here or there. Tonight his narcissistic babbles were about his deltoids followed by a discussion of all the men at the party who he thought had more money and were more accomplished than he—those who, in his estimation, had it better than he did.

As Kate tried to go to sleep, she worried about Adair. She decided the best way to control her was through Jack. Kate planned to call him as soon as Lorenzo left the house in the morning. She also decided she couldn't be married to Lorenzo anymore.

I just have to figure out a way to expose what he does to me, she thought. *No matter how unfit a parent Lorenzo tries to present me as in court, and I know he has a running list—my reliance on anti-depression and anxiety medicine, my lack of extended family members to help me in single motherhood—there is no judge who is going to award full guardianship to a man who regularly rapes his wife. Especially given that we have two daughters.* If nothing else, Kate's relationship with Jack had given her the confidence to rid herself of Lorenzo.

<hr />

The next morning, once Lorenzo left at seven o'clock to go to the gym for his Sunday morning workout, she called Jack.

"I'm sorry to bother you so early after the benefit," she said. "But I have to talk with you about Adair. She was at Le Beau Château the day you and I had sex. She saw us together. She saw Carly and I together. Last night before she threw a mirror at me, she threatened to tell Lorenzo everything. She said you canceled on her, so she went to the estate to find you."

"I think she may have already told Lorenzo about us," Jack said. "You heard him threatening me."

"If she had done more than insinuate, I would be dead," Kate said, and she explained what Lorenzo did to her when they got home from the party. She told Jack that she was leaving Lorenzo.

"Have you considered videotaping one of Lorenzo's sexual assaults?" Jack asked Kate. "The company Georgette Ark used to install the surveillance system at Le Beau Château, Secure, offers a discreet service that would record him in the act. If you hired the company, you would be assigned a security consultant, and a series of cameras would be installed when Lorenzo is out of the house. Once the cameras are in place, Secure offers a number of services, including monitoring your surveillance twenty-four hours a day. If they witness something on your recordings that they believe puts you in grave danger, they can anonymously call the police. Georgette doesn't have that service at the estate since she is there so infrequently and I check in on the home on a daily basis. The service she has just provides monitoring of the estate from the security room and the ability to record and have it uploaded to Secure's servers. The recordings taken in your home could be sent from their central office directly to your attorney's office."

"But how would I pay for it?" Kate asked. "Lorenzo watches our finances like a hawk, even the money I bring in from my catering. It's part of his total control over me."

"I'll pay for it," Jack said, "happily."

"Really?" Kate responded surprised. She wasn't used to men doing nice things for her.

"Absolutely," he said. "And the company's employees have to sign a confidentiality agreement, so your personal information would remain private until it's necessary for the divorce proceedings. You can also request that females monitor your home's surveillance."

"You think it's that easy?" Kate asked.

"Yes, I do," Jack responded. "I'll set it up."

One week later, after being assigned a security consultant and having the cameras installed, Kate prepared for a girls' night out.

"Lorenzo, I have plans tonight," Kate said as she looked in her closet for shoes.

"You do?" he responded. "So my mom is coming over?"

"I didn't ask her to," Kate said. "I figured you could handle the kids for one night on your own. I made dinner. It's in the oven. The kids are bathed, fed, and ready for bed."

"Kate, I had a long day," Lorenzo said. "I don't want you to go out. I need time to myself."

"I can't change my plans tonight, Lorenzo. I need time to myself, too. It's been weeks since I've had a night out with my girlfriends. I'll be home tomorrow night and you can do what you want."

"I can't deal with three kids right now," Lorenzo said. "Cancel your plans."

"No," Kate said.

Lorenzo moved toward her, and Kate turned around to face him. He grabbed her wrists.

"You are my wife," said Lorenzo. "When I say you can't go out, you can't."

"If you had your way, I would never go out," said Kate.

Lorenzo dropped her wrists, grabbed the collar of her blousy silk shirt, and pulled straight down, ripping it.

"Now do you want to go?" said Lorenzo with a smirk. "Look. Your best shirt is ripped."

"What is wrong with you?" Kate said, emboldened, knowing everything was being recorded. "You're acting like an animal!"

Lorenzo reached over and tore the entire shirt from her. She covered her chest and turned away from him. He pulled on her bra and it sprung open.

"Now you really can't go out, can you?" Lorenzo asked mockingly.

Kate said nothing more, not wanting to appear on tape as encouraging his bad behavior. She kept her back to him. He grabbed her and forced her into the bathroom. There he pushed her torso over the sink and lifted her skirt. Kate protested. She squirmed and kicked backward. He laughed and held firm.

"You can never get away from me," he boasted. "You try every time, but I'm stronger. I'll always be stronger than you, and there is nothing you can do about it. If you're going out, I'm going to give you a parting gift. Who are you to so blatantly disobey me? I'm your husband."

Given Lorenzo's proclivity for watching himself during sex, she had cameras installed in the bathroom. Lorenzo insisted that the room be filled with mirrors.

After Lorenzo was done, and as the cameras were still running, Kate asked, "Why do you repeatedly hurt me this way? Forcing me to have sex with you? Being so rough with me?"

"I don't hurt you," said Lorenzo. "You're my wife. It's what wives have to do in marriages."

"Is that how you want your mom treated?" Kate asked. "What about your daughters? Are you going to want Sarah and Maddy's husbands to force them to have sex? To fuck them against their will? Will that be Sarah and Maddy's wifely duties?"

"Shut up," Lorenzo said.

"Hit a nerve, didn't I, Lorenzo?" muttered Kate.

"Shut that big mouth of yours," Threatened Lorenzo, "or I will find something else for it to do."

"When did you get so crude?" asked Kate. "You didn't treat me this way when we were dating."

"You were fun when we were dating," said Lorenzo. "Just go. I don't want to see you anymore. Get out of my house."

But it was Lorenzo who left the room first, taking his iPhone from the dresser and calling his mother. As Kate heard him asking her to come over and watch the kids, she locked the bedroom door. Kate looked toward the cameras. If all went as planned, a woman named Freda Lombardi was watching the interaction from Secure's central office. She was instructed to call the police if Lorenzo appeared excessively violent. Kate had also turned on the sound recording mechanism on her iPhone. She emailed the audio recording to her lawyer with promises of the tapes to follow.

"Got him," Kate said to herself as tears ran down her cheeks.

38

The morning after the benefit, Adair was wild with worry trying to remember the events of the night before. She vaguely remembered a mirror breaking in the bathroom, but she didn't remember how it broke. Her foot throbbed and looked like it had been professionally bandaged.

Did I go to the hospital? She tried to remember. *I think I got stitches.* Adair was too hungover to investigate what was under the dressing. Her head throbbed and she couldn't focus. She continued to have waves of nausea after dry heaving on and off all morning. Her beautiful pink sari was in a ball in the corner of the room. The bottom of it was drenched in blood.

As she looked in the mirror, she saw a makeup-streaked face, and something was off about her hair. Adair didn't remember this, but one of her front hair extensions got caught on a hookah at the end of night, leaving her hair lopsided. She couldn't quite figure out what was wrong. Hugh wouldn't speak to her.

What did I say to him in the car on the way home? she wondered, though she was sure it wasn't kind. *Did I demand he have sex with me? Did I force myself on him? Did I call him a closeted homosexual?* Today was Sunday, which was typically their nanny's day off, but Hugh had called her and asked her to watch the kids before leaving for the day.

Adair's phone rang. She saw it was Jack and hesitantly picked up. *At what point in the night did I cut my foot?* she wondered.

"Hi, Jack," she said as brightly as she could muster given her pounding head.

"Adair," Jack said. "I'm disappointed in you."

"You are?" she asked.

"Yes," he responded. "Do you remember what you did last night? You got embarrassingly drunk and shattered the powder room's custom-designed, original mirror. Then you limped through the Glass House bleeding and didn't even realize it, which horrified the guests and sent many of them home. You told Lorenzo Musto that I'm sleeping with his wife, and I've since found out that you have been stalking me. What the fuck, Adair?"

"Oh, Jack, I'm so sorry," Adair said, apologizing quickly. "I just had too much to drink last night. I was so nervous about the party's success. You know I'm not supposed to drink on my meds, and I shouldn't have. Most of the night is a total blackout for me. I'm so sorry."

"And what about following me to Le Beau Château and spying on me? That's unforgivable," Jack said. "You've gone too far this time. I need to sever our professional and personal relationship."

"Jack, no!" Adair cried. "No, no, no. Please no." She felt a violent wave of nausea and realized she was about to dry heave again. "Wait," she said into the phone as she dropped it onto her bed and dashed into her bathroom, bracing over the toilet. Jack did not wait.

Adair tried to reach him the rest of the day as she remembered details from the party piece by piece. By three o'clock, she could get down a piece of dry toast and a Gatorade. An hour later, she thought she could drive. She got in her car and went looking for Jack. She couldn't find him at his apartment, the charity office, or the yoga studio. She couldn't enter Le Beau Château because there was a cop car blocking entry into the driveway.

She figured he must be there and looked at her watch. She knew he had an evening six thirty class to teach at his studio. She pulled into a neighbor's driveway—the Smiths, who wintered in Florida. Positioned a short distance into their driveway behind a row of evergreens, she had a view of the estate's entry gate and waited.

A half hour later, she saw Tory Blume's car exit followed by Jack and then two pickup trucks full of what appeared to be landscape help. The truck drove right past the cop car.

Isn't it illegal to drive with people in the cab? she wondered. *Those trucks are weighted down like refugee boats. Why didn't the cop pull them over?*

The following day, Adair set up at her surveillance spot again, this time writing down the license plates of the cars that came and went from the estate. She saw Cecily Morgan pull out just before Jack and two other cars.

The same routine took place the following day, but there were two occurrences of Jack coming and going with local women and a few men. That's when it dawned on Adair.

Jack is running a prostitution ring, she thought. *He's being paid for the private sessions, and he's providing sex partners for the women in town like he did for Kate! That's pimping!*

She decided to spend the next week videotaping the driveway. She saw close to ten prominent women in town going in and out of the château, but wasn't successful in identifying all of the men.

Carloads of guys pulled into the estate often, and Adair couldn't tell if they were landscapers, tradespeople who tended to the large home and property, or if they were involved with Jack and the sexual activities inside the home.

After downloading the videos, she emailed them to herself and attached them to an email she drafted to the managing editor of *Neighborly News*. Given the patrol cars stationed at the estate, she knew she couldn't go to the police with this evidence.

First, she called Jack. He didn't pick up or respond, so she went and waited for him at his yoga studio just before one of his classes. When he saw her, he tried to bypass her and walked toward his studio.

"Jack, I have recordings you will be interested in," Adair called, which stopped him. Adair told him about her surveillance. She threatened to go to the newspapers with the recordings. "You're running a prostitution business," she said. "I can expose and ruin you as well as your clients."

"What do you want, Adair?" Jack asked, playing along but already determined to destroy her if necessary.

"I want our private sessions to resume," she said. "I want access to you. I want to work for your charity again. Even though I now realize I have to share you with more women than I realized, I miss you and I need you. Without you, I can't function."

Jack agreed and then called the police.

～～～

On a crisp, cool day with a slight chance of snow, the following was front-page news in *Breaking News Today: Cannondale*:

MAN ARRESTED FOR SOLICITATION
OF A MALE PROSTITUTE

Hugh Burns was arrested last night for solicitation of a prostitute in the Commuter Park & Go near exit 39 off the Merritt Parkway, a long-rumored homosexual pick-up spot.

Police were conducting a routine survey of the parking lot when they observed Burns hand a man cash through the car window of a black BMW M5. The two men then moved into the rear of the vehicle. When the police approached the vehicle, Burns was partially undressed and engaging in sexual behavior.

Burns, who lives with his wife, Adair Burns, and their four children at 34 Merryweather Lane, Cannondale, was charged with solicitation of a prostitute, public sex act, and indecent exposure. The prostitute, who is an illegal immigrant, is being held pending charges.

Burns was released on bail. A court date is set for February.

"Well, I guess now we know why Adair Burns was so devoted to Yogi Jack," Elizabeth overheard Christine Bellow say to Helen Michaels in the Village Market checkout line.

"It's really shocking," said Helen. "Who would have guessed that Hugh was gay?"

"Not me," said Christine. "He plays squash with my husband.

I don't think anyone had a clue. It must be so hard to live with a man going through that. I heard Adair's dad was gay, too, as well as Hugh's."

"Really, wow!" Helen said.

"And you know what they say: you marry a version of your father," Christine said.

"I haven't seen her at school pick-up lately," Helen said. "Where is she?"

"I heard she rented a suite at the Mayflower Inn & Spa," said Christine.

"Good for her," Helen said. "I'm going to give her a call in a few weeks and see if she wants to get a drink."

Adair was, in fact, at NYU Langone Medical Center for what would become an extended stay. Adair didn't know that the anonymous tip that led to Hugh's very public and, for Adair, mortifying arrest came from Jack.

Several years before, she had told Jack that she suspected Hugh was gay. She explained about Hugh's father. "I think he only stays with me as a cover and because he wants to raise kids in a two-parent household," Adair told Jack in tears. "After his dad left his family when he was eight, he swore he would never do the same to his children."

Adair told Jack about her own troubled history growing up with a father who was a closeted homosexual and eventually died from AIDs. Jack stored that information away and knew that if he ever needed to blackmail or crush Adair and/or Hugh, all he had to do was have Hugh followed. Given Adair had told no one but Jack, she should have put two and two together, but she still had blinders on for him despite her upset.

To ensure Adair never revealed what she threatened, Jack visited her once a week at NYU. He played the concerned, trusted friend. He told her that given the circumstances, the stalking and drunken party incidents were behind them. He brought her kids to see her, who continued to live in the Burns' home with Hugh and his mother.

When the trial began, the kids would go to live with Hugh's mother until Adair felt strong enough to check herself out. "I can't be on the outside now," she told Jack. "I know my kids probably need me, but I'm too ashamed to be in that town until the sentencing is over."

39

Abigail Davis-Powers (Mobile):

Call me. I have news about Jack. XO

Elizabeth Kelly (Mobile):

Abby, if you can, come over. I'm home alone with the kids. ☺

When Abby got to Elizabeth's house, she told her the news. Abby had been out in Manhattan with college friends the night before and one of them had a sister who used to work for CANstruct. She said Jack had been her sister's boss before he was dismissed from the company—which was not what he'd told anyone in town. He'd been officially fired for performance issues, but that was widely rumored to be a cover for "inappropriate contact" with several females in India.

"While Jack worked at the company, he did have a fiancée die," Abby said as they sipped tea in Elizabeth's living room, "but then he supposedly took up with two married teachers who were employed by CANstruct. The first one's husband found out about the affair. He nearly beat her to death before casting her out of his home, essentially ruining her life. To avoid something like it happening again, CANstruct implemented a strict policy about interactions between its American employees and those the charity helps, including its paid teachers. Within two months, Jack was sleeping with another married teacher. When word got out about it at work, CANstruct's owner dismissed him for inappropriate behavior."

"That's a sleazy thing to do," Elizabeth said.

"I know. Those women essentially worked for him, and it's especially wrong given the cultural consequences for them. Funny how Jack neglected to tell me that part of the story.

"I really should have looked into his background," Abby continued. "I would have before Colin died. I'm totally off my game."

"Not totally," Elizabeth soothed.

"See, this is what happens when you're vulnerable," Abby said, growing increasingly upset. "You fall for bullshit like having an infinite dormant energy in the body and it all goes downhill from there."

"I think Jack does believe in kundalini," Elizabeth said.

"He probably does," Abby responded, "but he's also screwed up. Has anyone you know been to India with him and met the women who make the clothing he sells through the charity? Is he manipulating and fucking them, too?"

"No one I know of has traveled with him there," Elizabeth responded.

"Do we even know if his story about the charity is true?" Abby questioned. "That could be bullshit, too."

"I guess not," Elizabeth said. "Come to think of it, he could be conning everyone in town. The women are too mesmerized with him to notice, and the men are too busy to care as long as they get the donations' tax write-off."

"Do you still have access to his server?" Abby asked after a pause.

"I haven't checked recently," Elizabeth said, "and Adair is probably cut off from his system now, but there are a number of outstanding invoices from the benefit that I'm responsible for. I can talk to his assistant Leaha about getting access. And I still have the office key that Adair gave me."

"Are you free tomorrow morning at ten o'clock?" Abby asked. "Jack has a sexcapade with one of the clients I brokered for him. He'll be at the estate and should be gone for at least three hours given the number of participants. We can go through his office then. In the meantime, I'm going to run a criminal and financial background check on him."

"What about Leaha?" Elizabeth asked. "Every time I've been in Jack's office, she's there."

"Since she helped Adair with the benefit, she must have some free time coming," Abby said. "Given that Jack will be gone most of the day, let's see if she'll agree to go to True Grace Spa for a day of beauty—our treat. You can tell her it's a thank-you for being such a big help with the benefit. You've become friendly with her, haven't you?"

"Yes," Elizabeth said, grinning. "I've gotten to know her through Adair. I'll call her and the spa to set it up."

40

Le Beau Château

Jennifer Alder

The room was filled with attractive, well-dressed people sipping cocktails. The woman at the center of it all was in her midsixties. She was tall and thin and had dazzling pale-blue eyes accentuated by the gray of her chin-length hair. Her name was Jennifer Alder. Abby introduced her to Jack several weeks ago. He had then gone to her palatial home for a series of private sessions. Although Jennifer was polite, she had that steely, detached quality old school WASPs can possess—that "I'm better than you" carriage Jack knew so well from his own upbringing. Jack detested it.

Now, ensconced in a wing chair in the center of the safe room's master bedroom, Jennifer was looking at those hired for her entertainment with probing, calculating eyes. As Jack watched her on the safe room monitors, he wondered if he should have had a few more private sessions with her before introducing the sexcapade service. There was something about her that made him uneasy. He couldn't place it.

In recent months, Jack had opened up his sexcapades to more

and more women, some he had to admit he really didn't know well enough to allow into the service. Abby was a good broker and offered him a consistent stream of clients. These women were incredibly rich and willing to pay a lot for the service.

It's not like my clients will ever compare rates, Jack convinced himself, knowing that he had begun charging on a sliding scale. *Most of these women will never tell another soul about their encounters.* Jack didn't realize he was growing dangerously greedy. It made him increasingly careless.

Jennifer was from a wealthy Pennsylvania family and had married well. Several years ago, her husband had died in a Salzburg hotel room with a person Jennifer referred to privately as "the dirty whore." She had been blindsided by the affair and by her husband's death. It changed her. Made her angry. Made her cruel. Jennifer was trying to work through the betrayal and her grief and get back to who she'd been before. She had loved and trusted her husband.

While downsizing, Jennifer became friendly with Abby through her broker, Cecily. Abby was empathetic to her story. Eventually, Abby introduced Jack to her and what she called his "therapeutic" private sessions. Jennifer didn't buy into the kundalini part of Jack's yoga practice, but she liked yoga. And then she liked Jack. He reminded her of her son.

After a few private sessions—and after developing an infatuation with Jack—Jennifer found herself intrigued by his offer of sexcapades. She wanted to take him up on the offer as long as Jack agreed to be a participant in her fantasy. They hadn't been intimate yet, and Jennifer was disappointed. Abby had insinuated that they would be, but in the privacy of her home's exercise studio, Jack hadn't deviated from their yoga routine. So Jennifer thought about her fantasies. She thought about what she would want in a sexcapade.

She was turned on by both men and women, although with the exception of passionately kissing her best friend when she was thirteen, she had never been with a woman. She was turned on by watching sex.

I want an orgy, she decided.

Jack noted her upper-crust background and knew the crowd for her sexcapade had to be refined, at least in appearance: clean cut, well-groomed, fit, and with a limit of tattoos. In Fairfield County, finding participants who fit that bill was easy.

"I'll join you shortly," Jack told Jennifer after introducing her to the crowd he'd assembled. "Enjoy."

As Jack walked to the room of monitors, he realized that he couldn't be a part of her sexcapade. *She'll be all over me,* he thought. Having only seen Jennifer in her yoga attire prior to tonight, Jack was thrown off by her appearance. Wearing what was for many older WASPs a type of uniform, Jennifer was sporting a tailored button-down and belted wool trousers. *She looks too much like my mother or one of her friends,* he thought. *This feels wrong.*

As Jack continued to watch her through the monitor, he saw a young man begin to undress her. Reflexively, as if he'd just walked into his mother's dressing room while she was changing, he looked away. Jack stared into another monitor and saw two young, beautiful women on a chaise lounge making out. *This I can watch,* he thought. He pressed that monitor's RECORD button.

On another monitor, another couple moved across the screen hand in hand and joined Jennifer who was now partially naked on the bed with the young man. On the last monitor, Jack watched as a woman gave head to a boy barely old enough to vote. He quickly pressed RECORD. He continued to watch them, and then his eyes moved back to the two women.

This is hot, Jack thought, completely aroused now even with Jennifer in the middle of it. *I need to suggest orgies to more of my clients.*

41

The sisters were bidding Leaha farewell as she excitedly prepared to head to True Grace. "You totally deserve a day of beauty," Abby told her.

"Thank you so much, Elizabeth and Abby," Leaha responded. "I'm in dire need of a manicure and pedicure and haven't had a massage since my birthday."

"Elizabeth needs to finalize payments for the charity benefit anyway, and we'll man the phones while you're gone," Abby continued.

"Can I still log in using Adair's information?" Elizabeth asked.

"No," Leaha sternly replied. "That account has been cut off until further notice. But I'm authorized to create temporary IDs and passwords for volunteers. I can give you one for today."

"Okay," Elizabeth said. "Thank you!"

Elizabeth bolted the office door behind Leah after she left five minutes later.

"His filing cabinets are locked," Abby said as she angrily tugged on several drawers.

"Look for keys," Elizabeth said while she booted up Leaha's computer. "He may keep a set here."

Once online and logged into Jack's company's account, Elizabeth could only access the financial areas directly related to the Auntie Arts benefit. After she paid the requisite bills, she tried to find a log-in and password list but had no luck. Then she tried a few log-in and password combinations but was quickly locked out of the system. Abby scoured the office for filing cabinet keys but came up with nothing.

"What do you think are in these boxes?" Abby asked, pointing to a stack of cardboard boxes in the corner. She noted the return label's heading: BANGALORE TOURIST TRADE.

"Let's open one from the bottom," Elizabeth offered.

The package's contents were one of the products the charity sold: embroidered tunics in vibrant, sensuous colors of nectarine, turquoise, and raspberry.

Each tunic was wrapped in a plastic sleeve, and, as Abby removed a few, she closely examined them. "These are the Auntie Arts tunics," she said. "See the labels? The same product was on display at the benefit. The stitching is so intricate. An artisan must spend days on each one."

"Here's an invoice," Elizabeth said, removing it from the box. "There's a charge for each item. Why would that be? Jack said he pays the artisans a salary."

"Seems curious," Abby said. "Can you access Google on the computer? Google 'Bangalore Tourist Trade.' We'll delete our search history before we leave."

Elizabeth discovered images of the box's bagged tunics on the English-language version of the Bangalore Tourist Trade's website. They were categorized under the title "Custom Designed Products."

"Abby, look," she said pointing to photos of the tunics displayed on mannequins. Next, she clicked on the "Who We Are" Tab, which revealed interior photos of a large factory with rows and rows of seated women bent over tables, sewing by hand.

"That's a factory," Elizabeth exclaimed. "Jack's artisans don't need a factory built for them. They already work in one!"

"These 'artisans' look nothing like the women in the photos Jack's shown us," Abby commented as she knelt next to Elizabeth and peered at the computer monitor. "Where's the circle of rural women stitching on a dirt floor? Where are the kids roaming the countryside?"

"Bangalore is one of the largest cities in India, and it's in the Southern part," said Elizabeth. "It's not rural, and it's nowhere near Nepal. My friend Farah grew up there."

"Damn—how could I be so naïve?" Abby asked as she closed her eyes and let her head fall into her palms. "Jack *is* a con artist."

The sisters sat in silence for a minute. Elizabeth placed one hand on Abby's back as she continued to explore the Bangalore Tourist Trade website. "Short of going to India, how do we confirm it?" Elizabeth asked. "A few boxes of tunics aren't enough proof. Jack could talk his way out of it. And calling Bangalore Tourist Trade wouldn't reveal anything solid. They aren't going to talk to us."

"I know," said Abby as tears fell into her hands.

"Leaha must be involved," said Elizabeth. "I don't think Jack could do this without her knowing or, given his schedule, without her help. I wouldn't have guessed it. She doesn't seem like the type. She's shy and helpful and nice. Kind of sheltered. Immature in certain ways."

"She's exactly the kind of person who is extremely easy to manipulate," Abby said, regaining her composure. "But despite the manipulation, she must realize the seriousness of it if she's involved. That's got to scare her—a lot. She's not some hardened criminal."

"Jack told me he's planning to host another benefit," said Elizabeth. "He asked me to help. The next one will be at Waveny Park in the spring."

"Which would get Leaha in even deeper," said Abby.

"Yes."

"Let's take her to dinner tonight, and after a few glasses of wine, let's tell her what we found out," said Abby. "Let's tell her we're planning to go to the police with the information but are willing to give her the opportunity to go to them first so she can broker a deal."

"That might work," Elizabeth said, "or it might not. She could get up from the table and go directly to Jack, and then he could threaten you into silence given your involvement in the sexcapades."

"I'm going to convince Leaha that her only hope is to go directly to the police—because if she doesn't, we will," Abby stated. "I'm not going to let on that I'm afraid of Jack's retaliation...even though I am. Like you said, she's a nice person. I doubt she thought she would be involved in criminal activity when she accepted a job with a nonprofit. She probably wants out but thinks she's too enmeshed."

"Okay," Elizabeth agreed. "I'm going to let you do the majority of the talking tonight."

~~~

Later that day, Abby and Elizabeth went to True Grace Spa and requested the empty pedicure chairs next to Leaha, who had already had a South Pacific seaweed wrap, a Swedish heated-rock massage, and a European facial with additional microdermabrasion. She was settling in for an Oriental green tea spa pedicure and manicure when the sisters arrived.

"Enjoying your spa day?" Abby asked Leaha, who was sitting in a luxurious white bathrobe and having a sugar scrub applied to her feet.

"Absolutely," Leaha responded. "Thank you so much."

"We are going to Sushi Cosi for an early dinner after this," Elizabeth said. "Will you join us?"

"Sure," she said. "I don't have plans tonight. This is all so nice of you two."

Later, as Leaha neared the bottom of her second glass of wine, Abby started in on her. During the questioning, which started out mildly and grew more direct and intense, Elizabeth's mind flashed to a time when she was seven.

A boy who lived several neighborhoods away had stolen her brand-new bicycle. Abby asked around and found out who did it, then stormed over to the boy's home with Elizabeth in tow. After grilling him and threatening to beat him up, which she was very capable of doing, he admitted to stealing it. He returned the bike, apologized, and then, after Abby handed him a rake and pointed to their front yard, he raked up all the leaves in it. Over thirty years later, as Elizabeth observed Abby's interrogation of Leaha, she thought, *She's still got it.*

"When Jack hired me, he was working closely with buyers at Bendel and Saks to develop a product that would appeal to high-end clients," Leaha began once Abby had broken her. "He had thirty women in West Bengal making shawls. Given the level of detail, each woman could only produce two shawls a month. As demand for the product increased, Jack hired more women, but the output was still slower than he wanted. Eventually, he started to meet with factory owners so that the product line could be produced more quickly, at lower cost, and with fewer hassles. He chose to work with Bangalore Tourist Trade because its owner agreed that he wouldn't sell what they developed together to anyone else. The product would be exclusive to Jack and, as long as it wasn't appearing with other companies' labels in stores or online, he figured he could keep up the ruse."

"What happened to the artisans he'd been employing?" asked Elizabeth.

"He dropped them," Leaha said, lowering her head. "I don't know."

"That's harsh," responded Abby. "Giving those women a chance to make an income and then just dumping them. He could have had them continue to produce some of his products."

"Yes," agreed Leaha. "He just didn't want to deal with the hassle of it anymore."

"So, the proceeds from the clothing go to him," Abby pushed. "Not to anyone in India?"

"Yes, all the money goes to him," she replied, bowing her head, "and I get a small share in addition to the salary he pays me."

"What about the benefit at The Glass House?" Elizabeth asked.

"That was his biggest scam so far," Leaha divulged. "He has no plans to go back to West Bengal with the money at all. His plan is to show the Cannondale community photos of a school he oversaw the building of when he was at CANstruct and pretend it's the building the benefit's proceeds built. That school doesn't even exist anymore—it was destroyed by a monsoon and landslide more than ten years ago. Then, he told me he'll wait for a bad monsoon season, which he said happens every couple of years, and claim the building was destroyed. He believes the Cannondale community will be gullible enough to fall for it. He'll show everyone photos of a destroyed building and weeping

Indian women and children—photos he took when the school was wiped out. He believes they'll rally around the cause and donate even more money.

"When Jack planned the location where he would begin employing Indian women, he purposely picked a very impoverished, remote area of India," Leaha continued. "At that point his intentions were good, but he didn't want eyes on him. Given how things have developed, his decision worked in his favor. He knows no one from this town will ever travel there for work or for vacation. There are no hotels or office buildings around it for miles."

"What a fucking asshole," exclaimed Abby.

"Jack did start out with good intentions," Leaha muttered. "I did, too."

"You're in deep," Abby hissed.

"I know," Leaha said, tears welling in her eyes. "And when Jack told me he has plans to do more events like the benefit, I got really uncomfortable. I think it's just a matter of time before word spreads about his charity fraud and he gets caught."

"Like I said, if you go and speak with Police Chief Kevin Knight tomorrow morning and provide him with evidence against Jack, you may be able to broker some sort of deal," said Abby. "It's your only hope. Otherwise, I'm going to forward him the lengthy email we wrote that details Jack's illegal activities before we leave this restaurant."

Looking pensive, Leaha nodded her agreement.

"Now—what do you know about Jack's private clients and activities at Le Beau Château?" Abby asked.

"A lot," she said, rising her eyebrows. "Jack secretly tapes most of his private sessions and the sexcapades. He has at least one tape of every person who has participated in his sexcapade services."

A chill ran through Abby. *He can destroy me,* she thought. *I could have my real estate license revoked for sending the firm's clients to him. I could go to jail.*

"Do you know where he keeps the videos?" Abby asked.

"As far as I know, they're on his home computer, and he has hard copies all over the place—in his apartment, in Le Beau Château's basement safe, and in the yoga studio's safe deposit boxes," Leaha responded. "He may have sets elsewhere, but I only know about those three locations. I'm in charge of keeping his back-up copies up to date. I copy them and add them to the three libraries. "

"Anywhere else?" Abby asked.

"I also have a set," Leaha said. "I think that's it."

"You do?" Elizabeth said incredulously, glancing at Abby.

"Have you watched them?" Abby demanded.

"Some," Leaha admitted uncomfortably, "but I haven't watched yours yet. He has three of you, Abby."

"Three!" she echoed.

"They're titled *Cougar on Fire, Badges and the Babe,* and *The Tease,*" Leaha explained.

Oh my God, he gives them titles, thought Abby. *I'm such an idiot.*

"Bring those with you when you meet with Chief Knight," Elizabeth instructed. "He's going to want them."

"I will," said Leaha.

Abby looked at her watch then. "Oh no," she said. "I have to get home. My new au pair, Sabrina, has plans to go out tonight." The women paid the bill and, as they waited for their coats at the entry, finished their conversation. The coats were hung behind a ceiling-height, voluptuous velvet curtain.

The threesome didn't see Brianna Worth enter the restaurant, but she saw them. She was there to have dinner with Anastasia Barlow.

Brianna walked toward the ladies, hoping to chat and compare notes about the benefit. Given that there were a number of people in the vestibule, Brianna had difficulty maneuvering around one large group to reach them. As she drew closer, Brianna overheard Jack's name and the words "videos" and "sexcapades" in whispered tones. It stopped her dead in her tracks. Brianna moved right behind them but didn't say a word.

"If you try to go after him for fraud, he *will* go public with the videos," Leaha softly said to Abby. "He even has the police chief you're dating on video with you. Jack is very strategic. Between his private sessions and the sexcapade service, he has videos of most of the prominent people in town. He jokes about it. Yesterday, he was talking about how much fun it would be to reveal the tapes of all the Kings Lord Manor wives and then watch as the embarrassment led them to self-destruct."

Brianna felt sick. She had not only slept with Jack, but she had also foolishly trusted him to entertain a number of her fantasies, including her desire to play a stripper. *If a tape of my striptease gets out, I'll be a complete laughing stock once again,* she thought. *Edward will leave me. I'll probably lose custody of the kids. I'll have to leave town. I'll lose everything.*

Brianna exited the restaurant without speaking with Anastasia Barlow, who had been seated.

After receiving their coats a few minutes later, Abby, Elizabeth, and Leaha left the restaurant. Abby walked directly to her car and called Kevin Knight.

42

As the yoga class progresses, a rhythm develops. Like a skilled conductor, Yogi Jack directs his students into position, silently traveling through the studio and adjusting their stances. His touch is gentle and lingering. The corrections vary: legs widened or narrowed to mirror their hip width, knees repositioned above planted feet, rounded back stretches deepened, hips pulled back and up, twists enhanced. Some of his touches are straightforward and helpful to the pose, while others are all about contact.

Unlike other yoga instructors who explain the adjustment in process, Jack is silent. His students don't know why their positions were wrong, but the comfort of the new one he configures each into is answer enough—at least for that moment. Technical speak would interrupt the intoxicating feel-good vibe created in his class. It would force rational thought at a time when they welcomed the blurring of lines. Each student enjoys the dark, the music, the endorphin release. The women are old enough to savor moments when they can momentarily lose themselves without enhancements. Exercise, at least when not overdone, is nothing but good for them.

Touches that are more about contact than instruction are also welcomed by the regulars. Jack is the class bonus. His attractiveness

and emotional availability fuels their fantasies of an ideal man—
handsome, sensitive, evolved—while his attention staves off their
concerns about aging. Jack knows this and plays with them by selec-
tively doling out his touches. He understands that no matter how
assured they are, there is an insecure part in all of them—one that
craves attention to validate their waning attractiveness, to validate
their worth.

Jack exploits these insecurities; there are weeks when he ignores
students or only makes minor adjustments, and others when he
repeatedly returns to them in one class. He wants them to wonder
why they were ignored on some days and why they weren't on others.
He wants the women to long for his contact, to feel as though they
are his chosen adjustment.

These touches have nothing to do with proper yoga positioning.
They have everything to do with manipulation.

❧

As Abby allowed Sabrina her night out and waited for Kevin to
come over to her house to discuss what she and Elizabeth discovered, she was furious with herself for being taken advantage
of by Jack. *Why didn't I see this earlier?* she thought. Everything
was crystal clear to her now: the do-gooder persona and charity,
the yoga classes' manufactured sexual tension, the push for
private sessions and workshop registration, the encouragement
of kundalini growth, and ultimately, his sexcapades service. *It's*
all one big twisted business model, she thought. *And he set it up*
so he could easily destroy anyone who betrays him.

Once Kevin arrived, she explained what Leaha told her and
asked, "Can you arrest him on fraud charges?"

"Well, there are a number of things to consider," he responded. "For one, we need to destroy all incriminating evidence against you, me, the police department, and anyone else he's recorded. That stuff we can get with a 'no knock' warrant."

"What's that?" Abby asked.

"It's a warrant that allows you to enter a property without prior notice. It's typically done when there is concern for the safety of the officers, or when it's believed that the evidence could be disposed of between notice and execution of the warrant. In this case, I'll indicate the latter to the judge. And since we're going to destroy the recordings and they'll never be used in a court case, I'll instruct the officers to 'forget' to leave the notice of an executed search warrant behind. We'll trail Jack and only enter the locations where we think the recordings are stored when he isn't in them. I'll have to plan to confront him quickly before he realizes the videos are gone, and, possibly have the officers go back with dupes to put in the hiding spots. Jack can't find out about the search warrants before we want him to know."

"His assistant Leaha has a set of videos," said Abby. "She's going to bring them with her when she comes to see you tomorrow. Before executing the search warrant, your officers could buy the same kind of videos and duplicate the packaging to make them look like Jack's. That way if they're the same as Leaha's set, the officers could switch them then and not have to go back."

"That's good," said Kevin before continuing. "Secondly, even without the videos, if we arrest him for fraud, he could still go public with the sexcapades by convincing the people he hired for them to back up his claims. Some of them could even start a blackmail campaign against the women they were involved with. We don't want that to happen. I don't think we should arrest him. I think we need to find a way to scare him and run him out of town."

"But what would scare him?" Abby asked.

"That's what I need to figure out," Kevin said.

43

Brianna was in a panic when she returned from Sushi Cosi to her home at Kings Lord Manor. She saw Edward's car in the driveway.

That's funny, she thought. *After I told him I was having a girls' night out, he said he was going out, too. He must have been picked up.*

She entered the house but didn't know what to do with herself. She had completely lost her appetite but figured a large glass of wine would help calm her. She opened the wine fridge and was happy to see one of her favorite white wines—2007 Prager Grüner Veltliner—chilling and poured a generous amount into a large, bulbous wineglass, one typically reserved for red wine.

It can't be true, she tried to convince herself. *Jack wouldn't record my sexcapades, would he? We go way back. We're too close. He wouldn't do that to me, would he?*

Pacing through her house, she decided to take a swim and steam in their basement's hammam room. Although it had barely been used since its construction, Brianna realized that she should value it now. Once the house sold, it wouldn't be hers anymore.

Brianna descended the stairs. As she did, she heard music. *Maybe Edward is home and working out in the gym.* She swung open the door and heard the shower. Looking toward the large glassed-in space, she was shocked to see two intertwined forms.

Her eyes narrowed, trying to make out the faces through the steamed glass. She looked down at the discarded clothes on the floor. And then it hit her.

It's Edward and Leigh. She was sure of it.

Fury filled Brianna. She started to charge at them. She wanted to smash the glass walls down around them. But then, for some reason, she stopped.

After watching them for a few seconds longer, she retreated up the stairs and threw the wineglass into the kitchen sink, shattering it. Brianna grabbed her car keys and the entire bottle of wine and got back in her car. She was seething: Edward was her husband. Leigh was her best friend. Would Jack deceive her, too? Brianna drove to the Cannondale conservation land and, after finishing nearly the entire bottle, had a good, long, drunken cry. As she gazed at a neighboring spec house developed by Mitch Tallwall, she noted the dozens of evergreens and boxwoods and mountain laurel whose root balls were wrapped in burlap waiting for installation.

It was while studying all of this that she formulated her revenge.

◦～◦～◦

On the following Tuesday, just before Brianna knew Leigh would be at Le Beau Château for her monthly sexcapade—or Leigh's monthly minority fix, as they cruelly referred to it—she went to the Château's second, more concealed driveway and parked her car in a secluded spot. She then entered the house through a side door that Jack routinely left unlocked for the hired sexcapade participants to use.

The house was completely empty. No one had arrived for Leigh's gangbang yet, not even Jack. Brianna returned to her car and, over the course of a few trips, brought a number of red fuel canisters back to the house. She hid them in a cabinet in the mudroom.

Next, Brianna called Secure, which monitored the alarm system in the house, and gave them the required code—Jack had given it to her one day when he needed help at the estate. She explained to the Secure representative that they needed to temporarily shut down the fire and carbon monoxide alarm system in order to perform a routine test of the interior sprinkler system. She explained that the test would take several hours and that she would call them back when they were ready for it to be turned on again. After hanging up, Brianna double-checked to make sure no fire alarm error message was showing on the home's surveillance monitors.

She knew the third-floor safe room had six-inch-thick walls reinforced with steel bars, but it wasn't fireproof. *Jack shouldn't have shown off the security to me or trusted me to be his backup in an emergency,* she thought. *I know this house as well as I know my own.*

Just as she was making sure everything was in place, Brianna heard the front door unlock. She eventually heard Jack's voice, along with several men who sounded like they were speaking in a foreign language. Not long after, she heard the doorbell and then the sound of Jack letting Leigh in the home.

Leigh had told her that she generally tired of the men after about an hour and a half, so Brianna sat in her hiding spot in the mudroom for about thirty minutes. She worried that Jack might be monitoring the house from the security room. He typically moved between the two spaces during sexcapades, so she knew she was going to have to move quickly to avoid being seen on the monitors.

One by one, she took a canister of gasoline and walked along the perimeter of the largest first-floor rooms, pouring the flammable liquid. She made sure to saturate the bottom of every fabric window treatment. When all the canisters had been emptied, she walked through the house and ignited the window treatments.

If the fire burns well, she thought, *then I'll have rid myself of Brianna, Jack, and any potential sex video revelation. He told me he would never tape me. He shouldn't have taped me.*

Before exiting, Brianna stood for a moment and watched the flames engulf the gorgeous cream-colored velvet treatments and blacken the ceiling above them, completely satisfied by her work.

Unbeknownst to Brianna, Jack—who had observed Leigh during gangbangs and knew she could handle the men by herself—had exited the home just after the sexcapade started. He walked the property to see if any tree limbs had fallen and damaged the estate's outer buildings during the previous night's storm. In the distance, he heard a car engine start.

That sounds too close—like around the estate's second driveway, he thought.

Then he heard a long series of popping noises, similar to fireworks. Not soon after, the smell of smoke hit him.

Jack dashed back in the direction of the home and soon saw that the first floor was engulfed in flames. He was a thousand yards from it when he called 9-1-1.

Why isn't the fire alarm system working? he wondered. As he continued running toward the house, he saw four of the five men involved in the sexcapade run to the truck parked at the side of the house near the detached garage. They were naked and clutching their clothing.

Where's the other one? Jack thought frantically. *Where's Leigh?*

Where's her car? When he left the house earlier, he noted that both cars were parked together. Hers was gone.

One of the men got back out of the truck suddenly and ran back toward the house. Jack called to him, but he didn't hear Jack. In the distance, sirens started to ring out. The man quickly returned to the truck and then it sped away.

Jack tried entering the home from the back patio, but the heat and smoke were overwhelming. *Will there be a dead body in there?* he wondered. *Could one of the men have started the fire and then stolen Leigh's car? Is she trapped inside?*

～⌣ ⌣⌐

Leigh was, in fact, alive and well and speeding down Old Farm Highway. As the first one to realize something was amiss, she was nearly home. During the gangbang, Leigh had tired of the men faster than usual and had gone looking for Jack; she'd wanted him to join. But when she opened the surveillance room's door to see if he was there, she was surprised to see Brianna on one of the first-floor monitors, wielding a red gas can and wildly dousing the living room window treatments, the gas spilling in waves from the can's nozzle.

Shit, Leigh thought. *What the fuck is she doing?* And then realization hit her.

Oh God! Brianna *did* come back to her house when I was there the other night. *Oh fuck! She knows I'm sleeping with Edward. The broken wineglass in the sink. The missing bottle of white wine...*

Edward initially feared that Brianna had returned home early from dinner, but when he didn't see her car, he'd dismissed it. He'd said the cat must have knocked over the glass. That he must have forgotten to chill the wine. "Believe me, Leigh, if Brianna did come back and found us in the shower together, she would have tried to kill us on the spot," he'd joked.

Oh God! This is really bad! Leigh had quickly hit the first-floor monitors' RECORD buttons but didn't notice that the cameras in the bedroom had already been recording. She grabbed one of the white terry robes Jack provided for his clients and ran out of the safe room. She quietly crept down the home's back staircase to avoid Brianna. Once in the mudroom, she saw the pile of cans Brianna had brought with her and heard a splashing noise somewhere outside of the kitchen.

My God, Leigh thought, *she's going to burn down this entire home.* Leigh exited through the mudroom door and ran to her car. *She definitely saw us that night,* Leigh thought as she rummaged through her designer purse and jammed the car key into the ignition. As Leigh pulled out of Le Beau Château's driveway for what would be the last time, she thought, *Jack and the other men will hear the fire alarms and get out in time.*

But not all the men hired to please Leigh got out alive. Much of the first floor was burned before the smoke penetrated the safe room's six-inch walls. Having stopped to pull on his jeans, Miguel Ángel Diaz was behind the other men as they fled the safe room. He stumbled and fell at the top of the smoke-filled limestone-paved grand stairwell and, as he tumbled, cracked his head on the second-to-last step, rendering him unconscious.

By the time he stopped rolling down the stairs, the other men were already out the front door. His friend, Juan Jesús Emiliano, tried to go back in to find him, but the smoke had grown too strong.

44

At the end of Jack's Thursday evening kundalini workshop, Kevin Knight and four other police officers entered his studio. Most of the women were in the process of rolling up their mats and looked startled to see so many officers enter the building.

Jack was encouraging two of his students to sign up for private sessions when Kevin approached him. "We need to ask you some questions," he said loudly. Jack looked at him quizzically but decided to play along.

"Of course, Chief Knight," he said. "Ladies, if you would be so kind as to take your conversations outside, I would appreciate it." When they hesitated to leave, Jack explained, "As you know, I'm the caretaker of the Le Beau Château estate. You may have seen in the newspapers that its home burned down on Tuesday. Sadly, one of the town's last great homes is gone, and the officers have some questions for me." Two of the police officers started herding the Lululemon-attired crowd out of the building. They closed and locked the doors on their way back in.

"What's this about, Kevin?" Jack asked.

"Have a seat, Jack," Kevin responded.

One of the police officers placed a wooden chair in the middle of the yoga room. Jack hesitantly sat down.

"I have something to show you," Kevin said as he pulled out a portable DVD player. On the screen, he brought up a video of himself and two of the other cops in the room during their sexcapade with Abby.

Jack looked shocked. "Where did you get that?" he asked.

Kevin pointed to the yoga studio's old bank vault, where the safety deposit boxes were.

"When?" Jack asked.

"It doesn't matter, Jack," Kevin responded. "I have it, and it proves you broke a promise to me. Not only did you film us, but then you stored it away to use for whatever future purpose you had planned."

"I-I wasn't singling you out," Jack stammered as the two other officers on the tape moved in closely behind him. "I tape the sexcapades for my own private use. It's just a weird perversion. I'm not planning to do anything with the tapes."

"Bullshit. That's not what your assistant Leaha told us during questioning," Kevin said. "She even showed us a file you created listing your sexcapade clients' weaknesses. At some point, you were planning to blackmail us all."

Jack was speechless. *Leaha, you fat, pathetic bitch*, he thought.

"Given the fire that occurred during a sexcapade you orchestrated, you could be charged as an accessory to murder," Kevin started, deciding to list all the potential charges even though he knew he wouldn't pursue them, for fear of exposure. "We could find enough evidence for the charges to stick. We could also, given these tapes and the participants' testimony, charge you with pimping and prostitution. Based on Leaha's testimony, the files acquired during a 'no knock' search warrant, and your bank records, we could also charge you with fraud concerning your charity and the benefit.

With all of that… You're looking at a jail term of about fifteen to twenty years."

The other policemen moved close to Jack, surrounding him.

"What do you want?" Jack asked.

One of the officers pulled a cloth bag from his pocket. He placed it over Jack's head while another officer sharply pulled back Jack's arms and wrapped them in a monoglove behind the back of the chair. His ankles were cuffed.

From the darkness of the bag, Jack heard the studio's exterior door open and the tapping of what sounded like stiletto heels strutting across its wooden floors. A whip *crack*ed next to the chair. A match was struck. The bag was ripped from his head, revealing Stacy, his B&D sexcapade client.

"I get to have you tonight," she said as she pulled a long rattan cane from a thigh-high boot.

"No," Jack said as images of her sexcapade volunteers squirming in pain flooded his head. "No, no, no!"

"Enjoy your sexcapade, Jack. I'll be back to set you free so she can fuck you," Kevin said as he and the other officers exited the studio.

Forty-five minutes later, they returned to find Jack a bloodied mess. His face had been torn in several areas from contact with knuckle rings, one of his eyes was swollen shut and turning purple. All the exposed areas of his body had raised, bloody welts. He could barely hold his head up.

Kevin partially untied him and dropped him to the floor. Stacy then gingerly removed the monoglove and his clothing while kissing some of his lacerations. Jack flinched with each of her touches. Kevin had his men roll Jack onto his stomach and hogtie him with his hands and feet bound together.

"What are you going to do to me now?" Jack wearily asked. Stacy answered his question with splash of hot wax. She proceeded to cover him, walking in circles and dumping cups of melted wax on his backside. With each new splatter, he called out in pain. He begged her to stop.

"Stacey, dear, I don't think he's up for the finale," Kevin said as he kicked Jack in the ribs. Kevin stared down at Jack's exposed penis and asked the other officers if anyone was up for a castration. Jack's one unswollen eye was wild with fear.

"I didn't bring a drop cloth with me tonight," Kevin said finally. "Maybe we'll cut his dick off tomorrow? Guys, take him to the vault." Two of the four policemen took hold of Jack and dragged him on his stomach. Once at the vault door, they picked him up by the arms and legs and, after swinging him back and forth, threw him into the space with such momentum that he crashed against the back wall of safety deposit boxes and landed with a *thump* and a long groan. Before turning off the vault's lights and locking its door, they cut off his bindings and cuffed his hands and his feet.

"We'll water him tomorrow morning," Kevin said in jest as they locked up the studio's exterior door. "He'll survive the night." Kevin hung a "CLOSED FOR ASBESTOS REMOVAL" sign on the building, which he knew would send most of Jack's students into a complete panic. A photo of the sign would definitely be the lead in *Breaking News Today: Cannondale*, and the *Cannondale Mom's Group* chat room would be abuzz with comments.

"Where did you find Stacy?" one of the officers asked Kevin as they left the studio.

"Believe it or not, she's a local mom. I saw her on one of the sexcapade tapes we got from the vault, and when I showed a still of her to a few of our guys, one remembered meeting her during a routine traffic stop. Her house is the one on the market on Grassy Pastures Lane."

〜〜〜

The next day, Kevin entered the bank vault with his officers, two power bars, and bottles of Gatorade. Jack looked like shit. He was slumped against the far wall. His face was purple and swollen. His body was covered with crusted gashes. Urine was puddled inches from his feet.

"Jack, we're going to set you free on one condition," Kevin said, towering over him. "You are going to leave Fairfield County and never come back. From here, you'll have a police escort to your apartment, where you can pack one bag of belongings. The officers will then bring you to Stamford's Greyhound bus station, where we will provide a one-way ticket for you to Fort Lauderdale. You don't have to go all the way there, but you can never step foot in this town again. If you do, I will get word of it, and you will not survive the night. And if I ever hear of the sexcapade tapes going public, your mother will be the victim of an unfortunate accident. Stan Martin, the police chief of her town, is a close friend. I also know where your four brothers live with their families. We good?"

A terrified and cuffed Jack nodded.

"Lastly, just so you know, your assistant has been very helpful to us. She and I wiped out your computer's hard drive, but I have a copy of everything that could expose your charity's fraud. She's off-limits. You don't call her, text her—nothing. You really shouldn't have taped me and my men, Jack."

45

On a day of gale-force winds and pounding rain, the following was front-page news:

LOCAL WOMAN ARRESTED FOR FIRE AT LE BEAU CHÂTEAU

Brianna Worth of Cannondale is being held at Northern Correctional Institution after she allegedly set fire to Georgette Ark's Cannondale estate at 23 Old Farm Highway on December 1st, which resulted in the death of handyman Miguel Ángel Diaz of Bridgeport, CT.

Surveillance video showed Worth pouring canisters of gasoline in the home's first-floor living and dining rooms before igniting the fire and exiting the home. The fire spread quickly through the entire first and second floors, said Police Chief Kevin Knight.

An autopsy revealed that Diaz was knocked

unconscious during a fall down the home's main staircase. He died of smoke inhalation.

"[Worth] really wanted to destroy that house," Knight said. "She posed as the home's caretaker and called Secure, the resident's fire and security monitoring service, and had all the fire alarms temporarily shut down, claiming that a plumbing company was testing the home's connected interior sprinkler system."

During questioning, Brianna Worth admitted that she started the fire as a form of revenge against Leigh Gilding, whom she claims was having an affair with her husband, Edward Worth. Brianna Worth claimed the woman was inside the home when she began the fire.

The Cannondale Fire Department was alerted to the fire through a 9-1-1 call made by the home's real caretaker, Jack Turner. Turner couldn't be reached for comment, but Chief Knight confirmed that, during questioning, Turner said he was on the estate when the fire began. He was overseeing plasterwork and attending to repairs. Turner said there was no one other than himself and Diaz in the home prior to Worth's entry and the start of the fire.

Worth has a long history of run-ins with the

law. In 2006, she was arrested two times over a thirty-day period for assaulting two relatives, including her four-year-old son. She completed a court-ordered anger management program that year and has been an active anger management counselor and life coach in Norwalk for four years. A psychiatric evaluation was recommended by the chief prosecutor.

Brianna Worth is married to Edward Worth, a commodities trader with Standard Bearer, which is currently being investigated for insider trading. The couple's house is currently on the market with White's Realty for $3.7 million. The Worths have two children and have lived in the area for over ten years.

46

"Hi, Kate," Elizabeth said as she sat down to lunch at Mon Petite Café.

"Hi, Elizabeth," Kate replied. "It's so good to see you. I have some news."

"Oh, really?" Elizabeth responded as she placed a napkin on her lap.

"Yes: I have a new address," she said. "One with only four in the household."

"Wow! That is news," Elizabeth exclaimed.

"So you hadn't heard," Kate asked. "I thought Cecily might have told you. I used her as my agent."

"No," said Elizabeth. "I've been busy dealing with the closing of the March issue. Go on."

"The kids and I are now living on Rockrimmon Lane, and Lorenzo is living in our home—I mean, my *former* home—alone," Kate said, absolutely beaming.

"Based on your expression, it *is* very good news," Elizabeth said. "It's so nice to see you smiling."

Kate told her about the rape video, the legal separation, and the current custody arrangements.

"I'm proud of you," Elizabeth responded. "That took great courage."

"Jack gave me the idea of video surveillance and even paid for it," Kate further explained. "Lorenzo thought his abuse was too private to be exposed, but it backfired on him. It's proving to be very damning for him."

"How did you get custody of the kids until the mediation meeting?" Elizabeth asked. "Lorenzo is so possessive of them."

"My home video. My attorney told Lorenzo's attorney that we were considering pressing rape charges and definitely would if he didn't agree to my having full custody of the children prior to the divorce settlement," Kate said.

"That's smart. You have to be so clever in these situations," Elizabeth noted. "How are you and the kids doing on your own?"

"I'm taking it day by day, and the kids and I are adjusting to the change," Kate explained, taking a sip of water. "I'm so glad to be away from him. I don't how I functioned before. I was constantly worried about setting him off. I was so afraid of him and, no matter how much I tried to stay positive and hide it, I knew the kids sensed it. I knew they could feel all the stress between Lorenzo and me. I hated having them grow up in that environment; I felt like it was teaching Lorenzo Jr. to be a bad man and Sarah and Maddy to seek men who will abuse them. God, I hated being in that house. I hated being at home. Now, home is such a happy place for my kids and me."

"That's great!" responded Elizabeth.

"And I'm excited about dedicating more time to my career," added Kate. "Lorenzo limited how much I worked, how far I advanced. My success threatened him. Now I'm figuring out how to expand my catering business. I have aspirations of opening a café."

"Terrific!" Elizabeth enthused. "And what about Jack?"

"As you probably heard, Jack has fallen off the face of the earth," Kate replied, the smile disappearing from her face. "Even his assistant doesn't know where he is. No one knows, and he isn't responding to anyone's calls, texts, or messages. The yoga studio still has the asbestos notice out front."

"That's unusual," Elizabeth commented, already aware that Jack was gone and wouldn't be coming back. "Maybe the fire and the death was too upsetting for him to remain in town?"

"I'm actually pretty broken up about it," Kate admitted. "I think I'm in love with him."

"In love with him?" Elizabeth gasped. "No, you can't be."

"Yes, we had grown quite close recently," she said. "I think he loved me, too."

"Kate, you know how many other women he was sleeping with, don't you?" asked Elizabeth.

"Yes, but we had a deep connection," she said. "I'm positive we did. And, anyway, I'm married. Or was."

"Well, I'm sorry you're sad about Jack, but the really important thing is that you've finally gotten away from Lorenzo," Elizabeth stressed. "And even if Jack doesn't surface again, I don't believe you'll be alone for long. Once word gets out that you're unattached, single men will swarm to you."

"I don't think I want that, either," said Kate wearily.

"I understand," responded Elizabeth seriously. "Dating isn't easy. Not at all… But there is a new, single man who just joined Andrew's firm," she continued, quickly brightening. "He lives in Greenwich, but he's Australian. Andrew said he's good guy. I met him a few weeks ago and he was very charming. Witty. Attractive. Well-read. I'm going to introduce you to him. And I'm going to ask Andrew to think of other single men to introduce you to. He's in the city a lot with work. He must know of others. And he'll do a good job vetting them for you. He likes you, and he wouldn't want to set you up with a jerk."

"Elizabeth and Andrew, my match makers," said Kate with a sheepish smile. "I want all the first dates to be double-dates with you two."

"I'd love that!" exclaimed Elizabeth. "And after each date, we can analyze the man together. Thumbs-up or thumbs-down. Weed the bad ones out quickly. I know you won't be alone for long," she added, smiling broadly at Kate.

47

A week later, Abby was sitting down to lunch at a table at Brioche. "Hi, Michael," she said. "Thanks for meeting me."

"Of course, Abby," Michael Kat said. He was the hedge fund manager who provided the initial funding for Jack's yoga studio, and who lost the bid for the trip to Fiji at the Auntie Arts charity benefit. "It's always nice to hear from you. So are you finally going to agree to go on a date with me?"

"I would, but I'm already dating someone," Abby said, smiling politely. "I'm seeing Kevin Knight."

"Really?" Michael said. "Well then, I better back off. I don't want the town's police chief upset with me. Why did you want to meet with me today?"

"I want to discuss a business proposal with you," Abby said. "Since Jack appears to have disappeared and the yoga studio you funded is sitting empty, I'm wondering if you want to continue in the yoga business with new partners—specifically my sister Elizabeth and me."

"What are you considering?" Michael asked. "Jack had all the women in this town bewitched. His disappearance has left a huge void. I've been interviewing other male instructors, but no one's compared to Jack yet."

"I think it would be impossible to replace him," Abby said. "What Elizabeth and I have been discussing would take a different approach, but one that we think will still appeal to the studio's female clientele. We liked Jack's classes initially and got sucked in by him, but in truth, we were growing weary of him. Jack was constantly soliciting his students—asking us to sign up for private sessions, workshops, and retreats; or asking us to donate to his charity, buy his charity's products, and go to his charity functions— and part of why the women in town were so enthralled with him was because he was manipulating many of them by manufacturing a strong sexual tension in class.

"A true yoga practice isn't supposed to be about that," she continued. "It's supposed to be about the poses and *pranayama* and meditation. It calms the mind while improving strength and flexibility. When the practice is good, it ultimately offers a greater understanding of the self, which leads to emotional balance and well-being. The women will miss Jack at first, but if the new studio is good and the women start to experience what yoga is meant to do for them, then over time they'll be converted."

"But you and I both know that the women in his classes were either sleeping with him or wanted to sleep with him, and that's what largely kept them coming back," Michael objected.

"Again, that's not what yoga is supposed to be about," Abby stressed. "There are *always* going to be unfulfilled women looking for some kind of release, but Elizabeth and I think that many of the Cannondale women who became Jack's lovers were originally seeking the practice because they were looking for meaning in their lives beyond the local lifestyle and the societal roles assigned to them. Once they got into Jack's class, he started in with the manipulation, and so the yoga practice became confused and perverted.

"So what Elizabeth and I are proposing is to change your studio into a female-*only* yoga studio. Jack's clients were all female anyway, but we think it needs to have all-female instructors, too, to avoid a repeat of what happened with Jack and the women in this town. And regardless of the female teachers' sexual orientation, we would ensure that the teacher-student relationship remains professional. We would specify it in their contracts."

"I like your idea in concept," Michael said, nodding.

"And we would make sure it's an environment that supports women as mothers," Abby continue. "We would establish an excellent daycare to watch kids while the women are in class. Even those who have nannies want their kids to socialize, and we could market it as a fun experience for the kids. The bank vault entrance isn't big enough for a lot of kids to be dropped off, but the back of the building isn't utilized well. We could do a lot more with it.

"Another great addition would be a place where women can hang out before or after the class. We think the yoga studio should incorporate a café," Abby offered. "And I know Kate Musto is looking to open one."

"Heard she's separated now," Michael commented. "Pretty woman."

"Yes, and she is looking for more consistent work for her catering business," Abby said. "Also, I have a friend, Claudine Mead, who used to teach art classes for children in Pennsylvania. I know she would be willing to oversee a daycare and children's art space in your studio."

"Isn't she dating Eddie Silvio, who owns the Getty?" he asked.

"Yes," Abby replied. "She's Leigh Gilding's mother."

"No way," he chuckled. "I would have never guessed that."

"That's what Leigh was hoping for," Abby joked. "Anyway, word of the studio's improvements would bring back a lot of Jack's devoted students," Abby offered.

After a moment's consideration, Michael asked, "What would you call the studio?"

"We think it should be simple," Abby said. "Maybe the logo could be the Venus symbol, which would give the studio a bit of mystique while indicating it's only for women."

"Sounds like you and your sister have it all planned out," Michael said, sincerely impressed. "I like the idea. Let me think about it."

Epilogue

Natural light poured in through the newly added skylights, making the once-dark, cavernous space airy and bright. The mirrored walls, which had done nothing but distract, were gone, replaced by crisp, white paneling. The chatter that once filled the room prior to class had been silenced. Most of the women who had come here today were seeking relief. They craved the quiet, the peace. Their bodies craved the poses, the guided breathing. Once class was over, the chatter would begin again. At that point, they would crave it, too, the respite having provided a restorative break, a realignment, a calming.

The women sat in *padmasana*, lotus position, and waited for instruction. Soft new age music filled their ears and the faint scent of lavender hung in the air. Their teacher, a longtime yogi named Amy, was positioned in balasana, child's pose. She exuded a calm, nonthreatening authority. Shortly, Amy would ask her students to join her in balasana and, from there, move to other poses, rising her students up off the mats and building the intensity.

Meditation in motion. Releasing mind, body, and emotion.

There would be no lecture. No product pushed. No inappropriate adjustments or laying of hands. No manufactured sexual tension.

During shavasana, when the women moved to the prone

position, Amy would leave them alone with their thoughts. No judgmental interference. No conflicted messages. Their minds would be free to wander.

Some would take the time to remember. Counting stars with her brother, laughing with a best friend, a toddler's first ice cream cone, holding hands in a field of heather...

Ten minutes of stillness. Ten minutes to simply be.

Some would work through a difficulty: the frustration of an illness, a parent's death, a sudden job loss, the solitude of an empty nest...

Ten minutes of quiet, used for personal growth. Ten minutes of reflection.

And then there were those for whom yoga was only a form of exercise. They came to the remodeled studio, too—the classes were the best in town, after all. For them, the quiet of shavasana was for a different type of contemplation, for dealing with more "pressing" issues: choosing a nail color for their afternoon pedicure, deciding which designer dress to wear that night, settling on a new style of Louis Vuitton bag, picking the next far-flung locale for a girls' weekend away.

Despite all of Jack's shortcomings, he did try to encourage personal growth during his yoga classes. But, for those only there for exercise, that instruction always fell flat. And Amy's insights wouldn't penetrate either. There were no spiritual enlightenments, no mental developments, and no adjustments of their lives. They were who they were. They would exit the darkened room. They would turn their iPhones back on. They would walk to their luxury cars. They would return to their impressive homes.

Contentment just wasn't in the cards for them. Not yet. Maybe never.

Acknowledgments

I would like to thank my husband, Chris, who gave me the time to write this book, and my children, Alden and Hadley, for being as patient as they could be while I did. I'd like to thank my mother, Kathleen Sample, for instilling a love of reading and curiosity in me, and my siblings, Elizabeth and John, for always making me smile. I'm blessed with wonderful friends and additional family members.

In regards to this book, I want to acknowledge the following: Farah Soi, Roseann Munrow, Mara Lamanna, Heather Morello, Rita Santos, Sandi Blaze, Pam Pfeifer Fahey, Carolyn Nolan, Gina Ely, Caroline Hahn, Rachel Leung, Lauren Gibbons, Maureen McGrath, Anne Cronin, Amy Epes, my cousin Kate Corr, and my sister-in-law Meg Sample. A number of these women were side by side with me in the yoga classes that inspired my writing and offered me feedback.

I owe a special thanks to Christa Carr who, one night over drinks, helped me develop the book's concept and then gave feedback and other support to me while writing; Jen Wohl Jonson for editorial suggestions, including what became the title of the book; and friend and photographer Liz Godfrey for the author portrait.

Additionally, I have had the good fortune to work with terrific people at Wilton's Halstead Property, including John DiCenzo, Susan Byron, my mentor Anne Oliver, and my partner Claire Nichols. After spending hours alone at a keyboard, engaging with them is always entertaining, and they have been readers and strong supporters of my writing.

Lastly, I must thank James Frey and his wonderful staff at Full

Fathom Five, including Greg Ferguson and Kayla Overbey. James was kind enough to read my first draft and see value where others did not. He then spent his valuable time helping me improve it.

About the Author

Ann Lineberger is the author of *New Spaces, Old World Charm* and has worked as a reporter, editor, and writer for numerous publications, including *Fortune, Entertainment Weekly, Cottages & Gardens* and *Home Remodeling*. She earned a master's degree in journalism and mass communication from New York University and an associate's degree from the New York School of Interior Design. Her independent studies program undergraduate degree is from Providence College. In addition to writing, Ann is an interior designer and Halstead Property realtor. She lives in Connecticut with her husband, two daughters, and two very silly dogs.

Visit Ann on her website,
www.annlineberger.com